Longmeadow Press

*To Bob Kane, Jerry Robinson
and the legion of writers, artists,
colorists and editors whose efforts
have made The Joker a villain
worthy of The Batman*

*This edition published exclusively by
    Longmeadow Press
    201 High Ridge Road
    Stamford, CT 06904
under license from DC Comics Inc.*

ISBN 0-681-41015-9

*Printed in Canada,
bound in the United States of America*

First printing

0 9 8 7 6 5 4 3 2 1

*Cover illustration by Dean Motter
Book design by Bruning, Motter + Associates*

STACKED DECK

THE GREATEST JOKER STORIES EVER TOLD

EXPANDED EDITION

CONTENTS

KYLE BAKER

THE BEST OF THE BAD

*H*ere is one of the great secrets of writing heroic fiction: the bad guy is as important as the good guy. The hero's reaction to the villain defines him, gives him interesting things to do and, in fact, is usually what makes him a hero. A lame bad guy almost always results in a lame good guy who isn't around for long.

Batman recently celebrated his fiftieth birthday. That this particular good guy has been popular for over a half-century might be partially explained by his rogues gallery; he has gone against more and better villains than any other hero in comics. R'as al Ghul, the Penguin, Catwoman, Two-Face — world-class evil-doers, every one. But the Joker is the best (that is, the vilest) of the lot, as the book you're holding amply demonstrates. The Clown Prince of Crime was created in 1940 to be featured in the very first Batman comic book, about a year after Batman made his own debut in DETECTIVE COMICS. Many pop culture historians agree that he is not only the greatest of Batman's foes, he is in and of himself a major character. Liked his caped enemy, he has come full circle: after a ferocious start, he went through a rather benign period during which what he did wasn't all that terrible, and then returned to what he was originally — a grinning nightmare, an embodiment of the sheer, irrational hostility we all secretly fear life is really about.

Most of these stories were previously collected in THE GREATEST JOKER STORIES EVER TOLD — most, but not all. The three additions, full-length pieces from BATMAN #353, DETECTIVE #569 and #570, are not only worth reading for their entertainment value, but mark interesting points in the evolution of this greatest of bad guys. Think of them as bringing up to date the biography of a truly fascinating villain without whom Batman might be another mostly-forgotten guy in a cape and a cowl.

— Denny O'Neil
Group Editor/DC Comics
and noted Batman writer

THE JOKER'S DOZEN

*Y*ou'd think the guy was deserving of a rest.

After surviving the murder of his parents, training to become the Darknight Detective, meeting Dick Grayson and transforming him into Robin, the Boy Wonder, and dealing with such adversaries as Doctor Death, The Batman should have been pooped. All these adventures took place in less than a dozen issues of DETECTIVE COMICS — a handful of the most popular comics ever published. The Batman was so successful he was promoted to his own comic book title, a distinction shared with but one other comics character at the time... and it took Superman a couple more months to achieve spin-off status!

That historic first issue of BATMAN was a real killer: Batman met up with the Joker, Hugo Strange and Catwoman... and had a return bout with the Joker! Sixty-four pages of senses-shattering stories, to be sure.

When the publishers of DC Comics launched Superman and Batman, they had no idea those guys would become the all-time most popular continuing characters in the history of American fiction. But when the Joker came onto the scene, they knew they had a winner — not only was he brought back for an unprecedented second appearance in BATMAN #1, but he was "unkilled" (this might have been a first; the process since has become a comics tradition) and brought back several months later.

Producing all that Batman material was too much work for one artist, and that

64-page deadline must have hit Batman creator Bob Kane like a lead weight. There was a great deal of work to do, and it was artist Jerry Robinson, an assistant to Kane, who helped create the Joker for that classic first issue.

Whereas the Joker might be vaguely comedic in appearance, Jerry Robinson certainly is a man to be taken seriously. A past president of the National Cartoonists Society and a three-time winner of its coveted Reuben Award (once as best comics artist), Jerry has produced a number of syndicated features and books, is a respected educator, and the author of one of the best histories of the comic strip medium (in this writer's opinion): *The Comics*, published by Putnam in 1974. While his career in comic books was comparatively brief, the impact of his work is enormous: the Joker is among a handful of comics characters that have been continuously popular for nearly five decades.

So why is the Joker so successful? Why has he endured for so long while other great villains are also-rans?

Well, folks, for one thing, this guy's real scary.

Crime is scary, too. Chester Gould understood this, and made certain that the vast majority of his Dick Tracy villains looked as evil as they were. Most comics villains look powerful, or unusual, or threatening, but few — outside of the Joker — are anywhere near as scary.

The Joker started out doing real scary things: he killed people. Moreover, when he killed them, they died with a great big smile on their faces — a smile that resembled the unchanging grin of the Joker himself!

For another thing, the Joker is so weird his very presence virtually assures an unusual story. He looks so unusual, he acts in such an aggressively peculiar manner, and he is so darn happy about his work that he gives the stories in which he appears an edge that stories populated by more normal people cannot possibly have.

Finally, all great arch-villains have a particular "in" for the good guy who defeats them constantly; but, whereas the Joker clearly hates The Batman, that is not the sole reason for his existence. Criminal acts defy logic, even if criminals do not. But the Joker enjoys evil because evil is as deranged as he is.

Since his introduction, the Joker became the greatest and most enduring of comics villains, surpassing The Man of Steel's Lex Luthor in identifiability and sales appeal. Between 1940 and 1956, the Joker made an appearance in one of the many Batman titles nearly every month.

In those days, Batman held court in DETECTIVE COMICS, BATMAN, WORLD'S FINEST COMICS (solo stories from 1940 through 1954, team-ups with Superman after that point) and STAR-SPANGLED COMICS, which from 1948 through 1952 featured a monthly series of Robin stories, virtually all of which featured Batman. The Joker was a regular in all of these titles except the latter.

So what happened in 1956? Well, we're not really certain, but we do know this: the Comics Code Authority came into power at that time, there was a near-monthly stream of Joker stories prior to the Code, and that stream came to an abrupt end at the inception of the Comics Code.

Perhaps the Code, or the folks who were running DC at the time, found the Joker to be visually too offensive at a time when comics were seen as causing juvenile delinquency and comics creators were made to feel like pornographers.

Luckily, calmer heads prevailed — it's hard to keep a bad guy down. Unlike the vast majority of comics characters whose careers were cut short by the anti-comics mood of the time, the Joker made his reappearance the following year. While he never resumed his almost monthly appearances (with the exception of a nine-issue JOKER comic book series published in 1975 and 1976), it was understood exactly how valuable he was, and as a bad guy he was susceptible to overexposure.

Reducing his visibility helped make the Joker the awesome villain he is today. The near-monthly pace was stretching his credibility to the limit: he always had to lose, and in order to present a fresh challenge to The Batman, the Joker had to resort to increasingly silly gimmicks. It is no coincidence that the clear majority of Joker stories selected for this book come from the post-1956 period.

Too Much Batman, Too Little Space

In 1988, DC Comics published a hardcover book entitled THE GREATEST BATMAN STORIES EVER TOLD. This collection was reprinted the following year in trade paperback by both DC Comics and Warner Books, and it remains in print at comic bookshops and bookstores alike — the hardcover first edition already is commanding a rather stiff price on the collector's market.

Putting together THE GREATEST BATMAN STORIES EVER TOLD was no easy task. We set out to offer a representative sampling of the Batman legend, incorporating as many of the classic villains, supporting cast members and sundry bat-devices as possible. We also wanted to include the work of as many of the most significant Batman writers and artists as we could. To accomplish this, we assembled a nominating committee to recommend stories that met these criteria.

When we reviewed our nominations, we came upon a major problem: there were about one hundred Joker stories. To include even a small sampling of Joker stories meant we would deny exposure to characters and talent that was deserving. Luckily, our solution was simple: we added a GREATEST JOKER STORIES book to our schedule, and published a hardcover edition in 1988 and a softcover version the following year. We selected our stories from our "must publish" list of 19 Joker tales — a Joker's dozen, in the words of editor Brian Augustyn.

And we thought we were done with it.

But this year — 1990 — our friends at Longmeadow Press came to us with the desire to do an expanded, deluxe edition of THE GREATEST JOKER STORIES EVER TOLD — one that would reprint the contents of the original, along with some 60 pages of special material, plus new design and packaging. The foreward was contributed by Batman's editor, Denny O'Neil (a famous Batman writer himself) and Dick Giordano, one of the all-time classic Batman artists, graciously consented to write an afterword. Finding some unique Joker stories that weren't in the previous volume was an easy matter: we focused on the 1980s, a decade underrepresented last time around.

BRIAN BOLLAND

So what you're holding in your hands is truly a STACKED DECK.

Harvesting The Greatest

Giving credit where credit is due, the nominating committee for THE GREATEST BATMAN STORIES EVER TOLD consisted of Batman creator Bob Kane, artist Dick Sprang, writer/editors Jack Schiff and Dennis O'Neil, historians Jerry Bails, Gene Reed, Michael Fleisher, fans Jenette Kahn, Rick Stasi, and Joe Desris, and the editors who worked on that book: Dick Giordano, Robert Greenberger, Mark Waid, Brian Augustyn, and myself. Had we known our nominations would have gone into selecting stories for this book as well, we undoubtedly would have had an even longer list. Our heartfelt thanks to all.

This collection differs from our "GREATEST STORIES" volumes which featured Superman and Batman, respectively. In those books we felt an obligation to maintain certain balances: the need to represent each era of stories, the need to represent the most important characters, gadgets, locales and historical facets, and the need to represent the work of the most significant writers and artists involved in each series. Believe me, quite a number of painful trade-offs were made in editing down our list of nominations.

When it came time to put together THE GREATEST JOKER STORIES EVER TOLD, we felt no need to maintain the latter two balances. We recognized this book would appeal to a more elite and educated comics reader.

Of course, we wanted to represent each era in which the Joker operated, but this was quite easy to do: unlike The Batman, the career of the Joker can be divided into merely three stages: the earliest days, in which the Joker was a confirmed killer; the middle days, during which the Joker was less likely to actually murder people but instead resorted to pulling off astonishing crimes in ludicrous situations, often with preposterous gadgets; and the contemporary days, in which the Joker reverted to his more deadly guise — but now facing a darker version of The Batman.

While there was no need to represent the spectrum of Joker characters and facets — these were covered in THE GREATEST BATMAN STORIES EVER TOLD — several stories included in this book are significant from the standpoint of continuity: "The Man Behind The Red Hood" is, of course, the Joker's origin story; "Superman's and Batman's Greatest Foes" presents the first of the Joker's always ill-fated team-ups with Superman arch-enemy Lex Luthor; and "The Great Clayface-Joker Feud" is the saga of the Joker's teaming with another great Batman villain,

Clayface (the Joker's involvement with The Penguin was reprinted in our GREATEST BATMAN STORIES volume).

And whereas we do indeed have a representative sampling of Joker artists — it is unfortunate that the names of many of the pre-1964 stories are lost to history — quite frankly, this time around we decided to let the stories speak for themselves. With Neal Adams, Jim Aparo, Terry Austin, Steve Englehart, Bill Finger, Dick Giordano, Bob Haney, Bob Kane, Sheldon Moldoff, Jim Mooney, Dennis O'Neil, Charles Paris, Jerry Robinson, Marshall Rogers, Walter Simonson, Dick Sprang, and Len Wein among those represented herein, I think we covered the roster of Joker talent pretty well.

At least two recent major Joker stories were excluded, however, for reasons of space as well as the fact that both are still in print in book form: Frank Miller's THE DARK KNIGHT, and Alan Moore's and Brian Bolland's THE KILLING JOKE. Still, quite a number of great Joker stories went unreprinted; I direct you to Mark Waid's STACKING THE DECK end notes for a discussion of these stories.

The Joker has had a great career, and, undoubtedly, he will continue on in his merry way as long as the comics medium endures. As comics fans, we can take comfort in that.

As human beings, we can take comfort in the fact that the Joker's venue is the comic book page. Real life is scary enough as it is.

The editors would like to offer special thanks to Steven Bové, Joe Desris, Katie Main, Robert Greenberger, Todd Klein, Dick Sprang, Charles Paris, and Greg Theakston for services above and beyond the call.

— Mike Gold
Group Editor and
Director of Development
for DC Comics

Writer: Bill Finger / **Artist:** Bob Kane with Jerry Robinson / **Colorist:** Tatjana Wood

THEN ONCE AGAIN MUSIC....

HENRY, DID YOU HEAR? HENRY CLARIDGE, THE MILLIONAIRE, TO BE KILLED, THE FAMOUS DIAMOND STOLEN!

HAW! THAT'S JUST A GAG-LIKE THAT FELLOW WHO SCARED EVERYBODY WITH THAT STORY ABOUT MARS THE LAST TIME! HA! HA! PAY NO ATTENTION TO IT, DEAR!

RADIO STATIONS ARE SWAMPED WITH CALLS! OFFICIALS DECLARE THE STRANGE MESSAGE IS _NOT_ A PART OF THE PROGRAM, THE 'GAG' HAS BECOME A _REALITY_!

HENRY CLARIDGE, FRANTIC WITH FEAR, CALLS THE POLICE

YOU'VE GOT TO PROTECT ME! I'M GOING TO BE KILLED--ROBBED!

DON'T WORRY, MR. CLARIDGE. YOU AND THAT DIAMOND OF YOURS WILL BE SAFE ENOUGH! WE'LL ALL STAY IN THE SAME ROOM WHERE THE DIAMOND IS KEPT, AND WATCH YOU.

ELEVEN O'CLOCK! ONE HOUR TO GO!

BONG! BONG!

AN INFLEXIBLE CORDON IS FORMED ABOUT THE DOOMED MAN!

TIME DRAGS ON-- SECONDS MINUTES THEN THE FATAL HOUR... TWELVE O'CLOCK!

I'M STILL ALIVE! I'M NOT DEAD! I'M SAFE!...

THE JOKER HAS FULFILLED HIS THREAT, CLARIDGE IS DEAD!!

SLOWLY THE FACIAL MUSCLES PULL THE DEAD MAN'S MOUTH INTO A REPELLENT, GHASTLY GRIN, THE SIGN OF DEATH FROM THE JOKER

THEN WITHOUT WARNING!

..I'M SAAA-- AAGH! AAGH..!

DEAD...IT ISN'T POSSIBLE AND YET...

CHIEF! LOOK! HIS MOUTH!

IT'S...IT'S HORRIBLE!

GROTESQUE! THE JOKER BRINGS DEATH TO HIS VICTIMS WITH A SMILE!

WHAT NOW, CHIEF?

THE CLARIDGE DIAMOND!... IF THE JOKER KILLED CLARIDGE, HE MUST HAVE THE DIAMOND!

BUT HOW COULD HE? WE WERE IN THE ROOM ALL THE TIME!

THE DIAMOND! THE JOKER DIDN'T GET IT AFTER ALL!

HE DID GET IT! THIS IS A PHONEY! IT'S GLASS!

CHIEF! I FOUND SOMETHING IN HERE! IT WAS UNDERNEATH THE CASE!

THE SIGN OF THE JOKER!

NOT FAR AWAY SITS A MAN... A MAN WITH A CHANGELESS, MASK-LIKE FACE-BUT FOR THE EYES, BURNING, HATE-FILLED EYES!

THE CLARIDGE DIAMOND-MINE! THOSE BUNGLING POLICE- HOW THEY WOULD LIKE TO KNOW HOW I MANAGED IT! AND HOW I SHOULD LIKE TO SHOUT THE ANSWER INTO THEIR STUPID FACES!

A SOLUTION INJECTED INTO SLEEPING CLARIDGE AT TWELVE LAST NIGHT... A SOLUTION THAT KILLS IN EXACTLY TWENTY-FOUR HOURS SO THAT HE DIED AT TWELVE TONIGHT!

THEY FIND THE GLASS DIAMOND TO NIGHT, THAT I EXCHANGED FOR THE REAL ONE LAST NIGHT! A PREDICTION ON THE RADIO OF A CRIME THAT HAS ALREADY BEEN DONE!

A MAN SMILES A SMILE WITH-OUT MIRTH...RATHER A SMILE OF DEATH! THE AWESOME, GHASTLY GRIN OF... THE JOKER!!

IF THE POLICE EXPECT TO PLAY AGAINST THE JOKER, THEY HAD BEST BE PREPARED TO BE DEALT FROM THE BOTTOM OF THE DECK!

NEWSPAPERS-RADIOS ALL SCREAM THE STORY OF THE RUTHLESS CUNNING CRIMINAL THE JOKER! AT HOME BRUCE WAYNE, THE BATMAN, SPEAKS WITH HIS YOUNG AID, DICK GRAYSON, KNOWN AS ROBIN, THE BOY WONDER!

BUT BRUCE, WHY DON'T WE TAKE A SHOT AT THIS JOKER GUY?

NOT YET, DICK. THE TIME ISN'T RIPE, BUT WHEN WE DO...

13

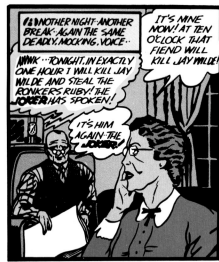

ANOTHER NIGHT. ANOTHER BREAK. AGAIN THE SAME DEADLY, MOCKING VOICE...

AWWK... TONIGHT. IN EXACTLY ONE HOUR I WILL KILL JAY WILDE AND STEAL THE RONKERS RUBY! THE JOKER HAS SPOKEN!

IT'S MINE NOW! AT TEN O'CLOCK THAT FIEND WILL KILL JAY WILDE!

IT'S HIM AGAIN. THE JOKER!

AGAIN A WALL OF HUMANS ENCIRCLES A DOOMED MAN!!

I'M GOING TO DIE! IN FIVE MINUTES I'M GOING TO DIE! DIE! DIE!

THE TOLL OF TIME... THE FATAL HOUR!

TEN! IT'S GOING TO HAPPEN NOW! THE CLOCK IS TICKING MY LIFE AWAY!

BONG BONG

A STRANGLED SCREAM... DEATH!!

AAUGH

...FOLLOWED BY A STRANGE GAS...

FROM THE ARMOR... THE JOKER!!!

LUCKY FOR THE POLICE THAT THE VENOM SPRAY ONLY PARALYSES FOR THE WHILE, ELSE THEY WOULD HAVE PERISHED LIKE WILDE! HE HAD NO SPRAY... BUT A BLOWN DART!

YOU HAD THE CONCENTRATED VENOM ON THE DART, EH WILDE? DIDN'T YOU, EH? ARE YOU SO HAPPY THAT YOU SMILE FOR JOY. EH? I'M GLAD I HAVE BROUGHT YOU SO MUCH CHEER.

THE DIABOLICAL JOKER REMOVES THE ARMOR - STEALS THE RONKERS RUBY.

THANK YOU ALL GENTLEMEN YOU HAVE ME HAPPY TOO! WE SHALL MEET AGAIN!

14

THE POLICE SEARCH EVERYWHERE FOR THE **JOKER** BUT TO NO AVAIL. BUT ANOTHER GROUP IS ALSO INTERESTED THE CRIMINAL! ··A HANGOUT NOTED FOR ITS CRIMINAL ELEMENT··

I TELL YA, BOYS, WE GOTTA GET THIS GUY, THE **JOKER**!

WE GET THE CLARIDGE DIAMOND LINED UP FOR AN EASY JOB AND HE PULLS THE JOB!

YOU'RE RIGHT, BRUTE, HE'S CUTTIN' IN ON OUR RACKET!

AND DON'T FORGET WE WERE GONNA TRY FOR THE RONKER'S RUBY!

WHAT'RE WE GONNA DO, TAKE IT LYIN' DOWN?

I GOT AN IDEA! YOU GUYS GO OUT AND PASS THE WORD AROUND THAT BRUTE NELSON IS GONNA GET THE **JOKER**··THAT HE THINKS THE **JOKER** IS A YELLER RAT!

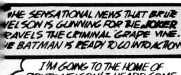

THE SENSATIONAL NEWS THAT BRUTE NELSON IS GUNNING FOR THE **JOKER** TRAVELS THE CRIMINAL "GRAPE VINE". THE **BATMAN** IS READY TO GO INTO ACTION!

I'M GOING TO THE HOME OF BRUTE NELSON! I HEARD SOME NEWS TODAY OVER THE "GRAPEVINE" THAT MAKES ME THINK THE TIME IS RIPE!··

WHERE ARE YOU GOING ALONE?

IT IS NIGHT··BRUTE NELSON SITS IN HIS PRIVATE HOUSE IN THE SUBURBS.

THE **JOKER**, EH. WHEN I GET THROUGH WITH HIM, HE'LL BE A JOKE ALL RIGHT!

SUDDENLY A DRONING DEADLY VOICE, A FUNEREAL FACE·· WITH EYES RADIATING HATE

TALKING ABOUT ME?

THE **JOKER**!

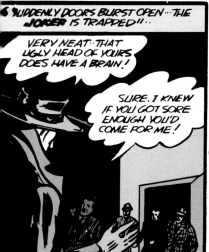

SUDDENLY DOORS BURST OPEN··THE **JOKER** IS TRAPPED"··

VERY NEAT··THAT UGLY HEAD OF YOURS DOES HAVE A BRAIN!

SURE. I KNEW IF YOU GOT SORE ENOUGH YOU'D COME FOR ME!

SUDDENLY THE SCRAPE OF A FOOT IS HEARD UP ON THE STAIR—THE MIGHTY **BATMAN**!

I'M AFRAID I WASN'T AS SILENT AS I HOPED TO BE!

THE **BATMAN**! HOW DID HE GET IN HERE?

THE **JOKER** IS MOMENTARILY FORGOTTEN AS THE **BATMAN** LEAPS DOWN THE STAIRS··

LOOK OUT!!··SHOOT HIM!

15

A HUMAN AVALANCHE STRIKES THE GUNMEN!

RATHER UNSTEADY ON YOUR FEET, AREN'T YOU?

A MASSIVE FIST CRASHES AGAINST A GUNMAN'S JAW!

THE JOKER TAKES ADVANTAGE OF THE FIGHT TO SETTLE AN OLD SCORE.

HAVE A SEAT BOYS! THERE'S ENOUGH ROOM ON THIS CHAIR FOR TWO!

I WON'T EVEN WASTE THE USUAL "JOKER" VENOM ON YOU, BRUTE, BUT GIVE YOU SOMETHING YOU CAN UNDERSTAND! LEAD!

LIKE A JUGGERNAUT THE BATMAN LEAPS AFTER THE RUTHLESS JOKER!!

THAT GUY ISN'T GETTING AWAY IF I CAN HELP IT!

EVEN AS THE CAR STARTS, THE BATMAN IS UPON IT LIKE AN AVENGING BLACK CLOUD!

HASN'T THIS BOY HEARD IT'S LEAP YEAR?

16

IT SEEMS I'VE AT LAST MET A FOE THAT CAN GIVE ME A GOOD FIGHT! HOWEVER I'M NOT LICKED YET!...NOT QUITE!

ONCE MORE THE JOKER DELIVERS HIS MESSAGE OF DOOM!

JUDGE DRAKE, YOU ONCE SENT ME TO PRISON...FOR THAT YOU WILL DIE! DEATH WILL COME AT TEN! THE JOKER HAS SPOKEN!

TWO HOURS!

IT'S NOW EIGHT O'CLOCK!

JUDGE DRAKE'S HOME...

NINE O'CLOCK! ONE MORE HOUR TO LIVE!

LISTEN JUDGE, I'VE GOT MEN POSTED OUTSIDE EVERY DOOR! NO ONE CAN GET IN! RELAX, LET'S PLAY SOME CARDS!

THE MINUTES FLY...

IT'S YOUR BET, JUDGE!

YOU WIN...I NEED THE ACE OF SPADES TO MAKE THE GAME!

THE JOKER!

YOU CAN'T WIN ANYWAY...YOU SEE, I HOLD THE WINNING CARD!

THE JUDGE IS AGHAST AS HE LOOKS AT THE SUPPOSED POLICE CHIEF!

YOU...THE POLICE CHIEF...THE JOKER!

YES! BUT NO! I QUITE THE POLICE CHIEF...THE REAL CHIEF...IS TRUSSED UP IN THE CELLAR! DISGUISE IS ALSO ONE OF MY MANY ACCOMPLISHMENTS!

THE CLOCK TOLLS THE DEATH KNELL FOR ANOTHER VICTIM OF THE JOKER!

TEN O'CLOCK! THE VENOM WORKS WELL! ADIEU, JUDGE...OUR LITTLE GAME IS FINISHED!

THE "POLICE CHIEF" GIVES ORDERS!!

JUDGE DRAKE IS DEAD! THE JOKER HAS WON AGAIN! WATCH THE BODY. I'M GOING TO HEADQUARTERS!

DEAD!...OKAY, CHIEF!

18

(1) BUT AS HE EXITS... HE IS SPIED, ROBIN, THE BOY WONDER!

BATMAN TOLD ME TO FOLLOW ANYONE THAT COMES OUT OF THE JUDGE'S HOUSE- SO HERE GOES!

(2) ROBIN TRAILS THE MAN TO AN OLD DESERTED HOUSE!

...GOING INTO THAT HOUSE!

THE BOLD YOUNG DARE DEVIL ENTERS THE SINISTER DWELLING!!...

CHEERFUL PLACE... I DON'T THINK!

IT'S QUIET...ALMOST TOO QUIET!

(4) CRUSHING BLOW FROM BEHIND!

SNOOPER, EH?

(3) BUT WHAT OF THE BATMAN? ...THE BATMAN, OUTSIDE OF THE JUDGE'S HOUSE, INSPECTS THE SCENE OF THE JOKER'S LATEST MURDER...

ROBIN...GONE...MUST HAVE FOLLOWED A LEAD! I'LL USE THE INFRA-RED LAMP!

(2) RED LIGHT FLASHES OVER THE GROUND...MIRACULOUSLY ROBIN'S FOOTSTEPS GLOW IN THE DARK!

THIS INVENTION OF MINE WILL COME IN HANDY NOW!

THE SOLES OF BOTH ROBIN AND THE BATMAN'S BOOTS ARE TREATED WITH A LUMINOUS CHEMICAL THAT GLOWS ONLY IN THE LIGHT OF THE INFRA-RED RAY!

NOW WE'LL SEE WHERE ROBIN WENT!

19

20

: BUT THE **JOKER** HAS NOT RECKONED WITH THE AMAZING RECUPERATIVE POWERS OF THE MIGHTY **BATMAN!**

ROBIN...TIED...GOT TO GET OUT OF HERE!

AN ESCAPE FROM A FIERY DEATH!

A FEW MOMENTS LATER...

THE **JOKER** IS GONE! I'D GIVE ANYTHING TO KNOW WHERE!

HE BOASTED INSIDE THAT HE WAS GOING TO GET THE CLEOPATRA NECKLACE NEXT!

THE CLEOPATRA NECKLACE!...THAT'S OWNED BY OTTO DREXEL! ...C'MON. THERE'S NOT A MOMENT TO LOSE...WITH A MANIAC ON THE LOOSE!

OTTO DREXEL LIVES ON THE PENTHOUSE IN THAT BUILDING ACROSS THE STREET!

IF WE CAN ONLY GET UP THERE BEFORE THE **JOKER** DOES!

ON THE PENTHOUSE, THE **JOKER** PREPARES TO ENTER.

BUT LEAPING FROM THE SCAFFOLD, THE COWLED **BATMAN**.

STILL AT IT, EH?

21

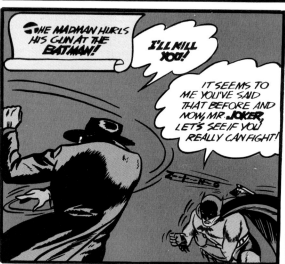

22

THE SMASHING KICK SENDS THE JOKER FLYING OFF THE SCAFFOLDING!

AS THE FRANTIC MAN FALLS PAST THE PENTHOUSE BALUSTRADE, A HAND REACHES OUT...

AAGH! I'M FALLING!

OH NO YOU'RE NOT!

THE STRONG ARM OF THE BATMAN HAULS HIM BACK TO SAFETY!

YOU'RE TOO VALUABLE A PRIZE TO LOSE!

YOU PLAYED YOUR LAST HAND, JOKER!

FINAL BLOW WITH ALL THE STRENGTH OF THE BATMAN BEHIND IT!!

NEXT DAY

DAILY STAR   2¢
FINAL
BATMAN CAPTURES JOKER
LEAVES JOKER I FRONT OF POLIC STATION, DRIVES A

UT WHAT I'D IKE TO KNOW S HOW HIS CTIMS' MOUTHS IRNED UP IN HAT TERRIBLE GRIN!!

SOME SORT OF DRUG THAT PULLED THE MUSCLES OF THE FACE! THE JOKER WAS A CLEVER BUT DIABOLICAL KILLER! TOO CLEVER AND TOO DEADLY TO BE FREE!

BUT EVEN AS BRUCE SPEAKS, AT THE STATE PRISON, THE JOKER IS PLANNING, PLOTTING FOR HIS ESCAPE!

THEY CAN'T KEEP ME HERE! I KNOW OF A WAY OUT—THE JOKER WILL YET HAVE THE LAST LAUGH!

BOB KANE

THE Amazing BATMAN

AMERICA'S MOST FAMOUS ADVENTURE-STRIP CHARACTER... WITH THAT SENSATIONAL NEW DISCOVERY, THAT LAUGHING YOUNG DARE-DEVIL

Robin THE BOY WONDER

WILL THRILL YOU EVERY MONTH WITH THEIR ASTOUNDING EXPLOITS IN DETECTIVE COMICS

23

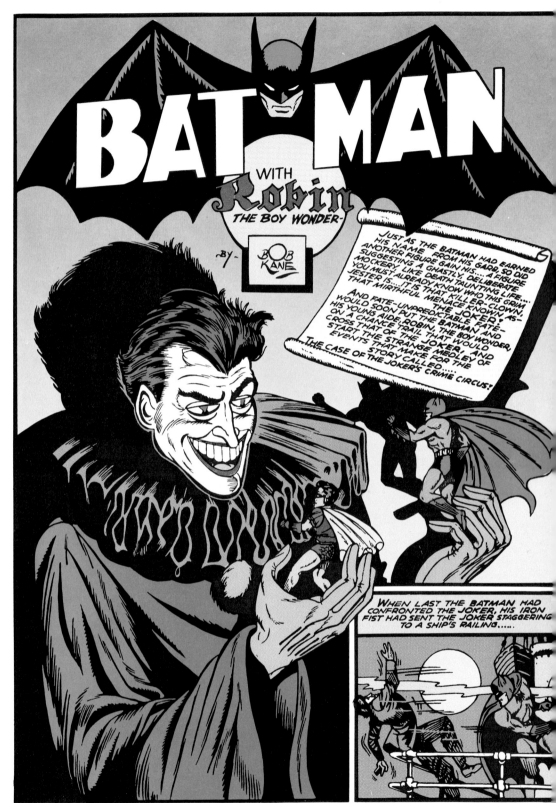

Writer: Bill Finger / Artist: Bob Kane with Jerry Robinson / Colorist: Adrienne Roy

.....THE JOKER PLUMMETED DOWN TO HIT THE WATERS AND REMAIN BELOW......

I WONDER IF THIS IS REALLY THE END OF THE JOKER AT LAST?

.....AS THE LIGHTS OF THE SHIP TWINKLE LIKE FIREFLIES IN THE DISTANCE, A FIGURE RISES TO THE SURFACE OF THE WATER... IT IS THE JOKER!

.....HOURS LATER, A YACHT MAKES OUT HIS BOBBING FORM...

MAN AHEAD, SIR—LOOKS LIKE HE'S CLINGING TO A BIT OF DRIFTWOOD!

GIVE THE NECESSARY ORDER TO PICK HIM UP!

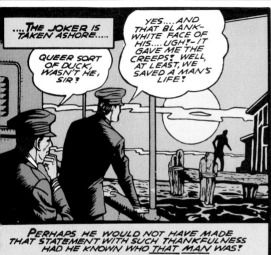

.....THE JOKER IS TAKEN ASHORE.....

QUEER SORT OF DUCK, WASN'T HE, SIR?

YES.... AND THAT BLANK-WHITE FACE OF HIS.....UGH!—IT GAVE ME THE CREEPS! WELL, AT LEAST, WE SAVED A MAN'S LIFE!

PERHAPS HE WOULD NOT HAVE MADE THAT STATEMENT WITH SUCH THANKFULNESS HAD HE KNOWN WHO THAT MAN WAS!

UNOBSERVED, HE STEALS TO THE EDGE OF TOWN TO A SEEMINGLY DESERTED, GLOOMY OLD MANSION DUBBED BY THE PEOPLE AS "HAUNTED".....

BUT THE STRANGE-LOOKING MANSION IS NOT REALLY "HAUNTED" AND DESERTED..... IN REALITY, IT IS THE HIDDEN SANCTUM OF THE JOKER...

.....THEN, THE JOKER LAUGHS. A WILD, JEERING LAUGH THAT MAKES THE VERY SILENCE OF THE ROOM CRAWL WITH MENACE...

I'M ALIVE! HA HA! I'M ALIVE! HA HA HA HA!

THE CLEVEREST AND THE MOST DANGEROUS CRIMINAL IN THE ANNALS OF CRIME WAS STILL AT LIBERTY!

THE BATMAN THINKS I'M DEAD. HE'LL KNOW DIFFERENTLY WHEN WE MEET AGAIN! ..... AND WE SHALL MEET AGAIN!

THE TIME WAS CLOSE WHEN NEW FACTORS WOULD BRING ABOUT AN ACTUAL DUEL BETWEEN THE BATMAN AND THE JOKER!

25

TWO MONTHS PASS

As night makes her entrance wearing her garments of blackness, two figures dart through the dark of her shadow....

② Suddenly, they see.....

LOOK, ROBIN!

THREE MASKED MEN! — THIEVES!

③ The three men bend their knees as soon as they hit the ground, and roll over.....

④ THEY ROLLED OVER TO ABSORB THE SHOCK OF HITTING THE GROUND.

JUST LIKE PROFESSIONAL ACROBATS WOULD DO IT!

⑤ The two crime-fighters strike!

PERHAPS YOU'RE NOT AWARE OF IT.... BUT THERE'S A LAW AGAINST STEALING!

⑥ As they battle, they do not notice the huge, hulking form that comes from the car parked nearby.....

A WEEK LATER, ANOTHER RICH HOME IS ROBBED...

GOTHAM CITY GAZETTE

VAN PLATT HOM ROBBED......

FIFTH RICH HOME LOOT IN LATEST ROBBERY EPIDEMIC

THOSE MYSTERIOUS BURGLARS, WHO HAVE BEEN STRIKING AT THE SOCIETY RICH THIS PAST MONTH, BRAZENLY ENTERED THE VAN PLATT MANSION VAN LAST NIGHT......

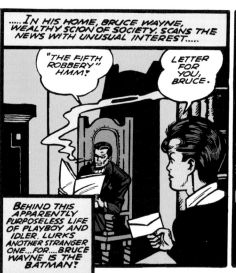

.....IN HIS HOME, BRUCE WAYNE, WEALTHY SCION OF SOCIETY, SCANS THE NEWS WITH UNUSUAL INTEREST.....

"THE FIFTH ROBBERY" HMM!

LETTER FOR YOU, BRUCE.

BEHIND THIS APPARENTLY PURPOSELESS LIFE OF PLAYBOY AND IDLER, LURKS ANOTHER STRANGER ONE...FOR....BRUCE WAYNE IS THE BATMAN!

THE LETTER...

You are cordially invited to attend a ball to be given this Saturday at eight o'clock
... and to
C.K. Darcey —

ACCORDINGLY.....THAT SATURDAY NIGHT......

AH, BRUCE — GLAD YOU COULD COME!

WILD HORSES COULDN'T KEEP ME AWAY, DARCEY.

BRUCE SEEMS TO GO OUT OF HIS WAY TO PROVE HE IS THE NO. 1 CANDIDATE FOR THE "IDLE RICH, BORED WITH LIFE —CLUB."....

THERE'S BRUCE, YAWNING AS USUAL! JUST LOOK AT HIM!

HE HAS NO MORE BRAINS IN HIS HEAD THAN THE HEAD OF HIS WALKING STICK HAS!

...SUDDENLY, THERE IS A ROLL ON THE DRUMS, AND DARCEY ADDRESSES HIS GUESTS...

FRIENDS — NOW I HAVE A TREAT IN STORE FOR YOU! THE BALL ROOM WILL BE CLEARED AND YOU WILL BE GIVEN SEATS SO THAT YOU MAY WATCH A CIRCUS!

....A MINIATURE CIRCUS SHOW IS PUT ON IN THE BALLROOM... ACROBATS PERFORM.

A STRONG MAN BENDS IRON BARS AND LIFTS TREMENDOUS WEIGHTS...

AJAX...THE STRONGEST, MIGHTIEST MAN IN THE WORLD!

REPLETE WITH ACROBATS, STRONG MAN, TRAPEZE ARTISTS, CLOWN, THE CIRCUS IS A HOWLING SUCCESS.....

HA HA!

HA HA!

ODD, HOW THAT CLOWN REMINDS ME OF SOMEONE!

THAT NIGHT, WHEN THEIR ENGAGEMENT ENDS, THE CIRCUS TROUPE TOILS UP THE LONELY ROAD THAT LEADS TO THE "HAUNTED HOUSE".....

INSIDE, THE PERFORMERS RID THEMSELVES OF MAKE-UP.... ESPECIALLY THE CLOWN....

EVERY TIME I DO THIS, IT REMINDS ME OF THAT OLD SONG THAT GOES " AT NIGHT I LAY MY MASK ON THE SHELF AND SEE MYSELF AS I REALLY AM!...."

.....BE A PUNCHINELLO... LAUGH, CLOWN, LAUGH! HA HA HA!

UNDER THE HUMOROUS MAKE-UP IS THE REAL CLOWN...THE KILLER~CLOWN....THE JOKER!......

..... AND EXACTLY THREE DAYS LATER....

BRUCE! BRUCE! THE DARCEYS- THE PEOPLE WHOSE PARTY YOU WENT TO-THEY'VE BEEN ROBBED!

WH-AT? THAT MAKES THE SIXTH RICH FAMILY ROBBED THIS MONTH!

BRUCE INVESTIGATES, AND AT THE END OF THE DAY ANNOUNCES S FINDINGS AND SUSPICIONS TO DICK....

..YOU MEAN O SAY YOU'VE FOUND OUT THAT EVERY RICH HOME HAT HAS BEEN OBBED HAS HAD HIS CIRCUS PLAY V ENGAGEMENT AT THEIR HOUSE?

YES .... AND REMEMBER WHEN WE HAD THAT RUN-IN THE OTHER NIGHT?.. THE CROOKS HOPPED AROUND LIKE PROFESSIONAL ACROBATS!

.... AND ONE WAS STRONG LIKE THE STRONG MAN OF A CIRCUS! NOW, WHAT'S TO PREVENT THIS CROOKED CIRCUS FROM PLAYING A RICH HOME AND "CASING" IT FOR A FUTURE ROBBERY? LOGICAL, ISN'T IT?

GOSH! THE SOCIETY COLUMN SAYS "THE MORGANBILTS' PARTY TONIGHT WILL FEATURE THE MINIATURE CIRCUS THAT IS THE CURRENT RAGE OF SOCIETY!"

WE CAN'T TELL WHEN THEY'LL STRIKE, SO WE'VE GOT TO PREVENT A FUTURE CRIME! DICK, WE'RE STEPPING OUT... TONIGHT!

THAT NIGHT.....IN THE "HAUNTED HOUSE"...... THE LAIR OF THE JOKER......

TONIGHT, WE PLAY THE MORGANBILT HOME. LOOK THE PLACE OVER, FIND OUT WHERE THEY HAVE THEIR SAFE HIDDEN. WORK FAST!

THIS IS TINO. HE HAS JUST JOINED UP WITH US. HE'LL BE OUR SURPRISE GUEST TONIGHT! NOW LET'S GO!

SO WAS THE STAGE SET, WITH THE BATMAN, ROBIN AND THE JOKER, TO BE THE PRINCIPAL PLAYERS!

EVENING, AT THE MORGANBIL HOME...... THE JOKER'S CRIM CIRCUS HOLDS THE CENTER C INTEREST......

THE HARLEQUIN OF HATE STEPS FORWARD.....

......AND NOW WE HAVE A SURPRISE FOR YOU. WE PRESENT....

RA TA TA-TA!

FANFARE, PLEASE!

LOOK! THE BATMAN!

AND ROBIN, THE BOY WONDER!

....AND AS IF ON CUE, THE DYNAMIC DUO LEAPS INTO THE ROOM......

LOOK! THEY'RE PUTTING ON AN ACT!

MAKING BELIEVE HE IS AFRAID, THE BOY WONDER RACES AWAY, FOLLOWED BY THE ACROBATS, AND....

"SWING", EH, CHUMS?

MIGHT WORK AGAIN!

AGAIN HE SIMULATES FEAR, RACES UP A LADDER AND IS FOLLOWED BY THE TRAPEZE ARTISTS.....

WITH A QUICK HOP, THE BOY WONDER SLIDES THROUGH THE LADDER RUNGS, GRASPS THE ANKLES OF HIS NEAREST PURSUERS, AND.....

ELEVATOR-GOING DOWN!

MEANWHILE, THE BATMAN HAS BEEN SINGLED OUT FOR COMBAT BY AJAX, THE STRONG MAN!

YOU-AGAIN? I MAKE SURE I KILL YOU THIS TIME!

COME AHEAD, BIG BOY!

31

32

WITH A SUDDEN, QUICK HEAVE OF HIS ARMS, THE BATMAN SLAMS THE GIANT BODY TO THE GROUND.....

....THE JOKER CHOOSES THAT MOMENT TO EFFECT HIS ESCAPE......

THE CLOWN?— NOW I KNOW WHY HE REMINDED ME OF SOMEONE.... HE'S THE JOKER-- ALIVE!

LOOK! THAT CLOWN—HE'S GETTING AWAY!

ONCE AGAIN, THE DARK KNIGHT HAS GIVEN PROOF OF THE OLD ADAGE......BRUTE STRENGTH CANNOT AVAIL AGAINST A QUICK MIND AND A QUICK BODY.

THE AUDIENCE LEARNS THE TRUTH...

...AND IF THE POLICE WILL QUESTION THESE MEN, YOU'LL FIND THIS ENTIRE CIRCUS IS RESPONSIBLE FOR THESE ROBBERIES!

DID YOU HEAR THAT?

NO WONDER THAT FIGHT LOOKED SO REAL!

C'MON, ROBIN!

KEEPING THE JOKER'S CAR IN SIGHT, THE BATMAN AND ROBIN FOLLOW HIM TO HIS LAIR!.....

SO, THIS IS HIS HIDEOUT!

SAY— THIS IS THE "HAUNTED HOUSE!"

AS THE BATMAN AND ROBIN DASH UP THE WINDING PATH, A FACE PEERS OUT AT THEM .....THE JOKER!

SO, THEY'RE COMING IN, ARE THEY? I'LL FIX THEM. I'LL SCARE THEM JUST AS I SCARE THE VILLAGERS WHEN THEY PRY INTO THIS HOUSE! HA HA HA!

AS THE BATMAN AND ROBIN ENTER THE MYSTERIOUS HOUSE, THE MASSIVE DOOR SUDDENLY SWINGS SHUT BEHIND THEM!

THE DOOR— LOCKED ITSELF!

SLAM!

THE TWO MOUNT CREAKY, OLD STAIRS.....

PLEASANT LITTLE PLACE, ISN'T IT?

YES— IT MAKES A LOVELY BREEDING GROUND FOR GHOSTS!

33

34

......THE BATMAN SLAMS HIS POWERFUL FRAME AT THE DOOR AGAIN AND AGAIN...... BUT IT DOES NOT EVEN BUDGE?

THIS DOOR — IT MUST BE STEEL, PAINTED TO LOOK LIKE WOOD? IT WON'T GIVE AN INCH!

SUDDENLY, THE LIGHTS GO OUT AND A SMALL LUMINOUS FACE GLOWS IN THE DARKNESS.... A WHISPERED LAUGH FILTERS THROUGH THE ROOM......

NOW WHAT?

HA HA HA HA

THE HEAD, HANGING DISEMBODIED IN THE DARKNESS, GROWS LARGER..... THE SNEERING LAUGH GROWS LOUDER.....

HA HA HA HA

JOKER!

LARGER, LARGER SWELLS THE EERIE, MISTY FACE, UNTIL IT SEEMS TO FILL THE VERY ROOM....THE MAD LAUGHTER GROWS LOUDER, LOUDER.....IT THUNDERS, POUNDS AT THE BATMAN'S EARDRUMS......

HA HA HA HA HA HA

WITH STARTLING SUDDENNESS THE BATMAN WHIRLS AND LEAPS AT THE WALL BEHIND HIM........

HE TEARS DOWN AN OBJECT FASTENED TO THE WALL....

I THOUGHT SO...... A MOTION PICTURE PROJECTOR THAT THREW THE IMAGE OF THE JOKER'S FACE ON THE WALL.... AND THERE MUST BE MICROPHONES HIDDEN ABOUT TO SEND OUT THAT LAUGH!

THEN, A VOICE....A SINISTER, MOCKING VOICE....THE VOICE OF THE JOKER!

QUITE RIGHT, BATMAN? AND NOW LISTEN, BATMAN— LISTEN FOR THE HISS OF GAS? IT MARKS YOUR END.... YOUR END?.... HA-HA-HA...

GAS? I'VE GOT TO GET OUT OF HERE!

THE BATMAN TAKES TWO PARTICULAR VIALS FROM HIS UTILITY BELT.....

35

PLACING THE CONTENTS OF ONE VIAL INTO THE OTHER, HE THROWS THE PELLET AT THE WALL....THERE IS A SHATTERING BLAST!....

THE BATMAN DARTS THROUGH THE RENT IN THE WALL TO SEE......THE JOKER AND ROBIN!

JUST IN TIME, EH, JOKER?

BATMAN!

CRIME-SMASHER AND ARCH-CRIMINAL MEET IN COMBAT!

I'LL MAKE SURE YOU DIE THIS TIME!

FIGHTING WITH MANIACAL FURY, THE JOKER UNLEASHES A BLOW THAT STUNS EVEN THE MIGHTY BATMAN....

AS THE JOKER LEAPS FORWARD, THE BATMAN THRUSTS UP HIS FEET IN A LIGHTNING MOVE....

....THE JOKER IS SENT SAILING OVER THE BATMAN'S HEAD.....

...AND DROPS INTO THE OPEN TRAP-DOOR.....DOWN....DOWN GOES THE JOKER, TO PLUNGE DEEP INTO THE SEWAGE WATERS RUNNING BENEATH THE MANSION!

PERHAPS....PERHAPS.... BUT HE ALWAYS SEEMS TO HAVE A WAY OF CHEATING DEATH! WELL.....IT'S ALL OVER ANYWAY. LET'S GO HOME!

LOOKS LIKE THE JOKER WON'T GET OUT OF THIS SO EASY!

THE END

IS THE JOKER ALIVE? IF THE PATH OF THE BATMAN AND THE JOKER CROSS AGAIN-WELL, THAT WILL BE ANOTHER STORY!

COPYRIGHT 1945 BY DETECTIVE COMICS, INC.
DIST. BY McClure NEWSPAPER SYNDICATE

BATMAN *AND ROBIN*

HA-HA! CLEVEREST IN GOTHAM, EH? THE FOOLS!

Gotham Gazette
UNKNOWN PUBLIC ENEMY BEHIND NEW CRIME WAVE BAFFLES POLICE

"THE SPARROW" DUBBED CLEVEREST CRIMINAL IN GOTHAM

IN A DISMAL CAGE SITS THE JOKER, FAMED CLOWN OF CRIME, AND BATMAN'S BITTEREST FOE, SCANNING THE LATEST STARTLING NEWS FROM THE OUTSIDE WORLD...

I'LL SHOW THIS UPSTART WHO'S THE REAL CRIME KING IN GOTHAM. LET'S SEE—A CODED LETTER TO FRIENDS OUTSIDE AND THE STAGE IS SET...

OH, GUARD!

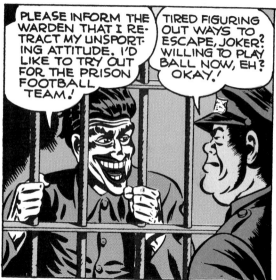

PLEASE INFORM THE WARDEN THAT I RETRACT MY UNSPORTING ATTITUDE. I'D LIKE TO TRY OUT FOR THE PRISON FOOTBALL TEAM!

TIRED FIGURING OUT WAYS TO ESCAPE, JOKER? WILLING TO PLAY BALL NOW, EH? OKAY!

SEVERAL DAYS LATER....

FROM THE POINT OF VIEW OF THIS IDIOTIC GAME, A POOR KICK! FROM MY POINT OF VIEW, PERFECT!

WHAT A HEADACHE! I GOTTA GO CHASE THE BALL!

Artists: Jack Burnley and Charles Paris / Colorist: Nansi Hoolahan

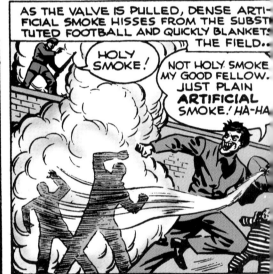

BATMAN
ROBIN
by BOB KANE

GENTLEMEN—NOW THAT I'M BACK, THE MYTH OF THIS MYSTERIOUS SPARROW'S SUPERIORITY IN CRIME SHALL BE ABRUPTLY SHATTERED!

IT'S ME—MINCEMEAT MULLIGAN. I GOT A MESSAGE FER DA JOKER.

HIS CRIMINAL REPUTATION AT STAKE BECAUSE OF WIDELY PUBLICIZED CRIMES OF "THE SPARROW", THE JOKER, FAMED FOE OF THE BATMAN, HAS JUST ENGINEERED A SUCCESSFUL JAIL BREAK...
105

MY BOSS, THE SPARROW, SENT ME TO BRING YA TO THE HIDEOUT. THE SPARROW THINKS YOU GOT TALENT AND WOULD LIKE TO PLACE YA IN THE ORGANIZATION!

WHAT COLOSSAL NERVE! SHOW THIS FOOL OUT—ON HIS EAR!!

PRESENTLY, IN ANOTHER PART OF TOWN...

AND DA JOKER DID NOT TAKE KINDLY TO YER OFFER, SPARROW. I T'INK HIS PRIDE WUZ HOIT.

I'LL SHOW THAT GRINNING COMEDIAN! I'LL MAKE HIM A PUBLIC LAUGHING-STOCK FOR REFUSING ME!

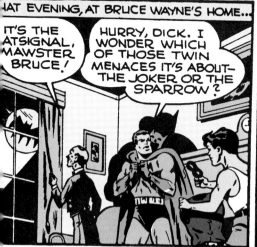

THAT EVENING, AT BRUCE WAYNE'S HOME...

IT'S THE BATSIGNAL, MAWSTER BRUCE!

HURRY, DICK. I WONDER WHICH OF THOSE TWIN MENACES IT'S ABOUT—THE JOKER OR THE SPARROW?

SHORTLY AFTER...

IT CAME THROUGH THE WINDOW TEN MINUTES AGO!

Dear Batman:
At precisely 10 tonight, I will steal Sascha Dreibitz' Stradivarius as he plays before a full house at the Concert Hall.
affectionately,
THE JOKER.

I'VE POSTED MEN ALL AROUND THE CONCERT HALL. EVEN PLANTED A FEW IN THE ORCHESTRA. HE'LL NEVER GET AWAY WITH IT.

JUST THE SAME, HE'LL TRY. THE JOKER ALWAYS KEEPS HIS WORD. I'LL BE THERE, IN ANY CASE...

LATER...

I DON'T UNDERSTAND. ALREADY FIVE PAST TEN AND NO JOKER! IT ISN'T LIKE HIM!

MAYBE HE REALIZED HE BIT OFF MORE THAN HE COULD CHEW THIS TIME..

BATMAN—A LITTLE LAUNDRY WAS JUST HELD UP AROUND THE CORNER. THE THIEF GOT AWAY WITH EIGHT SHIRTS. AND HE LEFT THIS.'

THE JOKER'S CARD! BUT—BUT I CAN'T BELIEVE IT. UNLESS HE REALLY LOST HIS NERVE!

WHY NOT? IT'S HAPPENED TO OTHER CROOKS. HE MUST'VE GOTTEN COLD FEET ON THE WAY AND PICKED ON SOMETHING NEARBY INSTEAD.

HA-HA! MAYBE HE DIDN'T WANT TO MAKE A PUBLIC APPEARANCE IN A DIRTY SHIRT!

— Gotham Gazette —

JOKER GETS COLD FEET, SCORNS STRAD FOR CLEAN SHIRTS!

LAUNDRY STICK-UP IS ANTI-CLIMAX TO BREAK OF MAJOR CRIME

I'VE BEEN FRAMED! I NEVER SENT THAT NOTE! I WASN'T NEAR THAT LAUNDRY! THE SPARROW! HE'S TRYING TO MAKE A FOOL OF ME! I'LL SETTLE WITH HIM IF IT'S THE LAST THING I DO!!

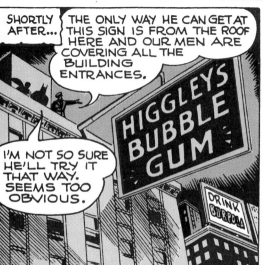

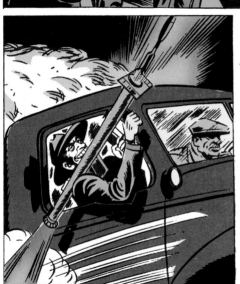

43

46

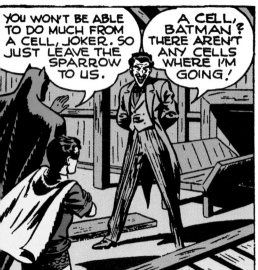

FORTUNATELY FOR ME, I KNOW THE CONSTRUCTION OF THIS OLD MILL FROM PREVIOUS EXPERIENCE.

LISTEN TO THEM SPLASHING ABOUT TRYING TO SAVE ME FROM DROWNING. HA-HA!

HA-HA! BY THE TIME THEY FIGURE OUT HOW I GOT OUT OF THE WATER, I'LL BE FAR, FAR AWAY!

THAT EVENING AT BRUCE WAYNE'S HOME...

SOME FUN—THE WAY THE JOKER GAVE US THE SLIP TODAY! BETWEEN HIM AND THE SPARROW WE'LL NEVER BE ABLE TO REST!

MAYBE IT'S JUST AS WELL HE DID ESCAPE, DICK.

HUH? WHAT DO YOU MEAN?

WELL— IN THIS CASE, IT TAKES A THIEF TO CATCH A THIEF! WITH THE JOKER STILL AT LARGE, WE'RE IN A POSITION TO LET HIM AND THE SPARROW HELP CATCH EACH OTHER! LISTEN..

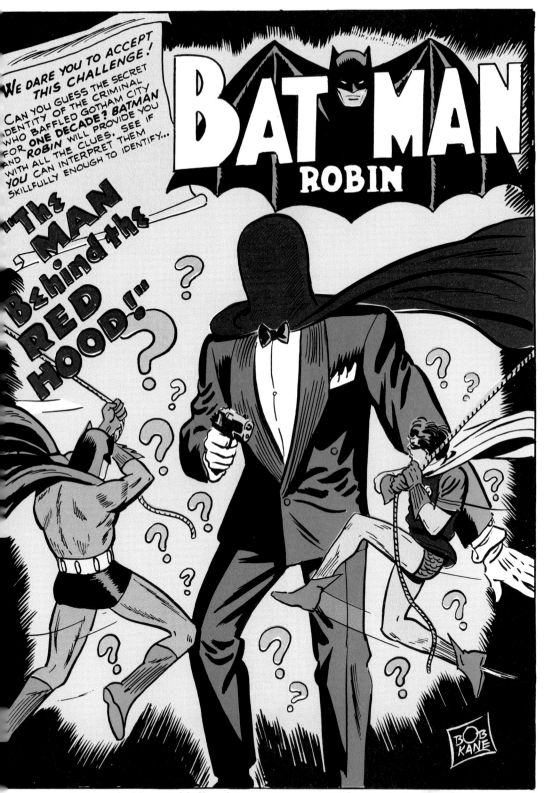

Artists: Sheldon Moldoff and George Roussos / Colorist: Anthony Tollin

NIGHTTIME IN GOTHAM CITY--AND TWO MANTLED FIGURES PLUMMET TOWARD THE ROOF OF POLICE HEADQUARTERS IN ANSWER TO THE *BAT-SIGNAL!*

BATMAN AND *ROBIN*, I WANT YOU TO MEET DEAN CHALMERS OF *STATE UNIVERSITY!* HE HAS A FAVOR TO ASK OF YOU!

YES, GENTLEMEN... THIS TERM, THE UNIVERSITY IS STARTING A COURSE IN *CRIMINOLOGY*, AND WE'D BE HONORED TO HAVE *YOU, BATMAN* AS *GUEST INSTRUCTOR!*

NEXT MORNING, AS *BATMAN'S* TALL FIGURE STRIDES ACROSS THE COLLEGE CAMPUS...

BOY, LOOK AT THOSE SHOULDERS ON *BATMAN!* WHAT A FULLBACK HE'D MAKE!

(SIGH) GOLLY, I'M SORRY I DIDN'T SIGN UP FOR THAT COURSE! (SIGH) ISN'T HE DIVINE?

TO UNDERSTAND HIS CLASS BETTER, *BATMAN* STARTS BY INTERVIEWING EACH STUDENT PRIVATELY!...

PAUL WONG, WHY DID YOU PICK THIS COURSE?

MY FAMILY LIVES IN HAWAII! SOMEDAY I HOPE TO BE A *MEDICAL EXAMINER* ON THE HAWAII POLICE DEPARTMENT!

YES, EACH STUDENT HAS HIS REASON, LIKE JIMMY KALE, FOR EXAMPLE...

MY FATHER WAS *CHIPS KALE, THE GANGSTER!* I SWORE I'D MAKE IT UP TO SOCIETY BY TAKING THE PLACE OF THE F.B.I. MAN HE ONCE KILLED! IT'S A DEBT I MUST PAY OFF!

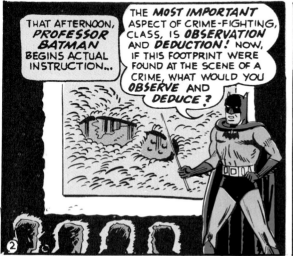

THAT AFTERNOON, *PROFESSOR BATMAN* BEGINS ACTUAL INSTRUCTION...

THE *MOST IMPORTANT* ASPECT OF CRIME-FIGHTING, CLASS, IS *OBSERVATION* AND *DEDUCTION!* NOW, IF THIS FOOTPRINT WERE FOUND AT THE SCENE OF A CRIME, WHAT WOULD YOU *OBSERVE* AND *DEDUCE?*

OBSERVATION: THE HEEL PRINT IS *UNCOMMONLY DEEP* WHEREAS THE SOLE PRINT IS *VERY LIGHT!* DEDUCTION: THE CRIMINAL TRIED TO FOOL THE POLICE BY WALKING AWAY *BACKWARD!*

RIGHT, JIMMY!

2

STUDY THIS PHOTOGRAPH! THE MAN, A GANGSTER, WAS FOUND DEAD! WAS HE A SUICIDE OR A MURDER VICTIM? **OBSERVE** AND **DEDUCE!**

OBSERVATION: THE **GUN HOLSTER** IS ON THE **RIGHT** SHOULDER, THEREFORE THE GANGSTER MUST BE **LEFT HANDED!** DEDUCTION: HE WAS **MURDERED!** HIS KILLER MADE THE MISTAKE OF PUTTING THE GUN IN HIS **RIGHT HAND!**

VERY GOOD, PAUL! WHAT ELSE?

DID I MISS ANYTHING?

YES! OBSERVATION: ALL THE CIGARETTES HAVE SMOOTH ENDS, EXCEPT **THIS ONE!** ITS **END IS CRIMPED!** DEDUCTION: IT WAS SMOKED BY HIS KILLER-- WHO USED A **CIGARETTE HOLDER!**

IN THE DAYS THAT FOLLOW, THE CLASS LEARNS MORE AND MORE TRICKS ABOUT CRIME FIGHTING...

WRAPPING A HANDKERCHIEF AROUND A MURDER GUN MIGHT SMUDGE FINGERPRINTS! THE **CORRECT** WAY TO LIFT THE GUN IS BY POKING A **PENCIL INTO THE MUZZLE!**

AND ONE MONTH LATER...

NOW, CLASS, YOU'RE READY FOR A **TEST CASE** --AN ACTUAL CRIME THAT EVEN **I** NEVER SOLVED! IN FACT, THE CRIMINAL WAS NEVER CAUGHT! HE CALLED HIMSELF -- **THE RED HOOD!**

"IT HAPPENED **TEN YEARS AGO!** HIS CRIMES STIRRED GOTHAM CITY, AND ALL HIS VICTIMS TOLD THE SAME STORY..."

HE WORE A HOOD OVER HIS HEAD! IT WAS RED, SHINY AND SMOOTH-- ALL **ONE PIECE!** IT DIDN'T EVEN HAVE CUTOUTS FOR **EYE HOLES!**

BUT THAT'S CRAZY! HOW COULD THE GUY **SEE?**

③

NEXT DAY, BATMAN'S STUDENTS MAKE FRONT PAGE NEWS...

SAY, LISTEN TO THIS-- "*BATMAN CRIME CLASS REOPENS RED HOOD CASE*"!

"*STUDENTS PROBE TEN-YEAR MYSTERY*"! GEE, WE CERTAINLY HIT THE HEADLINES!

AND THAT NIGHT, TWO BRILLIANT STUDENT SLEUTHS ANALYZE CRIME CLUES...

I MAY HAVE THE ANSWER TO HOW HE COULD *SEE THROUGH* HIS METAL HOOD!

I'VE ADDED THE AMOUNT OF MONEY HE STOLE, AND IT TOTALS *$1,000,000!* PAUL, I'VE A HUNCH THE *RED HOOD IS STILL ALIVE!*

AT THAT MOMENT, NEAR THE COLLEGE CASHIER'S OFFICE, A FANTASTIC FIGURE APPEARS... A FIGURE NOT SEEN IN A DECADE!

TH-THAT MASK-- THE ONE *BATMAN* TALKED ABOUT! Y-YOU'RE *THE RED HOOD!*

SMART FELLOW... NOW, IF YOU WANT TO LIVE, LET ME AT THE SAFE HOLDING THE *COLLEGE PAYROLL!*

BURSAR'S OFFICE

I ADMIRE YOUR COURAGE, WATCHMAN, BUT NOT YOUR STUPIDITY!

NO, I WON'T... OH-H-H...

CLANG CLANG CLANG CLANG

AS THE ALARM BELL RESOUNDS THROUGH THE CAMPUS, *BATMAN* AND *ROBIN* RESPOND SWIFTLY...

THERE GOES SOMEBODY, *BATMAN!* I'LL TAKE CARE OF HIM!

BUT WHEN *ROBIN* SWINGS AT THE SHADOWY FIGURE...

MY SUNDAY PUNCH, STRANGER! OWW! MY FIST!

CLANG!

55

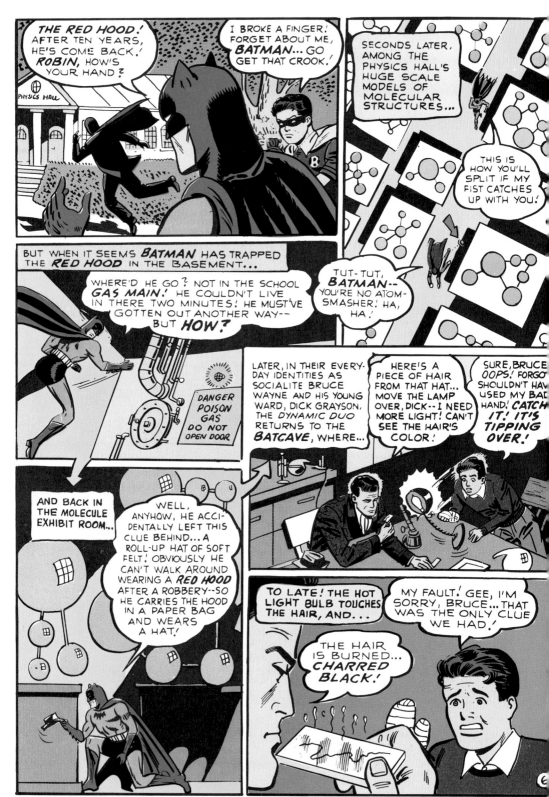

THE RED HOOD! AFTER TEN YEARS, HE'S COME BACK! ROBIN, HOW'S YOUR HAND?

PHYSICS HALL

I BROKE A FINGER! FORGET ABOUT ME, BATMAN... GO GET THAT CROOK!

SECONDS LATER, AMONG THE PHYSICS HALL'S HUGE SCALE MODELS OF MOLECULAR STRUCTURES...

THIS IS HOW YOU'LL SPLIT IF MY FIST CATCHES UP WITH YOU!

BUT WHEN IT SEEMS BATMAN HAS TRAPPED THE RED HOOD IN THE BASEMENT...

WHERE'D HE GO? NOT IN THE SCHOOL GAS MAIN! HE COULDN'T LIVE IN THERE TWO MINUTES! HE MUST'VE GOTTEN OUT ANOTHER WAY-- BUT HOW?

TUT-TUT, BATMAN-- YOU'RE NO ATOM-SMASHER! HA, HA!

DANGER POISON GAS DO NOT OPEN DOOR

LATER, IN THEIR EVERY-DAY IDENTITIES AS SOCIALITE BRUCE WAYNE AND HIS YOUNG WARD, DICK GRAYSON, THE DYNAMIC DUO RETURNS TO THE BATCAVE, WHERE...

HERE'S A PIECE OF HAIR FROM THAT HAT... MOVE THE LAMP OVER, DICK-- I NEED MORE LIGHT! CAN'T SEE THE HAIR'S COLOR!

SURE, BRUCE OOPS! FORGO SHOULDN'T HAV USED MY BAD HAND! CATCH IT! IT'S TIPPING OVER!

AND BACK IN THE MOLECULE EXHIBIT ROOM...

WELL, ANYHOW, HE ACCI-DENTALLY LEFT THIS CLUE BEHIND... A ROLL-UP HAT OF SOFT FELT! OBVIOUSLY HE CAN'T WALK AROUND WEARING A RED HOOD AFTER A ROBBERY--SO HE CARRIES THE HOOD IN A PAPER BAG AND WEARS A HAT!

TO LATE! THE HOT LIGHT BULB TOUCHES THE HAIR, AND...

MY FAULT! GEE, I'M SORRY, BRUCE...THAT WAS THE ONLY CLUE WE HAD!

THE HAIR IS BURNED... CHARRED BLACK!

WAIT, DICK! HOW ABOUT TRYING OUT THAT NEW CHEMICAL FORMULA YOU'VE BEEN DEVELOPING? EXPERIMENTING WITH?

YOU MEAN THE FORMULA THAT RESTORES THE *ORIGINAL COLOR* TO BURNED FIBRES? SURE--THAT SHOULD DO IT!

BUT AFTER THE CHEMICAL IS APPLIED...

HUH? THE HAIR TURNED *GREEN!* GOSH, I MUST'VE MADE A MISTAKE IN THE FORMULA! AND NOW I'VE RUINED EVERYTHING!

WELL, DON'T FEEL TOO BADLY, DICK... WE MAY GET ANOTHER BREAK SOON!

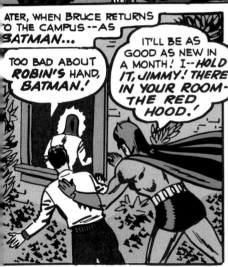

ATER, WHEN BRUCE RETURNS O THE CAMPUS--AS BATMAN...

TOO BAD ABOUT *ROBIN'S* HAND, BATMAN!

IT'LL BE AS GOOD AS NEW IN A MONTH! I--*HOLD IT, JIMMY!* THERE-- IN YOUR ROOM-- THE RED HOOD!

BUT AS HE LUNGES AT THE FIGURE...

WHY, IT'S *PAUL WONG!*

SURE... HA, HA! HE'S *NOT* THE *RED HOOD!* HE WAS ONLY WEARING A *REPLICA!* WE FINISHED IT TODAY!

WE'VE JUST FIGURED OUT HOW THE *RED HOOD* IS ABLE TO SEE *THROUGH HIS HEADPIECE!*

THE ANSWER IS A *TWO-WAY MIRROR!* THE TYPE OF MIRROR THAT *REFLECTS* ON ONE SIDE BUT IS *TRANSPARENT* ON THE *REVERSE SIDE!*

GET IT? HE OBVIOUSLY SET A PAIR OF *RED TWO-WAY MIRRORS* IN THE HOOD, WHERE HIS EYES COULD SEE THROUGH THEM! NATURALLY, THE SHINY MIRRORS BLENDED WITH THE SHINY METAL SO THAT HIS HOOD SEEMED TO BE *ONE BLANK PIECE OF METAL!*

⑦

BUT THE HEAD-PIECE ALSO HAS **ANOTHER** USE! THE REASON HE BURST THOSE AMMONIA PIPES, AND SURVIVED THAT CHEMICAL BATH IS BECAUSE IT'S ALSO A **GAS MASK** AND **DIVING HELMET!**

SO HE **DID** ESCAPE BEFORE THROUGH THE SCHOOL **GAS MAIN!**

RIGHT--AND I'LL BET THE **RED HOOD'S** ORIGINAL PLAN WAS TO STEAL EXACTLY $1,000,000, THEN **RETIRE**--WHICH HE DID!

BUT, JIMMY... WHY, THEN, DID DID HE COME OUT OF RETIREMENT AFTER TEN YEARS?

PROBABLY TO **DEFY** US... TO MAKE US A **LAUGHING STOCK** BECAUSE WE REOPENED THE CASE! AND SINCE HE WAS STOPPED THIS TIME, HE'LL RETURN... AND WHEN HE DOES, WE'LL GET HIM AND **UNMASK** HIM!

HOURS LATER, AS **SPOTTERS** -- EQUIPPED WITH **WALKIE-TALKIES**-- NOTICE A FIGURE STEALING THROUGH THE CAMPUS...

CALLING **BATMAN!** **RED HOOD** MOVING TOWARD UNIVERSITY MUSEUM!

CALLING **BATMAN! RED HOOD** HAS JUST PASSED ALPHA BETA FRATERNITY HOUSE!

INSTANTLY, THE FAMED **BATMOBILE** THUNDERS IN PURSUIT...

I'LL TAKE A SHORT-CUT ACROSS THE SCHOOL'S FOOT-BALL FIELD!

SOON, IN THE COLLEGE MUSEUM'S **MAYAN EXHIBIT**...

HERE'S WHERE I MELT **YOU** DOWN A LITTLE, MR. **RED HOOD!**

THIS THING'S MADE OF **SOLID GOLD!** I'LL MELT IT DOWN AN'-- HUH?? **BATMAN!**

59

61

BUT... BUT... WAS THE *REAL RED HOOD* EVER ON THE CAMPUS AT ALL?

YES--IT WAS THE *REAL RED HOOD* WHO TRIED TO ROB THE SCHOOL PAYROLL! HE ESCAPED BY THE SCHOOL GAS MAIN... REMEMBER? THAT'S WHEN BENSON TOOK OVER.'

YEAH--I SPOTTED HIM LEAVIN' THE GAS MAIN, SO I SURPRISED HIM AND TIED HIM UP, FIGURIN' ON A REWARD.' BUT THEN, I REALIZED *I* COULD WEAR HIS HELMET, COMMIT CRIMES AND LET HIM BE BLAMED FOR 'EM.'

BUT, *BATMAN.* THE HOOD *MASKED* BENSON! HOW YOU KNOW IT WAS HIM?

I *OBSERVED* AND *DEDUCED.'* REMEMBER HOW HE AVOIDED ENTERING THE GAS-FILLED CHAMBER IN THE MUSEUM? FROM THAT OBSERVATION, I COULD DEDUCE ONLY ONE POSSIBLE ANSWER--THAT THE MAN WEARING THE HOOD, THEN, DIDN'T KNOW HE WAS ALSO WEARING A *GAS MASK*... THEREFORE, HE WAS *NOT THE REAL RED HOOD!*

OBSERVATION AND *DEDUCTION!* REMEMBER, I TOLD YOU IN CLASS THAT THEY WERE THE MOST IMPORTANT ASPECTS IN CRIME-FIGHTING.'

THAT'S ONE LESSON WE'LL NEVER FORGET, PROFESSOR.'

AND HOW.'

OH, BY THE WAY... I MEANT TO TELL YOU, *ROBIN*--YOU *DIDN'T* MAKE A MISTAKE IN THAT CHEMICAL FORMULA! AND THAT'S WHY I KNOW THE *IDENTITY OF THE REAL RED HOOD!*

WHAT?

12

THE SHED'S DARK! I CAN'T MAKE' OUT THE MAN'S FACE, BUT I CAN SEE HE'S GAGGED.'

IT'S BEEN A LONG TIME-- TEN YEARS.' OKAY, JIMMY-- LET'S HAVE A LOOK AT THE FACE OF THE *RED HOOD!*

63

Artists: Dick Sprang and Charles Paris / Colorist: Greg Theakston

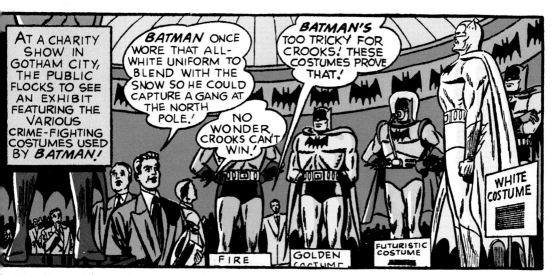

AT A CHARITY SHOW IN GOTHAM CITY, THE PUBLIC FLOCKS TO SEE AN EXHIBIT FEATURING THE VARIOUS CRIME-FIGHTING COSTUMES USED BY *BATMAN!*

BATMAN ONCE WORE THAT ALL-WHITE UNIFORM TO BLEND WITH THE SNOW SO HE COULD CAPTURE A GANG AT THE NORTH POLE!

NO WONDER CROOKS CAN'T WIN!

BATMAN'S TOO TRICKY FOR CROOKS! THESE COSTUMES PROVE THAT!

WHITE COSTUME

FIRE

GOLDEN COSTUME

FUTURISTIC COSTUME

...UT ONE ONLOOKER'S EGO HAS BEEN TOUCHED--ND WHY NOT?--FOR HE IS NONE OTHER THAN HAT CRIME CLOWN, *THE JOKER!*

...H! *BATMAN* ALWAYS GETS TALKED ...BOUT! MY TROUBLE IS THAT I'M *TYPED!* ...EOPLE ALWAYS EXPECT ME TO LOOK LIKE ...YSELF! I, TOO, SHOULD HAVE MANY COSTUMES--FOR *CRIME!*

AND LATER, IN THE MAD HARLEQUIN'S HIDEAWAY...

COSTUMES, EH? WHAT A HAPPY IDEA FOR A SERIES OF CRIMES! *HA! HA!* JOKER, YOU OLD RASCAL-- YOU *ARE* THE CLEVER ONE, AREN'T YOU! *HA! HA!*

...SEWHERE, IN THE HOME OF SOCIALITE BRUCE ...AYNE, AND HIS YOUNG WARD, DICK GRAYSON-- ...HO ARE IN REALITY, *BATMAN* AND *ROBIN* THE BOY WONDER!

GOT TO KEEP IN TRIM-- ESPECIALLY SINCE THE *JOKER* ESCAPED FROM JAIL!

I KNOW! THAT BURGLAR-BUFFOON ALWAYS KEEPS US ON THE MOVE!

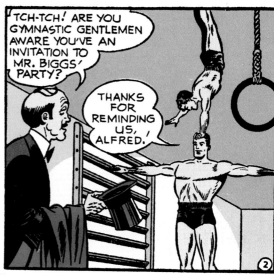

TCH-TCH! ARE YOU GYMNASTIC GENTLEMEN AWARE YOU'VE AN INVITATION TO MR. BIGGS' PARTY?

THANKS FOR REMINDING US, ALFRED!

2

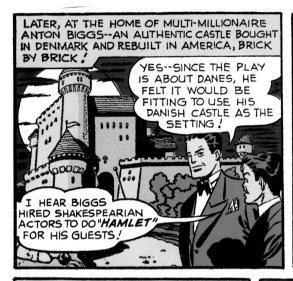

LATER, AT THE HOME OF MULTI-MILLIONAIRE ANTON BIGGS--AN AUTHENTIC CASTLE BOUGHT IN DENMARK AND REBUILT IN AMERICA, BRICK BY BRICK!

YES--SINCE THE PLAY IS ABOUT DANES, HE FELT IT WOULD BE FITTING TO USE HIS DANISH CASTLE AS THE SETTING!

I HEAR BIGGS HIRED SHAKESPEARIAN ACTORS TO DO "HAMLET" FOR HIS GUESTS!

AFTERWARD, IN THE GREAT COURTYARD, TENSE GUESTS WATCH THE FAMED SCENE WHERE "HAMLET" AWAITS HIS FATHER'S GHOST...

... THEN IT DRAWS NEAR THE SEASON WHEREIN THE SPIRIT HELD HIS WONT TO WALK!

MORE LINES ARE READ UNTIL THE IMPORTANT MOMENT ARRIVES--BUT NO GHOST APPEARS!

CONFOUND IT! HE'S MISSED HIS CUE LINE!

AND THEN THE AUDIENCE LAUGHS UPROARIOUSLY--FO INSTEAD OF THE GLOOMY SPECTRE, A FAT, CHUCKLING FIGURE WADDLES FORWARD...

HO! HO! WHO CALLS FALSTAFF A THIN, SICKLY GHOST? HO! HO!

HA! HA! FALSTAFF! HE'S IN THE WRONG PLAY! HE SHOUL BE IN "HENRY THE FOURTH" OR "-- FIFTH"! HA! HA!

HA! HA! HA! HA! HA!

YOU'VE RUINED MY PERFORMANCE --YOU IDIOT!

INSULT FALSTAFF, WILL YOU! FOR THAT, I SHALL RUN YOU THROUGH (PUFF-PUFF) IF I CAN EVER DRAW MY SWORD OUT! (PUFF-PUFF) STUBBORN, ISN'T IT! (PUFF-PUFF)

HA! HA! HA! HA!

EGAD! THE BLADE SHRANK!

HA! HA! YOU HIRED A GOOD COMEDY ACT, BIGGS!

BUT I DIDN'T!

LOOK!

THE BLADE'S GETTING LONGER!

IT'S GROWING LIKE A WEED!

AND WHEN THE BLADE STRETCHES TO A FANTASTIC LENGTH, FALSTAFF SUDDENLY FLIPS UP ITS HOOKED TIP, AND...

EEE! HE'S CAUGHT MY NECKLACE WITH IT!

AND SEE HOW PRETTILY THE LOOP OF GEMS RIDES DOWN THE BLADE TO MY WAITING HAND!

...STANTLY ALERTED, BRUCE AND DICK SHED ...HEIR GARB UNSEEN--AND SURGE FORWARD ... THE FIGHTING TOGS OF *BATMAN* AND *ROBIN!*

RING ...OWN THE ...URTAIN! HO! HO! THE PLAY IS ...INISHED!

NOT YET, TUBBY-- THERE'S ANOTHER ACT COMING UP!

ONLY ONE WAY TO MAKE A SHORT-CUT-- AND THAT'S BY USING THIS FOR *POLE-VAULTING!*

...HE *JOKER!* I HAD A HUNCH ... SEE YOUR UGLY FACE UNDER THAT HANDSOME MASK!

BEHIND YOU, *JOKER!*

I DON'T THINK YOU'LL LAUGH YOUR WAY OUT OF THIS TRAP, *FUNNYMAN!*

WANT TO BET? HA! HA! HA! HA!

ABRUPTLY--A HISSING SOUND, AND THE *JOKER'S* CORPULENT COSTUME BEGINS TO SWELL...

HA! HA! IT LOOKS LIKE I'M PUTTING ON WEIGHT!

SSS-SSS-SSS-

HE'S *FLOATING!* PULL HIM *DOWN!*

THE FAT FALSTAFF BLOATS TO BLIMP PROPORTIONS, UNTIL...

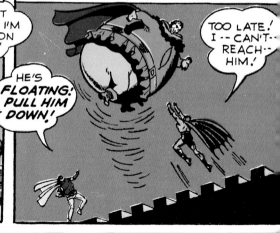

TOO LATE! I -- CAN'T-- REACH-- HIM!

HIS COSTUME WAS MADE OF RUBBER, AND HE PROBABLY HAD TANKS OF COMPRESSED *HELIUM GAS* CONCEALED INSIDE!

HA-HA HA-HA HA-HA HA-HA HA-HA

BOY, WHAT I'D GIVE NOW FOR JUST ONE OVER-SIZED PIN! THE BIG WIND-BAG!

IN DAYS FOLLOWING, THERE ARE TWO MORE ROBBERIES WHEN THE *JOKER* COSTUMES HIMSELF AS "MR. PICKWICK" FROM THE CHARLES DICKENS NOVEL--AND "THE CONNECTICUT YANKEE" AS PORTRAYED IN THE BOOK BY MARK TWAIN...

HO HO HO HA HA HEE HA HA HA

HA HO HE HI

AND *BATMAN'S* KEEN MIND SWIFTLY DEDUCES THE ONLY POSSIBLE EXPLANATION...

HE'S MAKING THE COSTUME FIT THE CRIME--AND IN EACH CASE THE COSTUMES ARE THOSE OF FAMOUS *COMEDY CHARACTERS* IN *FICTION!*

AND THERE ARE SO MANY OF THEM-- PUCK, MICAWBER, PAGLIACCI, FRIAR TUCK, SIMPLE SIMON--

GOLLY! NOW THE QUESTION IS -- *WHICH CHARACTER'S COSTUME WILL HE WEAR NEXT?*

NIGHT AFTER NIGHT, THE CAPED MANHUNTERS PROWL THE UNDERWORLD PATHWAYS, ALWAYS HUNTING...HUNTING FOR A LEAD, A CLUE! UNTIL...

BATMAN, THOSE THREE LOOK FAMILIAR!

THEY SHOULD--THEY'VE BEEN IN ENOUGH POLICE LINE-UPS! NOW WHY ARE THEY CARRYING VIOLIN CASES? THAT'S TOO CURIOUS FOR US TO OVERLOOK...

THEY WENT IN THROUGH THE FRONT DOOR! STRANGE!

VERY-- BECAUSE THAT'S THE TOWN HOUSE OF WEALTHY ELI TATE! HE OWNS SO MANY COAL MINES, THEY CALL HIM THE COAL BARON!

INSIDE, THE VIOLINISTS ARE WARMLY WELCOMED, FOR TATE HAS INVITED GUESTS TO PARTICIPATE IN AN OLD-FASHIONED SQUARE DANCE!

SWING YOUR PARTNERS —SASHAY 'ROUND—

SUDDENLY, A JOVIAL FIGURE ENTERS...

HO! HO! I LIKE SEEING MY PEASANTS AT A FROLIC! HO! HO! HO!

HUH? WHO'S THE FUNNY OLD GALOOT?

WHO INVITED YOU?

I NEED NO INVITATION--FOR I AM MORE ROYAL THAN YOU! YOU MAY BE A COAL BARON-- BUT I AM KING COLE! A GOOD PUN, EH? HO! HO!

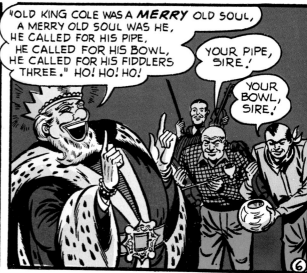

"OLD KING COLE WAS A MERRY OLD SOUL, A MERRY OLD SOUL WAS HE, HE CALLED FOR HIS PIPE, HE CALLED FOR HIS BOWL, HE CALLED FOR HIS FIDDLERS THREE." HO! HO! HO!

YOUR PIPE, SIRE!

YOUR BOWL, SIRE!

BUBBLES! HE'S BLOWING SOAP BUBBLES WITH HIS PIPE AND BOWL! HA! HA!

OLD KING COLE ISN'T JUST MERRY--HE'S PLAIN SQUIRRELY! HA! HA!

SUDDENLY, AS THE BUBBLES BURST...

HO! HO! TOO BAD I COULDN'T USE "COAL GAS"! HO! HO! WHAT A PUN!

INSTANTLY ADJUSTING NOSE FILTERS, TWO ACROBATIC FIGURES SWING IN...

BATMAN AND ROBIN! AHA! OLD KING COLE MUST CALL FOR HIS FIDDLERS THREE, AGAIN!

HE CALLED FOR HIS PIPE, SO HERE'S THE STEAM PIPE!

YOW!

SSSSSSSS

HE CALLED FOR HIS BOWL! HERE'S ONE WITH PUNCH IN IT!

SEEING THE BATTLE TURN AGAINST HIM, THE MAD HARLEQUIN DROPS A CHEMICAL IN THE SOLUTION AND BLOWS TWO GIGANTIC BUBBLES...

WOW! LOOK AT THE SIZE OF THEM!

IT'S A TRICK! ROBIN, LOOK OUT!

OO LATE! THE PROPELLED BUBBLES ENVELOP THE CRIME-FIGHTERS!

HA! HA! YOU'LL FIND THOSE BUBBLES WON'T BURST! THEY'RE MADE OF A NEW RELIABLE PLASTIC! HA! HA! HA!

LET'S TRY PUNCHING OUR WAY OUT!

NO USE! THE BUBBLE GIVES, BUT IT WON'T BREAK! WE'RE CAUGHT!

LIKE TWO FLIES! HA! HA! YOU CAN'T GET OUT--BUT I CAN--AND WITH PLENTY OF LOOT FROM OUR SLEEPING VICTIMS! HA! HA!

VAINLY, THE CRIME-FIGHTERS FIGHT THE STICKY SUBSTANCE, WHILE THE MIRTHFUL MOUNTEBANK ESCAPES...

YOU CAN EXTRACT A CAPSULE OF SOLVENT FROM YOUR UTILITY BELT...

BUT I CAN'T! THIS STUFF IS LIKE GLUE! ROBIN--THAT FIREPLACE IS OUR ONE CHANCE BEFORE WE SMOTHER TO DEATH!

FLAMES WRITHE ABOUT THE ENCASED BATMAN AND ROBIN AS THEY ROLL IN TO THE HUGE FIRE PLACE...

WE'RE LUCKY--THE PLASTIC IS SHIELDING US FROM MOST OF THE HEAT! NOW JUST CROSS YOUR FINGERS--AND HOPE!

I'M BEGINNING TO FEEL LIKE A ROAST POTATOE!

THEN, AFTER WHAT SEEMS AN ETERNITY, THE HEAT BEGINS TO HARDEN THE PLASTIC...

THE PLASTIC IS CRACKING OPEN! HURRY, ROBIN! OUR "EGGS" ARE BEGINNING TO "HATCH"!

CRACK! SNAP! CRACKLE!

AND SOON...

WE'RE JUST TOO LATE AGAIN! THAT CRIME CLOWN IS A LONG WAY FROM HERE BY NOW!

LOOK! HE DROPPED HIS "KING COLE" MANTLE! MAYBE IT CAN GIVE US A CLUE OR SOMETHING!

HERE'S SOMETHING FROM AN INSIDE POCKET! AN *OPERA* TICKET FOR TOMORROW NIGHT! FOR *"PAGLIACCI"!*

PAGLIACCI, THE CLOWN! THAT CERTAINLY FITS THE *CRIME CLOWN!* *ROBIN,* WE'RE GOING TO THE OPERA -- TO MAKE THE *JOKER* SING A DIFFERENT TUNE!

THE FOLLOWING NIGHT -- A GLORIOUS TENOR VOICE SINGS THE FAMED ITALIAN ROLE...

AS THE OPERA DRAWS TO THE CLOSE, *BATMAN* GETS WORRIED...

BATMAN, THE *JOKER* HASN'T SHOWN UP YET!

MAYBE THIS IS THE *JOKER* -- UNDER THAT CLOWN MAKE UP!

I *BEG* YOUR PARDON!

I -- I'M SORRY! IT WAS A MISTAKE! I THOUGHT YOU WERE SOMEONE ELSE!

LATER -- BAD NEWS....!

THE *JOKER* RIGGED HIMSELF AS *"MR. MICAWBER"* AND ROBBED THE DAVIS COPPER COMPANY!

"MICAWBER" OF *"DAVID COPPER*FIELD"! THE JOKER'S *PUN!* HE DELIBERATELY LEFT THAT OPERA TICKET FOR US TO FIND -- SO HE COULD COMMIT A ROBBERY SOMEWHERE ELSE! HE'S HAD A GOOD LAUGH -- ON US!

THE FOLLOWING NIGHT...

NICE TO FIND YOU HOME, SOUPY!

AND WHY AREN'T YOU, PRACTICING YOUR *FIDDLE* TONIGHT? DID OLD KING COLE GIVE YOU A NIGHT OFF?

(GULP) B-B-BATMAN AND R-R-ROBIN.

72

TALK, SOUPY! WHAT'S THE *JOKER* GOT PLANNED FOR TONIGHT?

I DON'T KNOW-- HONEST! THE *JOKER* SAID HE WAS *GONNA* DO TONIGHT'S JOB ALONE! HE SAID HE DIDN'T NEED US!

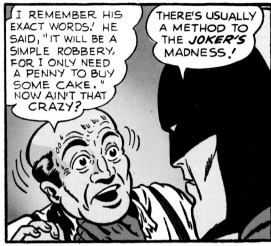

I REMEMBER HIS EXACT WORDS! HE SAID, "IT WILL BE A SIMPLE ROBBERY, FOR I ONLY NEED A PENNY TO BUY SOME CAKE." NOW AIN'T THAT CRAZY?

THERE'S USUALLY A METHOD TO THE *JOKER'S* MADNESS!

THE *JOKER* WAS LAUGHING AT SOUPY BECAUSE WHAT HE SAID WAS A RIDDLE! IF ONLY WE CAN FIGURE IT OUT...

HMM! "IT WILL BE A SIMPLE ROBBERY, FOR I ONLY NEED A PENNY TO BUY SOME CAKE." I WONDER-- I WONDER... HMM... I'VE GOT IT!

"*SIMPLE SIMON* MET A PIEMAN GOING TO THE FAIR, SAID SIMPLE SIMON TO THE PIEMAN, LET ME TASTE YOUR WARE. SAID THE PIEMAN TO SIMPLE SIMON, DO YOU HAVE A PENNY? SAID SIMON TO THE PIEMAN, NO, I DON'T HAVE ANY."

LATER, AT EXPOSITION HALL, WHERE GOTHAM CITY'S BAKERIES ARE HOLDING THEIR ANNUAL *BAKING FAIR!*

HA! HA! WHO'S THAT DUNCE? WILL YOU LOOK AT THAT OUTFIT!

TEE-HEE! HEE-HEE!

HOLIDAY ROOM

10

75

Artists: Dick Sprang and Charles Paris / Colorist: Glenn Whitmore

ONE EVENING, A WEIRD, EAR-SPLITTING LAUGH PIERCES THE STILLNESS OF A GOTHAM CITY MUSEUM! *THE JOKER* — THAT HARLEQUIN OF HATE-- *STRIKES AGAIN!*

HO-HO-HO! SO THEY FAILED TO INCLUDE *ME* IN THIS HALL OF FAME, EH!! *HA-HA!* THAT'LL JUST COST 'EM THEIR *NEW JEWEL COLLECTION!* HO-HO-HO!

GOTHAM MUSEUM of MODERN ART
COMEDIANS HALL of FAME

THE JEWELS ARE IN THE NEXT GALLERY, BOSS!

CHAPLIN

BUT THEN COMES AN UNWELCOME SURPRISE FOR THE *JOKER* --IN THE PERSONS OF *BATMAN* AND *ROBIN* --THE EVER VIGILANT LAWMEN!

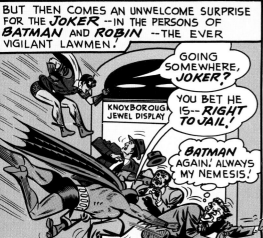

KNOXBOROUG JEWEL DISPLAY

GOING SOMEWHERE, *JOKER?*

YOU BET HE IS-- *RIGHT TO JAIL!*

BATMAN AGAIN! ALWAYS MY NEMESIS!

AND AS A FIERCE BATTLE RAGES...

A GOOD FIGHT, *JOKER* --BUT YOU'RE FINISHED NOW!

SUDDENLY, THE LARGE PAINTING OVERHEAD IS JARRED FROM ITS HOOK--AND COMES CRASHING DOWN ON *BATMAN!*

BATMAN! BATMAN! ARE YOU ALL RIGHT?

A RARE STROKE OF LUCK! HO-HO! GRAB THEM!

HA-HA-HA! TAKE THEM TO THE HIDEOUT--QUICKLY! I WANT TO TOY WITH THEM! *HA-HA!*

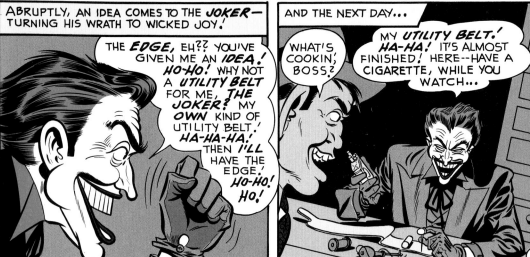

IN THE NEXT MOMENT!

HEY--AN EXPLODING CIGARETTE! WHAT GIVES, BOSS?

HO-HO! THAT'S ONE OF THE *GADGETS* FOR MY *BELT!* BATMAN MAY USE SCIENTIFIC DEVICES--BUT *THE JOKER* USES *JOKES* AND TRICK NOVELTIES! HO, HO, HO!

I SEE YOU'RE GETTING TOGETHER A LOT OF TRICK STUFF, *JOKER* --BUT WHAT'S THAT *CORK* FOR?? IS *THAT* GOING TO BE IN YOUR BELT-- AN *ORDINARY BOTTLE CORK?*

HO-HO-HO! THAT CORK IS THE *MOST IMPORTANT* UNIT IN MY BELT! IT WILL PROVE THE UNDOING OF *BATMAN* AND *ROBIN!* HA-HA-HA!

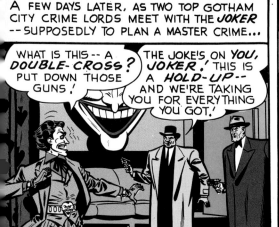

A FEW DAYS LATER, AS TWO TOP GOTHAM CITY CRIME LORDS MEET WITH THE *JOKER* --SUPPOSEDLY TO PLAN A MASTER CRIME...

WHAT IS THIS-- A *DOUBLE-CROSS?* PUT DOWN THOSE GUNS!

THE JOKE'S ON *YOU, JOKER!* THIS IS A *HOLD-UP*-- AND WE'RE TAKING YOU FOR EVERYTHING YOU GOT!

HE'S CLEAN, CHAMP! NO WEAPONS--NONE OF THEM JOKE GADGETS OF HIS! WE CAUGHT HIM BY SURPRISE!

NOT BAD, EH, *JOKER?* YOU GOT MORE *LOOT* HERE THAN ANY OTHER PLACE IN TOWN! WE ROB YOU, WE RUN NO RISKS! NO *BATMAN* AND *ROBIN* TO WORRY ABOUT!

UNNOTICED, THE *JOKER'S* HANDS SLIDE TOWARD HIS UTILITY BELT, PICK OUT A PAIR OF SMALL PILLS WHICH HE IGNITES WITH A CIGARETTE LIGHTER... AND A MOMENT LATER...

LOOK OUT-- SNAKES! UGLY MONSTERS!

HA-HA-HA! I'LL JUST TAKE THOSE GUNS, GENTLEMEN--AND RING FOR SOME OF MY BOYS!

SOON AFTER...

HO-HO! TOO BAD YOU DIDN'T KNOW *I* HAD A UTILITY BELT, TOO! *HA-HA!* AND WHAT AN AUSPICIOUS BEGINNING FOR MY BELT!--HO-HO-HO!

GEE, THEY SURE LOOK REAL, *JOKER!* IT'S TERRIFIC HOW THEY KIN EXPLODE OUTA THOSE LITTLE PILLS YOU CARRY!

4

NEXT EVENING IN THE PALATIAL HOME OF MILLIONAIRE BRUCE WAYNE AND HIS WARD, DICK GRAYSON...

BOY, THIS MODEL IS A BEAUTY, BRUCE! AS CHIEF STOCKHOLDER OF THE STEAMSHIP LINE, YOU CAN BE PROUD OF YOUR NEW SHIP!

I AM! AND I'M ALSO PROUD THAT BATMAN AND ROBIN WERE SELECTED TO CHRISTEN THE S.S. GOTHAM AT ITS LAUNCHING CEREMONY NEXT MONTH!

ALL AT ONCE, AN EERIE BEAM STABS THROUGH THE SKY--THE BAT-SIGNAL!

SPEAKING OF BATMAN AND ROBIN--LOOKS LIKE WE'RE WANTED RIGHT NOW!

RIGHT! AND I SHOULDN'T BE SURPRISED IF OUR FRIEND, THE JOKER, WERE THE REASON!

A QUICK CHANGE OF COSTUME, AND BATMAN AND ROBIN RUSH TO POLICE HEADQUARTERS!

THE JOKER, BATMAN! HE'S LOOTED THE BOX OFFICE AT THE CIVIC OPERA!

THEN WE'RE GOING TO THE OPERA, TOO!

MEANWHILE, AS THE JOKER FLEES BACKSTAGE AT THE OPERA...

I'VE BLUNDERED-- TOO MANY COPS AND GUARDS! THEY PROBABLY GUESSED I, THE GREAT CLOWN THAT I AM, COULDN'T RESIST AN OPERA LIKE "PAGLIACCI"!

THEN, AS THE JOKER RUNS INTO A DEAD END, AND IS CAPTURED...

I'VE STILL GOT A CHANCE--THANKS TO MY UTILITY BELT! I'LL MAKE BELIEVE I'M HITCHING UP MY TROUSERS...

THEY'RE UNARMED! PUT THE CUFFS ON THE JOKER, MAC! HE'LL PULL NO MORE TRICKS ON US!

5

AS THE POLICEMAN GRABS THE **JOKER'S** HANDS, READY TO SLIP ON THE HANDCUFFS...

OUCH! HEY, WHAT'S GOING ON!?

HA-HA! JUST THE **DIVERSION** I NEEDED! GET THEM, MEN! WE'VE THROWN THEM OFF-GUARD!

BUZZ!

THEN, AS THE **JOKER** AND HIS MEN MAKE GOOD THEIR ESCAPE...

HA-HA! MY **UTILITY BELT** PAYS OFF AGAIN! I FIND IT VERY USEFUL! HO-HO!

A HAND-BUZZER! BOY--IT SURE **STARTLED** THAT COP!

STAGE DOOR

AND WHEN **BATMAN** AND **ROBIN** HEAR THE STORY AT THE OPERA HOUSE...

HE DIDN'T HAVE THAT BUZZER ON, WHILE WE WERE CHASING HIM. HE PULLED IT OUT OF SOMEWHERE, AT THE VERY LAST MOMENT!

HMMM! LOOKS LIKE THE **JOKER** HAS A NEW ANGLE, **ROBIN!** I EXPECT WE'LL BE SEEING SOME MORE OF IT!

LATER...

YOU KNOW SOMETHING, BOSS? YOU NEVER **DID** SHOW US **ALL** THE STUFF YOU GOT IN THAT BELT! HOW ABOUT IT?

HA-HA! CERTAINLY, BOYS-- CERTAINLY! COME -- I'VE GOT A LARGE CROSS-SECTION DIAGRAM OF IT UPSTAIRS!

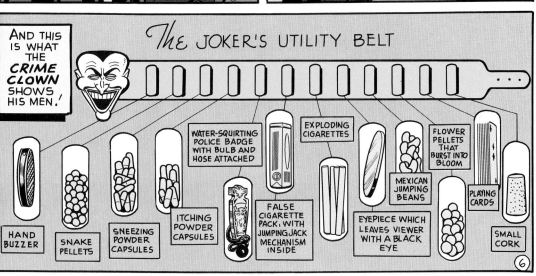

AND THIS IS WHAT THE **CRIME CLOWN** SHOWS HIS MEN!

The JOKER'S UTILITY BELT

HAND BUZZER

SNAKE PELLETS

SNEEZING POWDER CAPSULES

ITCHING POWDER CAPSULES

WATER-SQUIRTING POLICE BADGE WITH BULB AND HOSE ATTACHED

FALSE CIGARETTE PACK, WITH JUMPING JACK MECHANISM INSIDE

EXPLODING CIGARETTES

EYEPIECE WHICH LEAVES VIEWER WITH A BLACK EYE

MEXICAN JUMPING BEANS

FLOWER PELLETS THAT BURST INTO BLOOM

PLAYING CARDS

SMALL CORK

6

YOUR BELT IS WELL-EQUIPPED, *JOKER* --- BUT I STILL CAN'T FIGURE THAT CORK! HOW IS *THAT* GONNA FIX *BATMAN* AND *ROBIN!*

ALL IN GOOD TIME! *HA-HA-HA!* YOU'LL SEE!

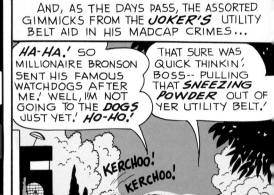

AND, AS THE DAYS PASS, THE ASSORTED GIMMICKS FROM THE *JOKER'S* UTILITY BELT AID IN HIS MADCAP CRIMES...

HA-HA! SO MILLIONAIRE BRONSON SENT HIS FAMOUS WATCHDOGS AFTER ME! WELL, I'M NOT GOING TO THE *DOGS* JUST YET! *HO-HO!*

THAT SURE WAS QUICK THINKIN', BOSS-- PULLING THAT *SNEEZING POWDER* OUT OF YER UTILITY BELT!

KERCHOO!
KERCHOO!

HA-HA! YOU STUPID ROOKIE! YOU COULD HAVE BEEN A HERO! YOU CAPTURED ME ALL BY YOURSELF! BUT YOU COULDN'T RESIST STARING AT THE BADGE I SLIPPED ONTO MY LAPEL! *HO-HO!*

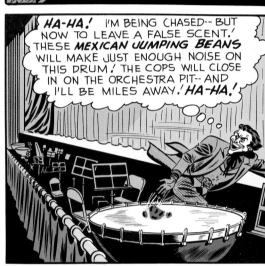

HA-HA! I'M BEING CHASED-- BUT NOW TO LEAVE A FALSE SCENT! THESE *MEXICAN JUMPING BEANS* WILL MAKE JUST ENOUGH NOISE ON THIS DRUM! THE COPS WILL CLOSE IN ON THE ORCHESTRA PIT-- AND I'LL BE MILES AWAY! *HA-HA!*

THAT EVENING...

Gotham Gazette

JOKER'S UTILITY BELT PLAGUES CITY!

Crime Clown Steals Leaf from Batman's Book!

ARTIST'S CONCEPTION OF BOTH UTILITY BELTS. THE BATTLE OF THE BELTS HAS BEGUN!! WHICH WILL WIN?

AND, IN THE *BAT-CAVE* CRIME LAB...

NOTHING ON THIS JUMPING BEAN THAT WOULD LEAD US TO THE *JOKER'S* HIDEOUT -- IT'S VOID OF CLUES...

ROBIN! LISTEN TO THIS! "PROF. J.J. LAUGHWELL RETURNED HOME TONIGHT FROM AN AFRICAN EXPEDITION WITH A PRICELESS COLLECTION OF RARE NATIVE MASKS! *LAUGHWELL!* WOULDN'T THAT NAME *INSPIRE* THE *JOKER*??

AN HOUR LATER, IN PROFESSOR LAUGHWELL'S PRIVATE STUDIO...

THERE HE IS, *ROBIN*-- WE WERE RIGHT!

AH, *BATMAN!* NOW TO HAVE SOME FUN-- IF EVERYTHING WORKS OUT! *HO-HO!*

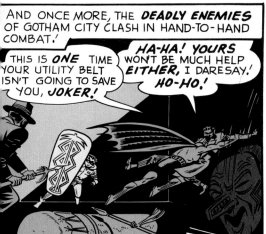

AND ONCE MORE, THE *DEADLY ENEMIES* OF GOTHAM CITY CLASH IN HAND-TO-HAND COMBAT!

THIS IS *ONE* TIME YOUR UTILITY BELT ISN'T GOING TO SAVE YOU, *JOKER!*

HA-HA! YOURS WON'T BE MUCH HELP *EITHER*, I DARE SAY! *HO-HO!*

SUDDENLY, THE AGILE *CRIME-JESTER* WRIGGLES FROM *BATMAN'S* GRASP! AND THEN...

HOLD IT, *ROBIN!* THIS HAS GONE FAR ENOUGH! TIME TO SHOW WHAT A UTILITY BELT CAN DO! PREPARE FOR GAS!

QUICKLY *BATMAN* SEIZES HIS GAS PELLETS, HURLS THEM THROUGH THE AIR! BUT THEN-- BEFORE HIS AMAZED EYES!

BATMAN! DID YOU SEE THAT!!? THOSE GAS-PELLETS *BURST* INTO FLOWERS!

HO-HO! I NEVER THOUGHT YOU'D THROW ME BOUQUETS, BATMAN! HA-HA!

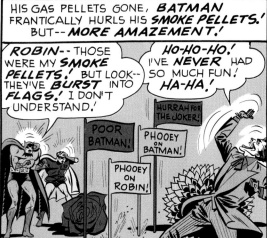

HIS GAS PELLETS GONE, *BATMAN* FRANTICALLY HURLS HIS *SMOKE PELLETS!* BUT-- *MORE AMAZEMENT!*

ROBIN-- THOSE WERE MY *SMOKE PELLETS!* BUT LOOK-- THEY'VE *BURST* INTO FLAGS! I DON'T UNDERSTAND!

HO-HO-HO! I'VE *NEVER* HAD SO MUCH FUN! HA-HA!

HURRAH FOR THE JOKER!

POOR BATMAN!

PHOOEY ON BATMAN!

PHOOEY ON ROBIN!

⑧

SUDDENLY, THE **JOKER** DARTS FOR A DARK CORNER! AND AS **BATMAN** FISHES FOR HIS POWERFUL UTILITY BELT FLASHLIGHT...

THIS IS **TOO MUCH!** A JACK-IN-THE-BOX!

BUT-- **HOW?** HOW COULD THE **JOKER** TAMPER WITH YOUR **UTILITY BELT?**

HO-HO-HO-HO! HA-HA-HA-HA.!!

AND THEN, AS THE SIMPLE ANSWER COMES TO THE DYNAMIC DUO...

LOOK! THIS **ISN'T MY BELT** ---BUT A CLEVER IMITATION WHICH FITTED RIGHT OVER MINE! THE **JOKER** MUST HAVE SLIPPED IT ON ME WHILE WE WERE STRUGGLING!

NO WONDER EVERYTHING WENT HAYWIRE! WELL-- IT'S TOO LATE NOW! THE **JOKER'S** GONE...

LATER...

I'M AFRAID WE WERE MADE TO LOOK LIKE FOOLS, **ROBIN!** BUT AT LEAST WE GAINED ONE OBJECTIVE. WE PREVENTED ANOTHER **JOKER CRIME!**

RIGHT! IT'S SMALL CONSOLATION-- BUT AT LEAST IT'S SOME-THING!

A FEW DAYS LATER...

MEN--THE DAY WE HAVE BEEN WAITING FOR IS ALMOST HERE -- THE DAY WHEN **THIS CORK** MARKS THE DOWNFALL OF **BATMAN AND ROBIN!** HO-HO!

BATMAN IS CLEVER-- BUT SO AM I! I KNOW THE ONLY WAY I CAN DEFEAT HIM IS TO CATCH HIM OFF-GUARD. THIS CORK WILL DO THAT-- **AS THE CORK IN THE CHAMPAGNE BOTTLE WITH WHICH BATMAN WILL LAUNCH THE S.S. GOTHAM TOMORROW!**

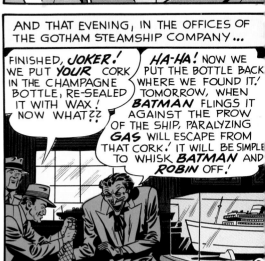

AND THAT EVENING, IN THE OFFICES OF THE GOTHAM STEAMSHIP COMPANY...

FINISHED, **JOKER!** WE PUT **YOUR** CORK IN THE CHAMPAGNE BOTTLE, RE-SEALED IT WITH WAX! NOW WHAT??

HA-HA! NOW WE PUT THE BOTTLE BACK WHERE WE FOUND IT! TOMORROW, WHEN **BATMAN** FLINGS IT AGAINST THE PROW OF THE SHIP, PARALYZING **GAS** WILL ESCAPE FROM THAT CORK! IT WILL BE SIMPLE TO WHISK **BATMAN** AND **ROBIN** OFF!

9

NEXT DAY, WITH THE LAUNCHING CEREMONIES ABOUT TO BEGIN...

HERE'S THE BOTTLE, *BATMAN.* WE SHOULD BE READY IN A FEW MINUTES.

THANK YOU...

HMM--THAT'S FUNNY.

ROBIN-- NOTICE THE COLOR OF THE WAX-- IT HASN'T FADED AT ALL. YET THIS IS 1936 CHAMPAGNE-- AND PARAFFIN WAX IS KNOWN TO DISCOLOR WITH AGE.

WHICH MEANS THAT BOTTLE MAY HAVE BEEN TAMPERED WITH --AND RE-SEALED. WE'D BETTER NOT TAKE CHANCES. I'LL GET ANOTHER ONE.

SOON AFTER...

WORSE LUCK! THAT SHARP-EYED *BATMAN* MUST HAVE SPOTTED SOMETHING! THEY'VE CHANGED BOTTLES--ALL MY PLANNING HAS FAILED!

THEN, AS THE GREAT SHIP IS LAUNCHED.

...AND I NAME YOU THE S.S. GOTHAM.

HURRAH! BON VOYAGE! GOOD LUCK!

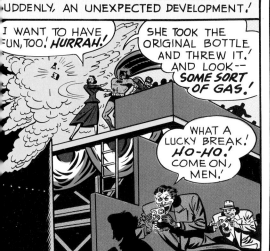

SUDDENLY, AN UNEXPECTED DEVELOPMENT.

I WANT TO HAVE FUN, TOO! *HURRAH!*

SHE TOOK THE ORIGINAL BOTTLE AND THREW IT. AND LOOK-- *SOME SORT OF GAS!*

WHAT A LUCKY BREAK! *HO-HO!* COME ON, MEN.

BEFORE THE VAUNTED LAWMEN TAKE ANY PRECAUTIONS, THEY ARE STRUCK BY THE POWERFUL GAS! AND AS THE *JOKER* TAKES ADVANTAGE OF THE CONFUSION...

HELP!

{GASP}

{COUGH!}

HURRY, MEN! I CAN'T WAIT TO GET BACK TO THE HIDEOUT WITH OUR *PRIZES!* I MUST DREAM UP A *SPECIAL* FATE FOR THESE TWO!

10

85

AND LATER, AT THE *JOKER'S* HIDEOUT, THAT SPECIAL FATE IS READY FOR THE TWO CAPTURED CRIME-FIGHTERS.'

HA-HA-HA! NOW THAT I'VE WON THE BATTLE OF THE *UTILITY BELTS--* I'VE GOT ANOTHER *BELT* FOR YOU, *BATMAN!* A CONVEYOR BELT! HO-HO-HO!'

WHAT A GAG! ONCE THEY'RE ON THAT BELT, THEY'LL RUN THEMSELVES RAGGED TRYIN' TO PREVENT BEING DRAGGED INTO THE FIRE!

HA-HA! LET'S SEE HOW *ROBIN* RUNS, FIRST! START THE MOTOR! START THE *BELT MOVING!* HO-HO!'

THE FIEND!

HO-HO-HO! I GET A *TERRIFIC BELT* OUT OF THIS!

POOR KID! I'VE GOT TO STRIP THAT MOTOR!

THE *JOKER'S* UTILITY BELT-- IF I CAN JUST SLIP MY HAND INSIDE IT WITHOUT BEING SEEN!

BATMAN'S STARING AT THE *JOKER'S* UTILITY BELT! HOW CAN *THAT* SILLY BAG OF TRICKS BE OF ANY HELP?

UNNOTICED, *BATMAN'S* DEFT FINGERS SLIP INTO A COMPARTMENT OF THE *JOKER'S* UTILITY BELT! A MOMENT LATER...

THE *SNAKE PELLETS!* NOW TO PROPEL THEM THE WAY A CHILD PROPELS A MARBLE! THE MOTOR'S HEAT SHOULD PRODUCE THE SNAKES!

IN THE NEXT MOMENT...

NOW, ROBIN! LEAP CLEAR!

MY BELT! BATMAN'S GRABBED MY BELT!

WHAT IN THE WORLD...! YOUR *TRICK SNAKES, JOKER!* THEY'VE FOULED UP THE GEARS--STOPPED THE MOTOR!

ONE EVENING, AS THE FAMOUS **CRIME-FIGHTERS**, **BATMAN** AND **ROBIN**, PAUSE IN THEIR LAW-PATROL THROUGH GOTHAM CITY...

LOOK, BATMAN-- THE **JOKER'S** CAR!

YES, HE'S FREE TO TRAVEL ABROAD, NOW THAT HE'S BEEN RELEASED FROM PRISON. APPARENTLY HE'S GONE STRAIGHT-- BUT IT'S HARD TO BELIEVE!

SUDDENLY, **BATMAN** GETS AN IDEA. AND MOMENTS LATER...

JUST A LITTLE PRECAUTION! IF THE **JOKER'S** GOT ANY CRIME-PLANS UP HIS SLEEVE, MAYBE WE CAN LISTEN IN TO THEM!

RIGHT! THIS TINY MIKE AND SENDING SET WE'RE INSTALLING WILL PICK UP ANY WORDS SPOKEN IN THIS CAR! LET'S HOPE THE **JOKER** DOESN'T NOTICE IT!

AND LATER, IN THE **BAT-CAVE**...

HO-HO-HO- HA-HA-

IT'S THE **JOKER**, BATMAN! HE'S GOTTEN INTO HIS CAR! **LISTEN!**

HO-HO-HO! SO THE COPS DON'T KNOW WHO PULLED THE GREGG JEWELRY ROBBERY!?? HA-HA! I DO! FIGURED IT OUT BY MYSELF!

THE WHOLE JOB--THE SAFE-CRACKING, THE GETAWAY-- ALL BEAR THE STAMP OF DINK DEVERS! THE COPS THINK HE DIED--BUT HE'S RIGHT HERE IN TOWN, AT THE BLAKE HOTEL! HA-HA-HA!

GOSH, BOSS--I BET YOU'RE RIGHT!

MEANWHILE...

HO-HO-HO! HA HA HO

DINK DEVERS-- ALIVE! THEN THE **JOKER'S** RIGHT! IT WAS DEVERS' TYPE OF CRIME--FROM BEGINNING TO END!

COME ON, **ROBIN!** WE'RE OFF TO THE BLAKE HOTEL-- THANKS TO OUR FRIEND **THE JOKER!**

2

89

SHORTLY AFTERWARDS...

BATMAN! HOW DID YOU EVER FIGURE **THIS** ONE OUT--HOW DID YOU KNOW IT WAS **ME?**

OH, **WE** DIDN'T SOLVE **THIS** CASE! GOT A NEW MAN ON THE FORCE! A FELLOW NAMED THE **JOKER!**

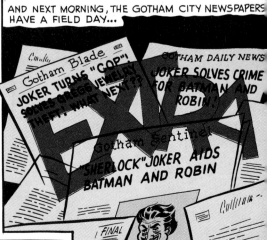

AND NEXT MORNING, THE GOTHAM CITY NEWSPAPERS HAVE A FIELD DAY...

Gotham Blade
JOKER TURNS "COP"! SOLVES GREAT JEWELRY THEFT! WHAT NEXT??

GOTHAM DAILY NEWS
JOKER SOLVES CRIME FOR BATMAN AND ROBIN!

EXTRA

Gotham Sentinel
"SHERLOCK" JOKER AIDS BATMAN AND ROBIN

FINAL

BUT WHILE ALL OF GOTHAM CITY CHUCKLES, THAT **CLOWN PRINCE OF CRIME, THE JOKER**, HAS LOST HIS SENSE OF HUMOR!

BATMAN HAS MADE A FOOL OF ME, BEFORE **ALL** OF GOTHAM CITY! IMAGINE! USING **ME** TO SOLVE A CRIME! TURNING THE **JOKER** INTO A **LAWMAN!**

I MUST **SAVE FACE**--BY **TURNING THE TABLES ON BATMAN!** I MUST MAKE **BATMAN A CRIMINAL!** HA-HA! THAT WOULD EVEN THE SCORE!

A FEW DAYS LATER, IN THE HOME OF MILLIONAIRE BRUCE WAYNE AND HIS WARD, DICK GRAYSON...

TIME FOR ME TO CHANGE INTO MY **ROBIN** IDENTITY. I'M TO SPEAK AT THE BOAT SHOW THIS AFTERNOON.

HAVE FUN! I'LL TAKE OVER ALONE AS **BATMAN,** SHOULD ANY CRIMES FLARE UP TODAY!

MEANWHILE, IN AN ALLEY NEAR THE HUGE GOTHAM AUDITORIUM WHICH ANNUALLY HOUSES THE BOAT SHOW..

THESE SOUTH AMERICAN SAILORS WERE TO BE THE GUESTS OF HONOR AT THE BOAT SHOW! DISGUISED AS THEM, WE SHOULD HAVE VERY LITTLE TROUBLE TRAPPING **ROBIN!** HO-HO-HO!

SHORTLY AFTERWARDS, WITHIN THE IMMENSE HALL ...

THERE'S *ROBIN!* I *KNEW* HE WAS TO SPEAK HERE TODAY! ALL RIGHT--GET YOUR GAS-MASKS READY! IN A MOMENT WE ATTACK! HA-HA.'

ALL AT ONCE, AS THE *JOKER* STRIKES WITHOUT WARNING! ...

UGH--FEEL SICK!

I'M DIZZY--THIS WHOLE PLACE MUST BE ROCKING!

HO-HO-HO! A SPECIAL *GAS* WHICH PRODUCES A STATE NOT UNLIKE *SEA-SICKNESS!* HA-HA! HOW PERFECT FOR A *BOAT SHOW!* AND NOW TO GRAB *ROBIN!*

A MOMENT LATER, BEFORE THE STUNNED CROWD CAN MOVE IN PROTEST...

NOTHING LIKE A *BOAT RIDE* NOW AND THEN, EH, *ROBIN?* HA-HA-HA! COME ON--LET'S GET HIM TO THE HIDEOUT!

I'M GROGGY--SICK! AND I SURE PUT MY FOOT IN IT *THIS* TIME!

HAT EVENING, IN COMMISSIONER GORDON'S OFFICE T POLICE HEADQUARTERS...

THIS IS BAD, *BATMAN!* MESSAGE FROM THE *JOKER*-- E HOLDS *ROBIN* PRISONER! OU'RE TO FOLLOW THESE IN-TRUCTIONS -- A CAR WILL CK YOU UP AND DELIVER OU TO THE *JOKER'S* HIDEOUT!

ROBIN'S UTILITY BELT! HE'S A PRISONER, ALL RIGHT! I'LL *HAVE* TO OBEY!--TO SAVE THE KID'S LIFE!

AND SOME TIME AFTER...

HERE HE IS, LADS! THE MAN WHO IS GOING TO MAKE *CRIMINAL HISTORY* IN GOTHAM CITY! OUR OWN *BATMAN*--WHO'LL BE AS *CROOKED* AS *WE!*

TROUBLE! *ROBIN'S* UNDER HEAVY GUARD-- ONE MOVE, AND HE'D BE SHOT! I'LL HAVE TO PLAY ALONG!

HURRAH for BATMAN-- THE MASTER CROOK!

WELCOME!

WELCOME TO GANGLAND'S OWN *BATMAN!*

4

91

BUT THEN, BEFORE THE HORRIFIED EYES OF THE SPECTATORS...

HIS 'CHUTE DIDN'T OPEN! HE'S A GONER SURE!

POOR BATMAN! COME ON-- LET'S GET A TRUCK AND GET OVER TO THOSE WOODS!

MEANWHILE, IN THE DENSE SECTION OF THE WOODS...

IT WORKED PERFECTLY! REMOTE CONTROL GUIDED THE PLANE ACCUR- ATELY--AND HAD THE BATMAN DUMMY PARACHUTE OUT AT JUST THE RIGHT INSTANT! NOW TO COVER UP ALL THIS EVIDENCE!

AND A FEW MINUTES LATER...

LOOK! BATMAN'S ALIVE! HE'S SCRATCHED AND BRUISED-- BUT HE'S ALIVE! IT'S A MIRACLE!

THE TREES MUST HAVE BROKEN HIS FALL! MAYBE HE HIT A SOFT SPOT-- A BOG! ANYWAY-- IT'S A GREAT DAY FOR GOTHAM CITY!

ROUTE 7

SOME TIME AFTER, IN THE CRIME CLOWN'S HIDEOUT...

HA-HA! BATMAN HAS BUT TWO HOURS TO ACHIEVE THE FIRST OF HIS CRIMES! HE'D BETTER HURRY!

JOKER-- THIS BOX JUST ARRIVED-- IT'S FOR YOU!

AND AS THE JOKER OPENS THE BOX...

BATS! UGH! IT'S FROM THE BATMAN!

LOOK, BOSS-- THERE'S A NEWSPAPER FRONT PAGE IN THAT BOX!

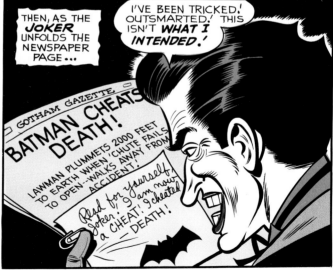

THEN, AS THE JOKER UNFOLDS THE NEWSPAPER PAGE...

I'VE BEEN TRICKED! OUTSMARTED! THIS ISN'T WHAT I INTENDED!

GOTHAM GAZETTE

BATMAN CHEATS DEATH!

LAWMAN PLUMMETS 2000 FEET TO EARTH WHEN 'CHUTE FAILS TO OPEN--WALKS AWAY FROM ACCIDENT!

Read for yourself, Joker. I am now a CHEAT! I cheated --DEATH!

AND WHEN **BATMAN** ARRIVES AT THE **JOKER'S** HIDEOUT...

IF THEY'D ONLY PUT THOSE GUNS AWAY! ONE FALSE MOVE ON MY PART AND ONE OF THOSE TRIGGER-HAPPY HOODS MIGHT SHOOT **ROBIN** ON THE SPOT!

AH, IT'S **BATMAN!** NOW OUR GAME CAN CONTINUE! YES, **BATMAN** --YOU OUTSMARTED ME-- BUT I MUST GIVE YOU CREDIT! IT WAS A MASTER STROKE **WORTHY OF ME!**

ROBIN'S LIFE IS STILL AT STAKE **BATMAN--** SO NOW YOU MUST **STEAL! HA-HA!** AND MAKE IT GOOD, **BATMAN!** IT MUST BE A **THEFT** THAT EARNS MY **RESPECT**--OR ELSE! **HO-HO-HO!** AGAIN--YOU HAVE 24 HOURS!

SOON AFTER, WHEN **BATMAN** HAS DEPARTED...

WHAT'S UP, BOSS? WE GOIN' ON A JOB?

HA-HA! YES! WE WILL ADD TO **BATMAN'S** PLIGHT! HE'LL BE CAUGHT BETWEEN TWO FIRES--ONE, HIS DESIRE TO SAVE **ROBIN** BY FULFILLING **MY** ORDERS--TWO, HIS RESPONSIBILITY TO GOTHAM CITY AS A LAWMAN!

LATER, IN THE **WAYNE** MANSION, AS **BATMAN** DISCUSSES THE SITUATION WITH HIS TRUSTWORTHY BUTLER, ALFRED...

BUT WHAT OF **ROBIN**, SIR? YOU HAVE ONLY 24 HOURS! YOU **MUST** SAVE HIM!

I KNOW, ALFRED! BUT I CAN'T IGNORE THE **BAT SIGNAL!** THIS IS UNDOUBTEDLY **THE JOKER'S** WORK! HE'S PULLING A CRIME TO ADD TO MY TROUBLES! BUT I'LL HAVE TO THINK OF SOMETHING!

LATER, AT HEADQUARTERS...

IT'S THE **JOKER!** HE BROKE INTO FARLEY'S DEPARTMENT STORE! HE'S PROBABLY AFTER THAT **PLAYING CARD** COLLECTION THEY HAVE ON DISPLAY!

FARLEY'S, EH? HMM! MAYBE THE **JOKER** ISN'T AS **SMART** AS HE THINKS HE IS!

AND AT THE DESERTED DEPARTMENT STORE ...JUST AFTER CLOSING HOURS...

the **GREENE** PLAYING CARD COLLECTION — PLAYING CARDS OF HISTORY

MY MEMORY WAS RIGHT! THE CARD COLLECTION IS NEXT TO THE SPORTING GOODS DEPARTMENT! NOW FOR SOME FUN!

SPORTS DEPARTMENT

IT'S **BATMAN**, BOSS! I THOUGHT YOU SAID HE'D BE **TOO BUSY!**

95

SOON AFTER... THE JOKER ESCAPED-- BUT WITHOUT ANY LOOT AND MOST OF HIS MEN! THIS NIGHT WILL HOLD HIM FOR A WHILE! AND NOW I MUST GIVE THE WHOLE STORY TO THE PAPERS.'

AND WHEN THE PAPERS REACH THE JOKER'S HANDS...

Gotham Gazette

BATMAN STEALS JOKER'S THUNDER!

CRIME-TRICKSTER FOILED WHEN LAWMAN DIPS INTO HIS OWN BAG OF TRICKS.'

HMM! AGAIN I UNDER-ESTIMATED *BATMAN!* HE HAS COMPLETED HIS *THEFT* AS PER OUR BARGAIN! HE REALLY *DID* STEAL MY THUNDER! HE IS INDEED A WORTHY ADVERSARY.'

YOU MAY BE HAVIN' FUN PLAYIN' GAMES, BOSS-- BUT I DON'T LIKE IT! *BATMAN'S* GONNA WRIGGLE OUT AGAIN-- AND THEN HE AND *ROBIN* GO FREE!

DON'T BE SILLY! I'LL ARRANGE IT SO THAT HE *CAN'T* WRIGGLE OUT-- *HO-HO!*

LATER... YOU'VE BEEN CLEVER, *BATMAN.'* YOU'VE *CHEATED* AND *STOLEN* AND YET YOU'RE NOT A CRIMINAL! IT IS STILL MY AIM TO *MAKE* YOU A CRIMINAL! SO NOW YOU MUST BECOME A *KILLER.'*

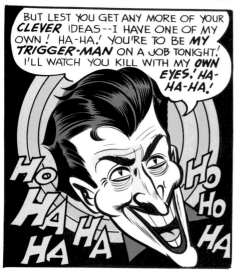

BUT LEST YOU GET ANY MORE OF YOUR *CLEVER* IDEAS--I HAVE ONE OF MY OWN! HA-HA! YOU'RE TO BE *MY TRIGGER-MAN* ON A JOB TONIGHT! I'LL WATCH YOU KILL WITH MY *OWN EYES!* HA-HA-HA!

HA-HA! COME ON, *BATMAN--* IT'S *KILL* OR *ROBIN* GETS *KILLED* TONIGHT! HA-HA! HO-HO!

FOR A WHILE IT LOOKED LIKE *BATMAN* MIGHT OUTSMART THE JOKER! BUT NOW...HE'S LICKED! THE JOKER HOLDS ALL THE CARDS.'

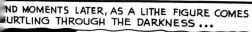

Artists: Dick Sprang and Charles Paris / Colorist: Glenn Whitmore

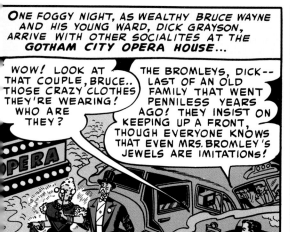

ONE FOGGY NIGHT, AS WEALTHY BRUCE WAYNE AND HIS YOUNG WARD, DICK GRAYSON, ARRIVE WITH OTHER SOCIALITES AT THE *GOTHAM CITY OPERA HOUSE*...

WOW! LOOK AT THAT COUPLE, BRUCE.. THOSE CRAZY CLOTHES THEY'RE WEARING! WHO ARE THEY?

THE BROMLEYS, DICK-- LAST OF AN OLD FAMILY THAT WENT PENNILESS YEARS AGO! THEY INSIST ON KEEPING UP A FRONT, THOUGH EVERYONE KNOWS THAT EVEN MRS. BROMLEY'S JEWELS ARE IMITATIONS!

SUDDENLY, FROM OUT OF THE THICK MIST...

EEEK!

HA, HA, HA!

MRS. BROMLEY! SOMEONE GRABBED HER, THEN DISAPPEARED INTO THE FOG! AND HE LOOKED LIKE--- LIKE---

LIKE THE *JOKER!* I'D KNOW THAT MOCKING LAUGHTER ANYWHERE! COME ON, DICK!

HA, HA, HA! HA, HA!

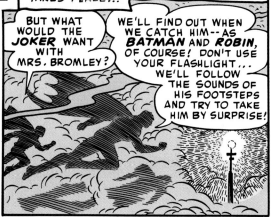

AND IN THE CONCEALMENT OF THE SWIRLING MIST, AN AMAZING TRANSFORMATION TAKES PLACE...

BUT WHAT WOULD THE *JOKER* WANT WITH MRS. BROMLEY?

WE'LL FIND OUT WHEN WE CATCH HIM-- AS *BATMAN* AND *ROBIN*, OF COURSE! DON'T USE YOUR FLASHLIGHT... WE'LL FOLLOW THE SOUNDS OF HIS FOOTSTEPS AND TRY TO TAKE HIM BY SURPRISE!

BUT JUST THEN...

CLUNK

OOPS! BUMPED INTO SOMETHING-- BUT I CAN'T TELL WHAT IT IS!

MAY AS WELL USE MY FLASHLIGHT NOW, BATMAN! THE JOKER MUST'VE HEARD THAT NOISE ANYHOW!

AND AS THE AMBER BEAM PIERCES THE FOG...

ULP! W-WE'RE TWINS!

WHY--IT'S A *MIRROR*... A HEAVY GLASS MIRROR THE *JOKER* MUST'VE SET UP HERE TO CONFUSE ANYONE WHO CHASED HIM! COME ON-- LET'S CIRCLE AROUND IT!

A MOMENT LATER...

LOOK! IT'S MRS. BROMLEY... BUT NO SIGN OF THE *JOKER!*

GUESS IT'S HOPELESS TRYING TO CATCH HIM IN THIS FOG! BESIDES-- WE'VE GOT TO ATTEND TO MRS. BROMLEY! HOPE SHE'S NOT HURT!

2

SHE'S ALL RIGHT...JUST FAINTED! BUT LOOK, *ROBIN*... SHE'S BEEN ROBBED OF ALL HER JEWELS! I GUESS THE *JOKER* DIDN'T KNOW THEY WERE PHONY-- ONLY *IMITATIONS!*

GUESS THE LAUGH IS ON THE *JOKER* THIS TIME!

BUT NOT THE LAST LAUGH! FOR ON THE VERY NEXT NIGHT, OUTSIDE THE GOTHAM CITY SAVINGS BANK...

THE *JOKER* HIMSELF-- TRYING TO BUST INTO THAT BANK! HERE'S MY CHANCE TO NAB HIM SINGLE-HANDED AND EARN ME A PROMOTION!

Gotham City SAVINGS BANK

SAVE REGULARLY AND SEE YOUR PENNIES GROW INTO A CASTLE OF GOLD!

BUT AS THE PATROLMAN REACHES FOR HIS GUN...

WONDERFUL STUFF, THESE QUICK-DRYING PLASTICS! PRESTO -- AND I'VE GOT A COP IN A COCOON! HA-HA-HA! WHEN YOU COME OUT, YOU'LL BE A BUTTERFLY... HA-HA... AND I'LL HAVE A CASTLE OF GOLD!

HUH? THAT STICKY STUFF'S JAMMED MY GUN!

LATER, AT POLICE COMMISSIONER GORDON'S OFFICE...

I'D BE A BUTTERFLY, HE SAID... AND WELL I MIGHT'VE BEEN, BECAUSE I THOUGHT I WAS LOSING MY MIND! HE *DIDN'T ROB THE BANK!* ALL HE TOOK WERE THOSE USELESS CHIPS OF WOOD, PAINTED TO LOOK LIKE GOLD COINS!

STRANGE... THE *JOKER* MUST'VE KNOWN THOSE COINS WEREN'T REAL, *BATMAN!*

THEN WHAT OF THOSE FAKE BROMLEY JEWELS HE STOLE LAST NIGHT? COULD HE HAVE KNOWN *THEY* WERE FAKES, TOO?

ALL I CAN SAY IS, IT LOOKS LIKE THE START OF A MAD *JOKER* SCHEME, COMMISSIONER-- BUT I CAN'T IMAGINE WHAT! WE'LL JUST HAVE TO WAIT FOR FURTHER DEVELOPMENTS!

AFTERWARD, IN THE SECRET BAT-CAVE.

IT'S NO USE! I'VE CHECKED ALL OUR TROPHIES OF OLD *JOKER* CRIMES, AND THERE'S NOTHING TO SUGGEST WHY HE'D BE STEALING WORTHLESS IMITATION VALUABLES!

HOPE WE FIND THE ANSWER SOON!

JOKER TRICKS TO ESCAPE LAW

SO NEXT DAY, AS THE **BAT-PLANE** HOVERS IN A WATCHFUL CIRCUIT OVER **GOTHAM CITY**...

WE'VE BEEN PATROLLING ALL DAY, BUT THERE'S NO SIGN OF TROUBLE ANYWHERE! MAYBE THE *JOKER* WAS JUST PULLING A COUPLE OF PRANKS JUST TO CONFUSE US -- WITHOUT ANY OTHER MOTIVE!

WAIT! DOWN THERE -- ON THAT BIG BILLBOARD! IT'S THE *JOKER*!

IMMEDIATELY, A ROPE LADDER IS RELEASED, AND...

WHAT?? THIS IS JUST *TOO* WILD! THE *JOKER* RISKING HIS NECK TO CUT A *PAPER COPY* OF THE *MONA LISA* OFF THAT BILLBOARD! WELL, WHATEVER HE'S UP TO, I'LL SOON GET AN EXPLANATION FROM HIM!

The MONA LISA the BEST in ART

STAFF'S BREAD the BEST in BAKING

BUT AT THAT MOMENT...

HA, HA TOO LATE, *BATMAN*! A ROPE'S A POOR MATTER COMPARED TO A LADDER!

HE'S GOING THROUGH THAT WINDOW! AND THAT BUILDING'S SUCH A MAZE, I'LL NEVER BE ABLE TO FIND HIM INSIDE!

LATER, BACK IN THE **BAT-CAVE**...

I SHOULD'VE KNOWN HE'D HAVE SOME TRICK GETAWAY PREPARED! AND IF WE DON'T GET TO THE BOTTOM OF THE *JOKER'S* CRAZY CRIMES SOON -- *I'LL* GO CRAZY!

BATMAN -- IT'S OUR BUTLER -- ALFRED -- PHONING FROM THE HOUSE! HE JUST HEARD A NEWS BROAD-CAST THAT THE *JOKER'S* BEEN CAUGHT!

THE STARTLING NEWS SENDS THE ASTONISHED PAIR TO COMMISSIONER GORDON'S OFFICE, WHERE THEY LEARN...

HE JUST WALKED INTO POLICE HEADQUARTERS WITH THOSE FAKE JEWELS, FAKE GOLD COINS AND THAT FAKE MONA LISA -- AND ASKED TO DEPOSIT THE STUFF, AS IF HE WERE IN A BANK! NATURALLY, THEY GRABBED HIM!

HE SOUNDS MADDER THAN EVER! BUT -- WE'LL LEARN MORE AT THE TRIAL TOMORROW!

NEXT MORNING, IN A GOTHAM COURTROOM, AS A PSYCHIATRIST REPORTS ON HIS EXAMINATION OF THE *JOKER*...

THE PRISONER SUFFERS FROM *HEBOPHRENIC SCHIZOPHRENIA*... IN NON-MEDICAL LANGUAGE, AN INSANITY MARKED BY EXTREMELY FOOLISH BEHAVIOR! EVEN HIS TWISTED SENSE OF HUMOR WAS MERELY A SYMPTOM OF THIS INSANITY THAT'S NOW OVERCOME HIM!

4

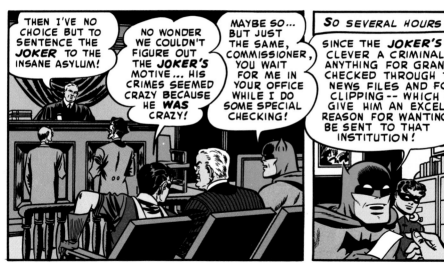

THEN I'VE NO CHOICE BUT TO SENTENCE THE **JOKER** TO THE INSANE ASYLUM!

NO WONDER WE COULDN'T FIGURE OUT THE **JOKER'S** MOTIVE... HIS CRIMES SEEMED CRAZY BECAUSE HE **WAS** CRAZY!

MAYBE SO... BUT JUST THE SAME, COMMISSIONER, YOU WAIT FOR ME IN YOUR OFFICE WHILE I DO SOME SPECIAL CHECKING!

SO SEVERAL HOURS LATER...

SINCE THE **JOKER'S** TOO CLEVER A CRIMINAL TO TAKE ANYTHING FOR GRANTED, I CHECKED THROUGH THE CITY'S NEWS FILES AND FOUND THIS CLIPPING -- WHICH COULD GIVE HIM AN EXCELLENT REASON FOR WANTING TO BE SENT TO THAT INSTITUTION!

LET ME SEE!

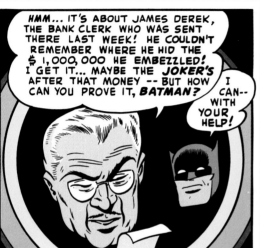

HMM... IT'S ABOUT JAMES DEREK, THE BANK CLERK WHO WAS SENT THERE LAST WEEK! HE COULDN'T REMEMBER WHERE HE HID THE $1,000,000 HE EMBEZZLED! I GET IT... MAYBE THE **JOKER'S** AFTER THAT MONEY -- BUT HOW CAN YOU PROVE IT, **BATMAN**?

I CAN-- WITH YOUR HELP!

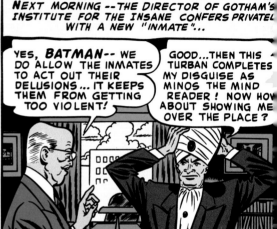

NEXT MORNING -- THE DIRECTOR OF GOTHAM'S INSTITUTE FOR THE INSANE CONFERS PRIVATEL WITH A NEW "INMATE"...

YES, **BATMAN**-- WE DO ALLOW THE INMATES TO ACT OUT THEIR DELUSIONS ... IT KEEPS THEM FROM GETTING TOO VIOLENT!

GOOD...THEN THIS TURBAN COMPLETES MY DISGUISE AS MINOS THE MIND READER! NOW HOW ABOUT SHOWING ME OVER THE PLACE?

PRESENTLY...

(WHISPER) THEY'RE ALL HARMLESS ON THIS FLOOR, SO THE DOORS AND WINDOWS ARE UNBARRED! BUT-- DON'T BE SURPRISED AT ANYTHING!

MORNING, DR. REED... HAVE YOU READ MY PAPER ON GRAVITATION YET?

ER--YES! MINOS-- MEET SIR ISAAC NEWTON, DISCOVERER OF GRAVITATION!

AND I'M CHRISTOPHER COLUMBUS-- DISCOVERER OF AMERICA!

AND I'M **BATMAN**

"BATMAN?"

"YES--BUT DON'T BREATHE IT TO A SOUL... MUST KEEP MY IDENTITY SECRET, YOU KNOW! SEE?... MY **BATMAN** COSTUME IS HIDDEN HERE--EVER READY FOR A CALL TO ACTION...THOUGH I MUST ADMIT THINGS HAVE BEEN QUIET LATELY!"

LATER, EN ROUTE TO THE NEXT WARD...

"NOW, THE FLOOR ABOVE HOUSES OUR MORE DANGEROUS CASES--INCLUDING THE **JOKER** AND DEREK, THE BANK CLERK! THAT'S WHERE I'M HAVING THE GUARD PUT YOU NOW! WATCH YOURSELF AND-- GOOD LUCK!"

"THANKS, DR. REED!"

*AND AS SOON AS THE DISGUISED **BATMAN** IS LOCKED IN THE UPPER WARD...*

"MINOS THE MIND READER, EH? WELL, I'M FRANZ THE STRANGLER... ONCE CHAMPION WRESTLER! CAN YOU READ WHAT'S ON **MY** MIND?"

"OH, OH... OBVIOUSLY THE WARD BULLY--AND HE'S TAKEN A DISLIKE TO ME!"

"ER...YES--AS LEADER OF THIS WARD, YOU'RE TESTING ME OUT!"

"YOU WERE RIGHT... AND THAT I DON'T LIKE! SO-- I'M GOING TO GET RID OF YOU!"

"DON'T, FRANZ! HE'S HARMLESS! DON'T START ANYTHING OR THE GUARDS WILL PUT US ALL IN STRAIT-JACKETS!"

*HEEDLESS OF THE **JOKER'S** WARNING, THE BRUTE LEAPS, AND...*

"HA-HA! PRETTY NEAT FOOT-WORK FOR A MIND READER! BUT EVEN **I** COULD READ THAT SIMPLETON'S MIND-- SO DON'T GET SWELL-HEADED, MINOS!"

"THEY ALL LAUGH AT MINOS AND SAY I'M CRAZY! YOU,TOO-- YOU CLOWN! BUT I CAN READ YOUR MIND AS EASILY AS THE REST!"

"**MY** MIND? HA, HA.. THAT'S A GOOD ONE! LET ME SEE YOU TRY IT... HA, HA, HA!"

"NOW'S MY CHANCE TO BAIT HIM!"

"JUST AS I READ IN FRANZ'S MIND WHERE HIS WEAKNESS WAS, I SEE THAT **YOUR** MIND IS ON THE MIND OF THIS MAN HERE-- AND HIS FORGOTTEN SECRET!"

"YOU MEAN HIM? DEREK? SECRET? **WHAT** SECRET, MAY I ASK?"

6

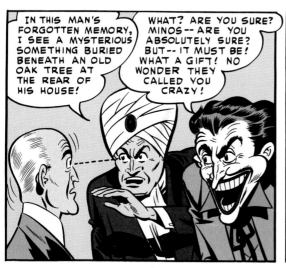

IN THIS MAN'S FORGOTTEN MEMORY, I SEE A MYSTERIOUS SOMETHING BURIED BENEATH AN OLD OAK TREE AT THE REAR OF HIS HOUSE!

WHAT? ARE YOU SURE? MINOS -- ARE YOU ABSOLUTELY SURE? BUT -- IT MUST BE! WHAT A GIFT! NO WONDER THEY CALLED YOU CRAZY!

PSST -- I'M BREAKING OUT TONIGHT! WANT TO COME WITH ME? WHAT A TEAM WE'LL MAKE!

PERFECT! WITH ROBIN WAITING AT THAT OLD OAK TREE -- THE JOKER'S WALKING RIGHT INTO OUR TRAP! WHICH WILL PROVE MY CONTENTION THAT DEREK'S MONEY WAS HIS REASON FOR PRETENDING TO BE INSANE!

SO THAT NIGHT, WHILE THE OTHERS SLEEP...

I MADE THIS SKELETON KEY MYSELF! THIS DOOR LEADS TO A PADDED CELL THEY'VE STOPPED USING -- BUT BETTER LET ME GO IN FIRST AND SEE IF ALL'S CLEAR!

SURE... I'LL WAIT!

BUT SUDDENLY, AFTER A BRIEF WAIT BESIDE THE OPEN DOOR...

SAY, ARE -- OOF!

AND SECONDS LATER, AS THE DAZED CRIME FIGHTER OPENS HIS EYES...

HA-HA-HA-HA! INGENIOUS, THIS BATMAN OUTFIT I FOUND NEATLY PACKED UNDER YOUR SHIRT -- COMPLETE WITH UTILITY BELT AND RADIO! YOUR FALSE TIP ON DEREK'S HIDDEN WEALTH MADE ME SUSPICIOUS, BECAUSE LAST NIGHT DEREK REVEALED THE REAL HIDING PLACE BY TALKING IN HIS SLEEP!

NOW, BEFORE LEAVING FOR MY TREASURE HOARD, I'LL TURN THIS WATER ON! IT'LL FILL THIS ROOM LIKE A BATH-TUB -- JUST TO REMIND YOU THAT YOU'RE A WASHOUT AS A MIND-READER! HA-HA-HA!

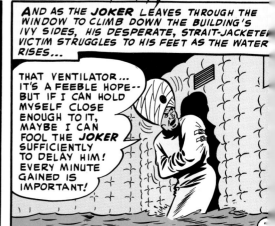

AND AS THE JOKER LEAVES THROUGH THE WINDOW TO CLIMB DOWN THE BUILDING'S IVY SIDES, HIS DESPERATE, STRAIT-JACKETED VICTIM STRUGGLES TO HIS FEET AS THE WATER RISES...

THAT VENTILATOR... IT'S A FEEBLE HOPE -- BUT IF I CAN HOLD MYSELF CLOSE ENOUGH TO IT, MAYBE I CAN FOOL THE JOKER SUFFICIENTLY TO DELAY HIM! EVERY MINUTE GAINED IS IMPORTANT!

A MOMENT LATER, AS THE **JOKER** PASSES THE OPEN WINDOW OF THE WARD DIRECTLY BELOW...

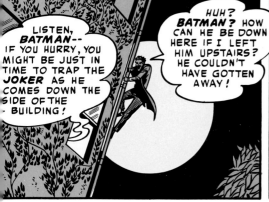

LISTEN, **BATMAN**-- IF YOU HURRY, YOU MIGHT BE JUST IN TIME TO TRAP THE **JOKER** AS HE COMES DOWN THE SIDE OF THE BUILDING!

HUH? **BATMAN?** HOW CAN HE BE DOWN HERE IF I LEFT HIM UPSTAIRS? HE COULDN'T HAVE GOTTEN AWAY!

I KNOW **I'M** NOT CRAZY -- BUT NEITHER AM I CRAZY ENOUGH TO TAKE CHANCES! IF SOMEONE'S READY TO NAB ME AS I COME DOWN, WHY RISK THAT WHEN I CAN CLIMB UP AGAIN AND FIND ANOTHER WAY OUT?

BUT UPON RETURNING TO THE ROOM WHERE HE LEFT HIS TRAPPED VICTIM, THE **JOKER** GETS THE BIGGEST SHOCK OF ALL!

WHAT? CAN I BE LOSING MY MIND? Y-YOU'RE **BRUCE WAYNE** -- THE PLAYBOY! BUT I LEFT **BATMAN** HERE! WHERE IS HE?

LUCKY I MANAGED TO WASH OFF MY DISGUISE AND SCATTER THE PARTS IN THE WATER BEFORE HE GOT BACK! NOW TO REALLY DRIVE HIM DAFFY!

WHAT DO YOU MEAN--- WHERE'S **BATMAN?** I'M **BATMAN**--! ME-- BRUCE WAYNE! YOU JUST TIED ME UP HERE YOURSELF!

NO-- YOU **COULDN'T** BE **BATMAN!** IT'S A PLOT... A TRAP!... A WILD, CRAZY TRICK! BECAUSE I HEARD **BATMAN** IS DOWNSTAIRS!

BUT-- IF IT WASN'T REALLY **BATMAN** I TIED UP -- IT WASN'T **YOU** EITHER! THIS PLACE-- HAS IT AFFECTED MY MIND? CAN **I** BE GOING CRAZY?

BUT WAIT!...THIS VENTILATOR! YOU COULD'VE SHOUTED THROUGH IT SO THAT YOUR VOICE WOULD EMERGE DOWNSTAIRS! AND, IN MY EXCITEMENT, I'M FORGETTING SOMETHING ELSE -- THAT **BATMAN** ALWAYS WEARS A DISGUISE TO PROTECT HIS IDENTITY! YOU COULD'VE **REMOVED** YOUR DISGUISE!

HA, HA... FOR A MOMENT, I WAS WORRIED ABOUT MY MIND! BUT NOW-- IT'S OBVIOUS! AND WHAT'S MORE-- I'VE FINALLY LEARNED THE SECRET OF **BATMAN'S IDENTITY!**

OF COURSE, **JOKER**... I'M **BATMAN!**

8

108

I SAW HIM CLIMBING FROM HIS WARD WINDOW AS I APPROACHED, BUT HIS CLUMSINESS TOLD ME HE WASN'T--- COULDN'T--- BE THE REAL *BATMAN!* STILL, HE WAS HELPFUL!

HE'S ALSO A VERY LUCKY MAN! THE DOCTORS TELL ME THAT BLOW ON THE HEAD MAY HAVE BROUGHT HIM BACK TO HIS SENSES!

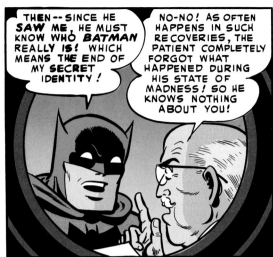

THEN -- SINCE HE *SAW* ME, HE MUST KNOW WHO *BATMAN* REALLY *IS!* WHICH MEANS THE END OF MY *SECRET* IDENTITY *!*

NO-NO! AS OFTEN HAPPENS IN SUCH RECOVERIES, THE PATIENT COMPLETELY FORGOT WHAT HAPPENED DURING HIS STATE OF MADNESS! SO HE KNOWS NOTHING ABOUT YOU!

BUT WHAT ABOUT THE JOKER -- WOULDN'T HE KNOW THE SECRET? AT THIS VERY MOMENT, IN A PADDED CELL...

IF WAYNE IS *BATMAN* -- THEN *BATMAN* COULDN'T BE *BATMAN!* BUT SINCE WAYNE COULDN'T BE *BATMAN* -- THEN MAYBE *I'M BATMAN!* BUT -- THAT'S CRAZY! HA-HA-HA-! SO OBVIOUSLY-- *I'M* CRAZY!

HA HA, HA, HA, HA, HA, HA, HA!

SEVERAL DAYS LATER, AS BRUCE AND DICK HAVE THEIR BREAKFAST...

I SEE WHERE THE *JOKER'S* RECOVERED FROM THE CONFUSING NIGHT WE GAVE HIM! THEY'RE TRANSFERRING HIM TO THE *STATE PRISON!*

YES -- HE FINALLY HAD TO TELL THE AUTHORITIES WHERE DEREK'S MONEY WAS HIDDEN, IN ORDER TO PROVE THAT HE HIMSELF WAS SANE!

THE END

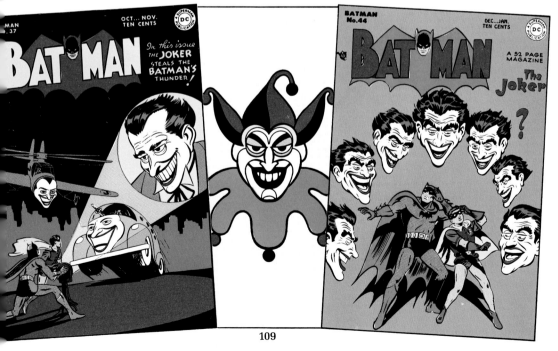

109

Artists: Dick Sprang and Stan Kaye / Colorist: Glenn Whitmore

MY PARTNER WILL SIGN HIS NAME, TOO... **THE JOKER!**

YES, HA--HA-- I, TOO, AM GOING HONEST! I CAME HERE FROM GOTHAM CITY, TO GET A NEW START!

WH-WHY... YOU'RE **LUTHOR**, THE NOTORIOUS CRIMINAL-SCIENTIST! **YOU** WANT A MANUFACTURING LICENSE?

YES, I'VE SERVED MY TERM AND AM GOING TO USE MY SCIENTIFIC GENIUS AS AN HONEST BUSINESSMAN!

IT DOESN'T TAKE LONG FOR SENSATIONAL NEWS LIKE THIS TO REACH THE **DAILY PLANET**...

GREAT CAESAR'S GHOST! OUR CITY HALL REPORTER PHONED THAT **LUTHOR** AND **THE JOKER** ARE THERE TOGETHER, RIGHT NOW!

WHEN REPORTERS CLARK KENT AND LOIS LANE REACH THE SCENE...

WOW-- HEAR THAT, CLARK? LET'S GO...

WE'VE NOTHING TO HIDE, NOW THAT WE'RE GOING STRAIGHT! THIS AFTERNOON, WE'LL DEMONSTRATE THE NEW INVENTION WE'RE GOING TO MANUFACTURE, OUTSIDE OUR FACTORY!

YOU AND **THE JOKER** IN BUSINESS? THIS I'LL HAVE TO SEE!

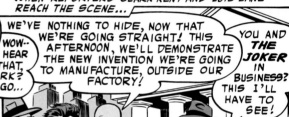

BUT AS **THE JOKER'S** FLASHY CAR, THE **JOKERMOBILE**, ROLLS AWAY...

I'M SURE OUR NEW CAREERS WILL INTEREST OUR OLD FRIENDS **SUPERMAN** AND **BATMAN**, TOO!

YES-- HA, HA-- AND WHAT A SURPRISE THEY'RE IN FOR... HO, HO, HO!

AREN'T YOU COMING WITH ME, CLARK?

SORRY, LOIS, I...ER...JUST REMEMBERED ANOTHER ASSIGNMENT!

I HEARD WHAT **THE JOKER** SAID, WITH MY **SUPER-HEARING**! I DON'T LIKE THE SOUND OF THAT AT ALL!

2

FOR HIS OTHER "ASSIGNMENT," MILD-MANNERED CLARK KENT SECRETLY SWITCHES TO-- **SUPERMAN**, THE **MAN OF STEEL**...

WITH THOSE TWO CROOKS TEAMED UP, ANYTHING COULD HAPPEN! AND SINCE **BATMAN** KNOWS **THE JOKER'S** TRICKS BETTER THAN ANYONE...

...I'LL PAY HIM A QUICK VISIT, AND LET HIM KNOW WHAT'S GOING ON!

ONLY MOMENTS LATER, IN THE GOTHAM CITY MANSION OF WEALTHY BRUCE WAYNE AND HIS YOUNG WARD, DICK GRAYSON...

BRUCE! SOMETHING'S SHAKING THE WHOLE HOUSE-- FROM UNDERNEATH!

SOMEONE MAY BE TRYING TO BREAK INTO THE **BAT-CAVE!**

DOWN THEY RACE TO THEIR SECRET **BAT-CAVE**, ONLY TO DISCOVER...

IT'S **SUPERMAN!** HE DRILLED UP FROM UNDERNEATH!

SORRY IF I STARTLED YOU, BUT I DIDN'T WANT TO CHANCE ANYONE SEEING ME ENTER! I'VE GOT NEWS FOR YOU...

TO THE **DYNAMIC DUO**, IT'S OMINOUS NEWS INDEED...

THE **JOKER** AND **LUTHOR** IN PARTNERSHIP? THAT'S BAD! GOTHAM CITY IS QUIET-- SO WE CAN COME TO METROPOLIS AT ONCE!

GOOD...I'LL TAKE YOU THERE THE **FAST** WAY!

BACK IN METROPOLIS, OUTSIDE THE NEW PARTNER'S FACTORY...

AH...THERE COME **SUPERMAN, BATMAN** AND **ROBIN**, AS WE EXPECTED! WHAT A JOKE ON THEM THIS WILL BE!

YES... HA, HA...THE GREATEST JOKE OF MY ENTIRE JESTING CAREER, THANKS TO YOUR SCIENTIFIC GENIUS, LUTHOR!

NO, NO, MY DEAR FELLOW! IT WAS THROUGH YOUR BRILLIANT SENSE OF HUMOR THAT THIS WHOLE SCHEME WAS CONCOCTED!

3

SHORTLY...

THAT FACTORY IS LINED WITH **LEAD**, THE ONLY SUBSTANCE THAT CAN BLOCK MY **X-RAY VISION!** WHAT ARE YOU TWO TRYING TO HIDE?

WE MUST PROTECT OUR MANUFACTURING SECRETS, TILL WE PATENT THEM, THAT'S THE ONLY REASON!

WHEN REPORTERS ARRIVE...

THERE'S THE INVENTION WE INTEND TO PROMOTE-- A GREAT BOON TO THE WORLD!

WHERE IS IT?... I ONLY SEE THREE WORKMEN...

YOU MEAN **MECHANO-MEN**, CONSTRUCTED OF A SUPER-STRONG METAL I DEVELOPED! I CAN CONTROL THEM ABSOLUTELY!

BECAUSE THEY ARE INVULNERABLE TO ANY AMOUNT OF HEAT AND PRESSURE, THEY CAN BE USED FOR TASKS IMPOSSIBLE TO ORDINARY WORKMEN!

AS SOON AS WE'VE TESTED THEM COM-PLETELY, WE'LL START MAKING THEM FOR SALE!

SO THAT NIGHT, AS **BATMAN** AND **ROBIN** MAINTAIN A RELENTLESS VIGIL...

AND FOR **THE JOKER**, TOO! THERE HE IS NOW, UP TO HIS OLD TRICKS!

AND AS THE AMAZING DEMONSTRATION ENDS...

AN IMPRESSIVE INVENTION... BUT I STILL FEEL IT'S A COVER-UP FOR SOME BIG THEFT!

WE CAN'T PROVE IT, THOUGH! ALL WE CAN DO IS PATROL METROPOLIS, IN SHIFTS, 24 HOURS A DAY, TILL THEY STRIKE!

METROPOLIS IS A NEW FIELD FOR US!

HA, HA... MY STEEL *JOKER-NET* WILL SURELY HOLD HIM!

LOOK! IT'S *BATMAN* AND *ROBIN*, FROM GOTHAM CITY! THEY MUST HAVE CAUGHT SOME BIG CROOK!

SAME OLD *JOKER!* JUST AS I FIGURED, YOU HAD NO INTENTION OF GOING STRAIGHT!

REALLY, *BATMAN*—HA, HA, HA, HA--THIS IS AN UNWARRANTED INTRUSION! I WAS ONLY PERFORMING A TEST...

..ON ONE OF THE *MECHANO-MEN*, TO MAKE SURE NO OBSTACLE OF THIS TYPE COULD STOP THEM!

GEE--IT *IS* ONLY A *MECHANO-MAN!* WE'LL HAVE TO LET HIM GO!

AND NOW I HAVE MORE WORK TO DO! I'LL BE SEEING YOU, *BATMAN*... HO, HO, HO!

THAT STUNT WAS STAGED DELIBERATELY, TO MAKE US LOOK FOOLISH! HE'S GOT SOMETHING UP HIS SLEEVE...BUT *WHAT?*

*Y*ET THIS IS ONLY THE BEGINNING--FOR AWHILE LATER, AS *SUPERMAN* TAKES OVER THE PATROL...

WHATEVER *LUTHOR* AND *THE JOKER* ARE PLANNING, I'VE GOT TO--OH, OH--TROUBLE DOWN BELOW!

5

LOOK-- THAT CRAZY CAR... IT'S GOING TO HIT THAT MAN!

NOT SO FAST THERE, *JOKER!* BY DRIVING RECKLESSLY, YOU ALMOST HIT THIS MAN!

BUT-- HA, HA-- I *WANTED* TO HIT HIM, *SUPERMAN!*

NO-- HERE COMES *SUPERMAN!* JUST IN TIME!

SCREEE

T'S ONE OF OUR MECHANO-MEN, ND I WAS PERFORMING N EXPERIMENT TO LEARN OW MUCH A CAR WOULD DAMAGE IT!

AND I WAS IN SUCH A RUSH TO SAVE HIM, I NEVER NOTICED!

NOW I'LL HAVE TO DO MY EXPERIMENT ELSEWHERE-- IF YOU'LL ALLOW ME, *SUPERMAN...* HA, HA, HA!

I CAN'T STOP HIM, SINCE HE BROKE NO LAW--BUT I STILL THINK THERE'S SOME- THING BIGGER BEHIND THESE JOKES!

OIS LANE HAS THE SAME OPINION-- AND NEXT MORNING, SHE SETS OUT O PROVE IT...

HERE GOES *LUTHOR*-- ND I INTEND TO FIND UT WHAT HE'S UP TO! T COULD BE A BIG COOP!

*T*HE ANSWER COMES SHORTLY AFTERWARD, AT A LONELY PLACE OUTSIDE METROPOLIS...

ONE OF HIS SCIENTIFIC INVENTIONS! IT HURLS ELECTRIC BOLTS THAT SHATTER THE ROCK CLIFF... BUT *WHY?*

6

115

116

GOOD... THAT'LL KEEP HER OUT OF TROUBLE! OF COURSE, IT WASN'T REALLY HER FAULT...THE MECHANO-MEN FOOLED US, TOO!

LUTHOR'S INGENIOUS INVENTION, AND THE JOKER'S WARPED SENSE OF HUMOR, ARE MAKING US ALL LOOK A BIT FOOLISH!

THEY MUST BE PULLING THESE TRICKS SO WE WON'T BOTHER THEM ANY MORE... THEN THEY CAN TRY A BIG CRIME!

BUT WHAT ARE THEY PLANNING? IF I COULD SEE INSIDE THEIR FACTORY, I MIGHT FIND OUT... BUT I CAN'T!

MAYBE YOU CAN, SUPERMAN... I JUST GOT AN IDEA! THOSE TWO WOULDN'T ALLOW US PAST THE DOOR OF THEIR FACTORY... BUT WHAT ABOUT WEALTHY BRUCE WAYNE? THEY'VE NO REASON TO SUSPECT HIM!

THUS A LITTLE LATER, IN THE FACTORY'S WEIRD OFFICE...

HA, HA... WE'VE MADE SUPERMAN AND BATMAN LOOK UTTERLY RIDICULOUS! AND THEY DON'T KNOW THE REAL JOKE ON THEM IS YET TO COME... HA, HA, HA!

QUIET, JOKER-- WE HAVE A CALLER!

AND AS THAT "CALLER" STATES HIS "BUSINESS"...

I'M BRUCE WAYNE, A DIRECTOR OF THE WAYNE MINING COMPANY! I READ OF YOUR NEW MECHANO-MEN, AND WOULD LIKE TO HIRE THEM FOR A TOUGH JOB!

WE DON'T PLAN TO RENT THEM OUT UNTIL AFTER TOMORROW'S BIG PUBLIC SHOWING OF THEIR ABILITIES!

TOO BAD... WHEN A MINING-BARGE SANK OFFSHORE RECENTLY, WE LOST SOME VALUABLE INDUSTRIAL DIAMONDS! HUMAN DIVERS CAN'T GO THAT DEEP!

OH...WELL--ER--SHOW ME THE LOCATION! WHEN WE OPEN OUR BUSINESS, WE'LL HAVE OUR MECHANO-MEN RECOVER THEM FOR YOU!

8

AND AS A FAST TRUCK SPEEDS BACK TO METROPOLIS...

WITH **TELESCOPIC VISION**, I CAN SEE THE **BATMOBILE** FOLLOWING! NOW, WITH ANY LUCK, I'LL GET INSIDE THAT FACTORY AND FIND OUT WHAT THEY'RE PLANNING!

PRESENTLY, IN THE PLANT...

THERE'S NOTHING HERE TO SHOW WHAT THEY'RE UP TO! NO BIG CRIME-MACHINES, LIKE **LUTHOR** HAS MADE IN THE PAST...

BUT JUST THEN...

EH--? ONE OF THE **MECHANO-MEN** MOVED HIS HEAD, LOOKING AROUND! I GLIMPSED IT AS I TURNED!

BUT I DIDN'T TOUCH THE CONTROLS! HMM... ONE OF THEM COULD BE AN IMPOSTOR! WE'D BETTER FIND OUT...

AND AFTER TESTING THE HUMAN-LIKE MACHINES, ONE BY ONE...

THE OTHER **MECHANO-MEN** ARE JUST METAL--AND THIS ONE IS, TOO! OTHERWISE, THE MALLET WOULD AFFECT IT!

YES, EVEN THIS DRILL DOESN'T MARK HIM! I GUESS I WAS MISTAKEN, AFTER ALL!

BUT, **ONCE** ALONE IN THEIR OFFICE...

THIS SPECIAL DRILL COULD DENT **ANY** METAL, BUT IT DIDN'T DENT **HIM**! THAT MEANS IT'S **SUPERMAN**, DISGUISED!

DON'T LET ON WE KNOW IT! I'VE GOT A SCHEME!

LATER...

NOW'S THE TIME TO TAKE THE **MECHANO-MEN** AND CARRY OUT OUR PLAN OF ACTION!

AND **BATMAN ROBIN** AND I WILL BE THERE TO STOP THEIR PLANS!

10

119

AFTERWARD, IN AN ALLEY BEHIND SOME OFFICE BUILDINGS...

THEY'LL SMASH INTO THE BUILDING FAST!

AND THEY CAN EASILY CARRY OUT THAT SAFE!

ABRUPTLY...

SO THAT'S IT! WE'VE GOT YOU COLD THIS TIME, FOR ROBBERY!

WHY, IT'S SUPERMAN-- AND BATMAN AND ROBIN! BUT YOU'VE NO RIGHT TO STOP US!

WE JUST BOUGHT THAT SAFE FOR OUR OFFICE, AND GOT PERMISSION TO OPEN THE WALL TO GET IT OUT! HERE'S THE PROOF!

AND NOW-- HA, HA-- IF YOU'LL LET TWO HONEST BUSINESSMEN ALONE, WE'LL GO BACK AND GET READY FOR OUR BIG SHOW!

BILL OF SALE
ONE (1) SAFE

THEY MUST'VE SEEN THROUGH MY DISGUISE, AND SET UP THIS STUNT TO MAKE US LOOK BAD AGAIN! I'M AFRAID OUR PLAN BACKFIRED!

AND YOU SAW NOTHING IN THEIR FACTORY TO INDICATE THEIR REAL PLANS?

WAIT A MINUTE... THE EXTRA CLOTHES I SAW HANGING THERE MAY BE A CLUE TO THEIR PLANS! IT WOULD TIE IN WITH THIS BIG MECHANO-MAN SHOW THEY'RE STAGING!

THAT AFTERNOON, IN A RENTED STADIUM, THE BIG EXHIBITION COMMENCES...

THEIR MECHANO-MEN SHOULD MAKE THEM A FORTUNE!

I GUESS SUPERMAN AND BATMAN ARE STILL SUSPICIOUS...THERE THEY ARE, WATCHING EVERYTHING!

Artists: Dick Sprang and Charles Paris / Colorist: Shelley Eiber

124

127

LATER, AS POLICE TAKE THE THIEVES AWAY...

WHAT I CAN'T FIGURE OUT IS WHY THESE CROOKS SHOULD DO **THE JOKER'S** WORK FOR HIM!

THIS CARD EXPLAINS IT... ONE OF THEM DROPPED IT WHEN YOU KNOCKED HIM DOWN!

176 MEMBERSHIP IN THE **CRIME-OF-THE-MONTH-CLUB**

Blinky Dean

The Joker

SO THAT'S IT, EH? **THE JOKER** HAS BEEN **SELLING MONTHLY JOBS** TO THE UNDERWORLD!

JUST WHAT I'D EXPECT OF HIM! AND IF I KNOW **THE JOKER**--AS SOON AS HE HEARS HOW WE'VE FOILED HIS PLAN, HE'LL PULL ANOTHER JUNE CRIME, JUST TO SAVE FACE!

RIGHT... AND I HAVE AN IDEA WHERE IT'LL BE, TOO! COME ON, **ROBIN**...

UPON REACHING THEIR DESTINATION, HOWEVER...

I THOUGHT IT MIGHT HAVE SOMETHING TO DO WITH THIS JUNE GRADUATION AT **GOTHAM UNIVERSITY**-- BUT I WAS WRONG! NOW WHAT?

I THINK **I** KNOW, **BATMAN!** LET'S GET TO THE RAILROAD TERMINAL FAST!

BUT AT THE STATION, THEIR LUCK PROVES NO BETTER...

THESE KIDS ARE TAKING OFF FOR **PINE GROVE**, THAT SUMMER CAMP FOR WEALTHY CHILDREN! I THOUGHT **THE JOKER** MIGHT STRIKE HERE!

GOOD TRY, **ROBIN!** GUESS WE'D BETTER HEAD HOME AND **WAIT** FOR HIS NEXT MOVE! I CAN'T THINK OF ANY OTHER POSSIBLE...

WAIT A MINUTE! THIS NEW MOVIE, OPENING TODAY... THAT'S THE ANSWER!

IT--IT IS? I DON'T UNDERSTAND, **BATMAN!**

CHARITY Premiere

LLET THEATER

"**JUPITER'S BRIDE**"

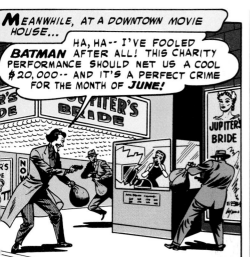

Artists: Jim Mooney and Sheldon Moldoff / Colorist: Helen Vesik

131

AND NOW... HAGEN'S ON THE LOOSE AGAIN! BUT HE CAN'T PULL ANY *CLAYFACE* CRIMES NOW THAT HIS POWER IS GONE FOREVER!

EVEN SO, WE'LL KEEP A SHARP WATCH ON ALL UNDERWORLD HAUNTS...

THE NEXT NIGHT, AS THE CRIME-FIGHTERS CONTINUE THEIR PATROL...

LOOK! A HUGE BIRD -- A GIANT *EAGLE* -- HEADING FOR THAT OPEN WINDOW OF THE *EXPOSITION BUILDING!*

THAT EAGLE COULD HARM SOMEON WE'VE GOT TO GO IN AND CAPTURE IT!

SHORTLY, ON THE FLOOR HOUSING A MODEL FUTURISTIC CITY THAT IS PART OF THE *ARCHITECTS EXPOSITION...*

CLAYFACE! SOMEHOW HE GOT HIS POWER BACK! HE BECAME AN "EAGLE" SO HE COULD FLY INTO THE MANAGER'S OFFICE!

STOP HIM! HE FORCED ME TO OPEN THE SAFE CONTAINING THE GATE RECEIPTS...

QUICK AS THOUGHT, *BATMAN* SEIZES A WOOD-AND-PLASTER "BUILDING" AND...

MY ONLY CHANCE IS TO TAKE HIM BY SURPRISE-- KNOCK HIM OUT FAST!

BUT *CLAYFACE* INSTANTLY CONCENTRATES- HIS MENTAL COMMAND MOULDING HIS BODY LIKE PLIABLE CLAY INTO THE SHAPE, COLO AND MASS HE DESIRES!

OUT-FOXED *BATMAN!* BY BECOMIN A FAN WITH SPIKED BLADES, I'VE CHOPPED THE "BUILDING" TO BITS!

ONCE AGAIN, **CLAYFACE** COMMANDS HIS BODY TO ALTER--AND BECOMES A RAGING MAMMOTH TRAMPLING THE MOCK CITY UNDERFOOT!

BATMAN! WE CAN'T FIGHT **THAT!**

THEN--THE UNEXPECTED!

WHA-AAT? I THOUGHT I HAD PLENTY OF TIME! IT'S ONLY BEEN **FIVE** HOURS SINCE I BECAME **CLAYFACE**-- YET MY POWERS ARE EBBING!

ONLY **FIVE** HOURS? BUT THE TIME-LIMIT WAS ALWAYS FORTY-EIGHT...

INSTANTLY, **CLAYFACE** CONCENTRATES FIERCELY-- SUMMONING UP HIS WANING POWER, AND...

GREAT SCOTT! HE'S BECOME A FIERY METEOR, SETTING THE MOCK CITY AFLAME!

I CAN ONLY KEEP THIS FORM FOR SECONDS --BUT THAT WILL BE LONG ENOUGH!

SECONDS LATER, HIS **CLAYFACE** POWERS GONE, MATT HAGEN MAKES HIS ESCAPE!

FORGET HIM FOR THE MOMENT! WE'VE GOT TO PUT OUT THIS FIRE BEFORE IT SPREADS THROUGH THE BUILDING!

WE CAN'T GET TO HIM NOW!

HOW? HOW COULD HAGEN BECOME **CLAYFACE** AGAIN? YOU DESTROYED THE POOL!

TRUE! BUT HAGEN MUST'VE BEEN CUNNING ENOUGH TO HIDE SOME OF THE POOL LIQUID AS A PRECAUTIONARY MEASURE! HE OBVIOUSLY WENT STRAIGHT TO WHERE HE HAD IT HIDDEN AFTER HE BROKE OUT OF JAIL!

4

BATMAN'S DEDUCTION IS CORRECT--FOR HAGEN HAD DONE EXACTLY THAT UPON ESCAPING FROM PRISON...

GOOD THING I HAD THE FORESIGHT TO HIDE THIS BOTTLE OF POOL LIQUID IN THE REAR SECTION OF THE GROTTO'S CAVERN! LUCKILY, THIS SECTION WASN'T BURIED BY THE EXPLOSIVE BATMAN SET OFF!

WITH SOME OF THIS LIQUID-- AND WHAT I'VE LEARNED OF CHEMISTRY--I'LL MAKE ENOUGH SYNTHETIC LIQUID TO ENABLE ME TO BECOME CLAYFACE AGAIN!

THUS, CLAYFACE WAS REBORN! AND NOW, IN THE BAT-CAVE...

WHAT SURPRISED ME IS THAT CLAY FACE MUST RENEW HIS POWER EVERY FIVE HOURS NOW!

IT SURPRISED CLAYFACE, TOO! I'LL WAGER HE'S SOMEHOW MADE SYNTHETIC LIQUID-- BUT HE DIDN'T EXPECT THAT THE SYNTHETIC HAS A SHORTER TIME-LIMIT THAN THE ORIGINAL LIQUID!

MEANWHILE, THE HEAD-LINE NEWS OF CLAYFACE'S RETURN IS DISCUSSED IN AN UNDERWORLD HANGOUT...

CLAYFACE DID IT AGAIN! NOT EVEN BATMAN CAN STOP CLAYFACE!

YEAH! CLAYFACE IS THE TOP CRIMINAL IN THE COUNTRY!

CLAYFACE STEALS GATE RECEIPTS

AREN'T YOU FORGETTING ME?

THE JOKER!

MY CUNNING HAS MADE ME BATMAN'S GREATEST FOE! WITHOUT HIS FREAK POWERS, CLAYFACE IS A BLUNDERING THIRD-RATER--INCAPABLE OF MATCHING CRIMES OF MY CALIBRE! AND I CAN PROVE IT ANYTIME!

5

CONTINUED IN CHAPTER 2

139

EVEN WITHOUT **CLAYFACE'S** POWER, I CAN ALSO CHANGE INTO A WINGED CREATURE! HA, HA! BY THE WAY, **BATMAN,** IT WAS **I** WHO MADE THAT PHONE CALL TO HEADQUARTERS!

I WANTED YOU HERE--SO I COULD PROVE TO **CLAYFACE** THAT EVEN **WITHOUT** HIS POWER, I STILL COULD DUPLICATE HIS FEATS AND OUTSMART YOU, WHEREAS HE COULDN'T CONTINUE AS THE **JOKER** WHEN HE TRIED TO MIMIC ME! HA, HA!

SO--THE **CLAYFACE-JOKER** FEUD IS STILL RAGING!

HMM! **ROBIN,** MAYBE WE CAN USE IT TO OUR ADVANTAGE...

LATER, HAGEN FUMES AS HE READS NEWS HEADLINES OF THE **JOKER** TRIUMPH OVER **BATMAN**...

THE **JOKER** HAS MADE ME THE LAUGHING STOCK OF THE UNDERWORLD! SOMEHOW, I'VE GOT TO PULL A BIG COUP THAT WILL REGAIN ME MY PRESTIGE! BUT HOW? **HOW?**

JOKER APES CLAYFACE AND OUTWITS BATMAN!

Gazette

IT IS A TV NEWSCAST--AN INTERVIEW WITH **BATMAN**--THAT GIVES HAGEN HIS ANSWER...

BATMAN, IT'S REPORTED THAT TOMORROW NIGHT THE RAJAH TAJORE IS HONORING YOU WITH A GIFT OF A FABULOUS GEM KNOWN AS THE "KING OF DIAMONDS"!

THAT'S TRUE!

12

141

YOU AND *ROBIN* WILL HAVE TO BE ON GUARD WHEN YOU LEAVE THE RAJAH WITH SUCH A VALUABLE GEM!

I'LL BE ABLE TO DO THAT BY MYSELF! I COULDN'T INSULT THE RAJAH BY NOT APPEARING, SO *ROBIN* WILL BE ON MORE IMPORTANT BUSINESS! *ROBIN* WILL BE PATROLLING THE CITY, LOOKING FOR THAT MASTER CRIMINAL, *CLAYFACE!*

THE *JOKER* WILL BE FURIOUS BECAUSE *BATMAN* CONSIDERS *ME* THE MASTER CRIMINAL! THE *JOKER* WILL TRY TO DISPROVE THAT-- BY TRYING TO STEAL THE *"KING OF DIAMONDS"*! IT'S SUCH A NATURAL *JOKER-THEME* CRIME, THE *JOKER* WON'T BE ABLE TO RESIST! HMM...

CLICK

THE FOLLOWING NIGHT...

IT'S IN THE CARDS, *BATMAN*--SINCE I'M THE *JOKER* IT'S ONLY NATURAL THAT I TAKE THE *"KING OF DIAMONDS"*! BIG JOKE, EH? YOU'LL LAUGH--AS SOON AS THIS *LAUGHING GAS* AFFECTS YOU!

NO PARKING

UNEXPECTEDLY...

THEN THE "STANCHION" ALTERS SWIFTLY -- TO BECOME *CLAYFACE*...

HA! NOW I'VE NOT ONLY GOT THE DIAMOND -- BUT ALSO THE *JOKER* AND *BATMAN!*

ANOTHER MENTAL COMMAND--AND ANOTHER CHANGE TO FIT THE NEEDS OF *CLAYFACE!*

NOW WITH MY NEW FORM AND STRENGTH, I CAN EASILY CARRY MY HOSTAGES TO MY HIDEOUT!

13

143

OKAY, *JOKER*--HERE GOES! LET'S SEE WHAT THE REST OF *BATMAN'S* FACE IS LIKE!

HUH! THE REST OF HIS FACE--IT'S LIKE MY FACE LOOKS WHEN I'M *CLAYFACE!*

STUNNED BY SURPRISE--*CLAYFACE* IS THEN STUNNED UNCONSCIOUS BY A SLEDGE-HAMMER BLOW!

NOW! I KNEW THE SHOCK OF SEEING THAT FACE WOULD DISTRACT YOU LONG ENOUGH FOR ME TO GET IN THIS KNOCKOUT PUNCH!

NOW I'LL GIVE *CLAYFACE* A SEDATIVE THAT WILL KEEP HIM SLEEPING PAST THE FIVE-HOUR TIME LIMIT SO THAT HIS POWER WILL BE GONE! WHEN HE AWAKENS, HE WON'T LIKE KNOWING THAT *I* IMPERSONATED THE *JOKER* AND THAT THE "*BATMAN*" HE UNMASKED WAS MY *BATMAN-ROBOT* WITH CLAY ON ITS FACE!

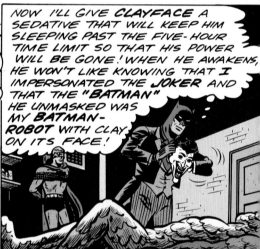

LATER, WHEN HAGEN AWAKENS IN PRISON AND IS TOLD THE TRUTH...

BUT IF YOU IMPERSONATED THE *JOKER*, WHERE IS THE *REAL JOKER*?

THE *JOKER'S* BEEN IN JAIL SINCE THE NIGHT OF THE ROBBERY IN THE MUSEUM'S AFRICAN ROOM! YOU SEE, WHEN HE PHONED IN HIS FAKE TIP THAT *CLAYFACE* WAS GOING TO ROB THE GOLD IDOL, I MADE SOME HURRIED PLANS...

"I SWIFTLY CONTACTED *BATWOMAN* AND *BAT-GIRL*, LENT THEM TWO *WHIRLY-BATS*, HAD THEM HIDE NEAR THE MUSEUM."

THIS TIME, IF *CLAYFACE* ESCAPES FROM *BATMAN* AND *ROBIN* BY CHANGING TO A WINGED CREATURE, WE CAN TRAIL HIM IN THE *WHIRLY-BATS!*

IF *BATMAN'S* PLAN WORKS, *CLAYFACE* MAY LEAD US TO THE CACHE OF LIQUID THAT GIVES HIM HIS POWER!

15

"TO THEIR SURPRISE, THEY RECOGNIZED THE FLYING FIGURE AS THE *JOKER*, SO THE PLAN HAD TO BE SCRAPPED!"

YOU WEREN'T THE PERSON WE WERE EXPECTING, JOKER-- BUT WE MIGHT AS WELL HAUL YOU IN!

BATMAN WILL NEED A NEW IDEA NOW TO CAPTURE CLAYFACE!

AND I GOT MY IDEA -- FROM YOUR OWN *CLAYFACE-JOKER* FEUD! WITH THE HELP OF THE POLICE, WE KEPT THE JOKER'S CAPTURE SECRET, AND INSTEAD HAD FAKE NEWS STORIES OF HIS "SUCCESS" PRINTED! THEN THE TV STATION COOPERATED WITH A FAKE INTERVIEW THAT WOULD BAIT YOU INTO "CAPTURING" *BATMAN* AND THE JOKER!

AND THE TRICK WORKED.. BECAUSE HERE YOU ARE!

SO WHAT! YOU DIDN'T FIND MY CACHE OF LIQUID BECAUSE IT WASN'T IN MY HIDEOUT! I HID IT IN *ANOTHER* PLACE -- AND WHEN I GET OUT, IT'LL MAKE ME *CLAYFACE* AGAIN!

LATER

GOSH, *BAT-GIRL*, IT WAS SWELL OF YOU TO CALM ME DOWN WHEN I WAS SO WORRIED ABOUT *BATMAN* TACKLING CLAYFACE ALONE...

YOU LOOK WORRIED ABOUT *CLAYFACE*, *BATMAN*... SO WHY DON'T YOU FOLLOW *ROBIN'S* EXAMPLE AND LET ME SOOTHE *YOU*?

GULP!

THE END

145

Artists: Sheldon Moldoff and Charles Paris / Colorist: Jerry Serpe

GOTHAM CITY-- WHERE, AFTER COMMITTING A CRIME, THE **JOKER** TRIES TO ELUDE THE POLICE...

IF I CAN LOSE THEM AROUND THE CORNER, I'LL HAVE A CHANCE TO MAKE IT BACK TO MY HIDEOUT...

SWIFTLY, THE **JOKER** SENDS HIS CAR CAREENING AROUND A STREET CORNER, BUT...

BAH! OF ALL THE ROTTEN LUCK! I'M BLOCKED BY TRAFFIC BECAUSE OF THE FIRE DEPARTMENT!

AS THE POLICE CLOSE IN, THE **JOKER** IS FORCED TO ATTEMPT HIS ESCAPE ON FOOT...

JUST ONE CHANCE-- THAT TRUCK!

HA! HA! IT WAS THE CITY'S **FIRE DEPARTMENT** THAT ALMOST STOPPED ME-- BUT BECAUSE OF THE **DEPARTMENT OF PUBLIC WORKS**, I'LL MAKE GOOD MY ESCAPE! AND THAT GIVES ME A NEW JOKER THEME!

LATER, AT POLICE HEADQUARTERS...

A LETTER FROM THE **JOKER** TO **BATMAN!** HE SAYS THE CITY'S DEPARTMENTS WILL SERVE AS A BASIS FOR HIS FUTURE CRIMES! THAT CONCEITED **CLOWN** HAS EVEN ENCLOSED A **CLUE** TO CHALLENGE **BATMAN!**

SOON AFTER, THE CAPED MANHUNTERS ARRIVE...

HIS MESSAGE SAYS, "I'M GOING TO USE MY OWN **SANITATION DEPARTMENT** IN A NEW WAY BECAUSE I'M A FAIR-MINDED MAN."

HMM... SANITATION DEPARTMENT MUST REFER TO CLEANING UP. AS FOR "FAIR-MINDED"-- IF I KNOW THE JOKER, I THINK I KNOW WHAT HE'S UP TO!

2

AT THE GOTHAM CITY **INTERNATIONAL FAIR**, A STRANGE VEHICLE DRAWS UP BEFORE AN EXHIBIT BUILDING...

HEY! LOOK AT THAT! A GIANT VACUUM CLEANER!

I WONDER WHAT EXHIBIT THAT CAME FROM?

GEMS OF THE ORIENT

SUDDENLY, THE DRIVER OF THE UNIQUE VEHICLE TOUCHES REMOTE CONTROL BUTTONS AND...

WHAT...? THAT VACUUM CLEANER GADGET--IT'S SUCKING UP ALL THE PRECIOUS GEMS!

HA! HA!

WHOOOSHH!

HOLY SMOKE! THE **JOKER** WASN'T KIDDING WHEN HE SAID HE WAS GOING TO CLEAN UP IN HIS OWN WAY!

BATMAN AND ROBIN!

IT'S ABOUT TIME I DUSTED OFF THAT LITTLE BRAT!

ROBIN--LOOK OUT! THE **JOKER'S** SPOTTED YOU! HE'S TURNING THE VACUUM EXTENSION IN OUR DIRECTION!

BUT **BATMAN'S** WARNING IS TOO LATE...

HA! HA!

GREAT SCOTT! **ROBIN'S** BEING SUCKED UP RIGHT INTO THE VACUUM CLEANER!

WHOOOSHH!

148

THE **JOKER**--STARTING TO DRIVE OFF--WITH **ROBIN** INSIDE! I'VE GOT TO FREE **ROBIN** BEFORE HE SUFFOCATES!

GEMS OF THE ORIENT

A FLIP OF THE WRIST-- AND A **BAT-ROPE** LOOPS INTO PLACE...

THANKS, PAL -- I'LL NEED THIS!

GEMS

LIKE A SWOOPING, SLASHING HAWK, **BATMAN** LANDS ATOP HIS TARGET...

I CAN SEE **ROBIN** INSIDE! HE'S STILL A LITTLE DAZED-- BUT OKAY!

WITHOUT WARNING...

I'M ALWAYS READY FOR TROUBLE, **BATMAN**-- THAT'S WHY I HAD THE REAR SECTION OF MY "VACUUM CLEANER" GIMMICKED SO THAT I CAN DITCH IT WHEN NECESSARY! HA! HA!

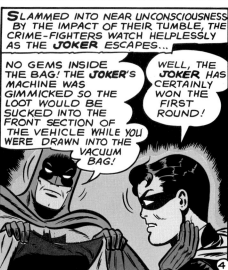

SLAMMED INTO NEAR UNCONSCIOUSNESS BY THE IMPACT OF THEIR TUMBLE, THE CRIME-FIGHTERS WATCH HELPLESSLY AS THE **JOKER** ESCAPES...

NO GEMS INSIDE THE BAG! THE **JOKER'S** MACHINE WAS GIMMICKED SO THE LOOT WOULD BE SUCKED INTO THE FRONT SECTION OF THE VEHICLE WHILE YOU WERE DRAWN INTO THE VACUUM BAG!

WELL, THE **JOKER** HAS CERTAINLY WON THE FIRST ROUND!

4

NEXT DAY, TO POLICE HEADQUARTERS COMES ANOTHER CHALLENGING CLUE FROM THE *CRIME-CLOWN*...

HMM! THE WAY TO SUCCESS IS USUALLY CALLED A *ROAD*! I'LL WAGER THE *JOKER'S* REFERRING TO THE *DEPARTMENT OF ROADS AND HIGHWAYS*!

The way to success can sometimes be three!

BUT WHY DID HE SAY IT WAS "*THREE*"?

OBVIOUSLY HE MEANT A *THREE-LANE* ROAD! THAT HAS TO BE IT! AND I KNOW THE PLACE WHERE THE *JOKER* CAN MAKE HIS CRIME A SUCCESS! LET'S GO!

AT THAT MOMENT, AT THE CONSTRUCTION SITE OF A NEW THREE-LANE HIGHWAY...

OKAY, JOE--LET'S GET THIS PAYROLL TO THE FOREMAN!

SUDDENLY...

WHAT...?

HA! HA! THAT SPECIAL CEMENT IS AS STICKY AS GLUE! IT WILL HOLD YOU WHILE I GRAB THE CASH!

IT IS AT THAT MOMENT THAT *BATMAN* AND *ROBIN* ARRIVE...

GREAT SCOTT! THE *JOKER'S* GIMMICKED THAT MACHINE NOT ONLY TO DISABLE THE GUARDS--BUT ALSO TO GRAB THE PAYROLL! HMM... THERE'S ONLY ONE WAY TO STOP HIM FROM GRABBING THE PAYROLL...

INSTANTLY, *BATMAN* LEAPS AT THE DANGLING HOOK OF A HOIST CRANE AND...

TWO CAN PLAY AT THIS GAME, *JOKER*!

BATMAN! YOU'VE FOILED ME THIS TIME, BUT NOT FOR LONG!

5

INSTANTLY, THE **JOKER** DASHES TO A WAITING CAR AND...

I'M RETURNING TO MY STRONGHOLD, BUT I'LL BE BACK AGAIN!

GET IN, **BATMAN!** THE **BATMOBILE** WILL OVERHAUL HIM EASILY!

BUT, AS THE TWO VEHICLES REACH A BUSY MAIN HIGHWAY INTERSECTION...

WE'LL BE ABLE TO GET TO HIM ONCE THESE TWO TRUCKS MOVE OUT OF THE WAY!

UNEXPECTEDLY, THE TRUCKS COME TO A HALT--SNARLING TRAFFIC HOPELESSLY...

THE TRUCK DRIVERS-- THEY'VE ABANDONED THEIR TRUCKS AND ARE RUNNING OVER TO THE **JOKER**'S CAR!

THEY'RE THE **JOKER'S HIRELINGS!** NOW THAT THEY'VE STOPPED US, THEY'LL ESCAPE IN HIS WAITING CAR! WELL-- AT LEAST THE **JOKER** GETS AWAY EMPTY-HANDED THIS TIME!

LATER, AT POLICE HEADQUARTERS, THE ABANDONED TRUCKS ARE CAREFULLY EXAMINED...

NOT A CLUE SO FAR!

HERE'S SOMETHING-- A NAIL IN THE THICK TRUCK TIRE! BUT IT'S A VERY UNUSUAL NAIL!

POLICE DEPT. GAR

NOTICE THE NAIL HEAD, **ROBIN**--IT'S RECTANGULAR- SHAPED! NAILS LIKE THIS WERE MADE IN **MEDIEVAL TIMES!**

GOSH! WHERE COULD A MODERN TRUCK TIRE PICK UP A NAIL CENTURIES OLD?

REMEMBER THE **JOKER'S** COMMENT ABOUT GETTING BACK TO HIS **"STRONGHOLD"**? A STRONGHOLD MEANS A FORTRESS--A CASTLE! I'VE A HUNCH...

151

SOMETIME LATER, SOME DISTANCE FROM *GOTHAM CITY*...

HOLY SMOKE! A *CASTLE*!

NO TRESPASSING

YES, *ROBIN*-- THIS PROPERTY ONCE BELONGED TO AN ECCENTRIC MILLIONAIRE WHO HAD AN ENGLISH CASTLE SHIPPED HERE BRICK BY BRICK! NOTICE THE WOODEN DRAWBRIDGE!

I GET IT NOW! THAT ANCIENT NAIL COULD'VE POPPED OUT OF THE WOODEN DRAWBRIDGE AS A TRUCK PASSED OVER IT!

EXACTLY! NOW LET'S SEE IF THIS REALLY IS THE *JOKER'S* STRONGHOLD! WE MIGHT BE SPOTTED ON THE OPEN ROAD-- SO WE'LL APPROACH THROUGH THE THICK BRUSH INSTEAD!

LATER, AS THEY MOVE WARILY THROUGH THE BRUSH, SUDDENLY...

LOOK! A JOKER HEAD-- COMING UP OUT OF THE GROUND!

TWO MORE-- EACH ONE POPPING UP LIKE A DEADLY *JACK-IN-THE-BOX*! WE'RE TRAPPED!

ROBIN-- THIS WAY!

AS THE DUO DASHES TO THEIR ONLY AVENUE OF ESCAPE...

THAT CUNNING CLOWN! THE ENTIRE SETUP WAS RIGGED TO DRIVE AN INTRUDER INTO A TRAP!

152

TUMBLING HEAVILY, **BATMAN** AND **ROBIN** SLIDE DOWN A LONG CHUTE -- AND INTO UNCONSCIOUSNESS...

WHEN THE CRIME-FIGHTERS FINALLY AWAKEN...

AS YOU CAN SEE -- I'VE REMOVED YOUR **UTILITY BELTS!** YOU ARE NOW HELPLESS PRISONERS IN THE DUNGEON OF MY STRONG-HOLD!

THIS CASTLE, THIS PROPERTY IS MY "CITY" -- AND HERE I AM JUDGE AND JURY! THEREFORE, **BATMAN** -- IN A SHORT WHILE YOU WILL STAND TRIAL NOT FOR TRESPASSING -- BUT FOR YOUR CRIMES AGAINST ME!

SHORTLY, AS **BATMAN** IS SUMMONED FOR TRIAL...

THE **JOKER** -- DRESSED AS A JUDGE!

THE JURY -- ALL **JOKERS!** HE'S PUT HIS HIRELINGS IN MAKEUP! THE **JOKER** WASN'T KIDDING WHEN HE SAID HE WAS BOTH JUDGE **AND** JURY!

THE CASE OF **JOKERSVILLE VS. BATMAN!** THE HONORABLE JUSTICE **JOKER** PRESIDING!

LET THE TRIAL BEGIN!

153

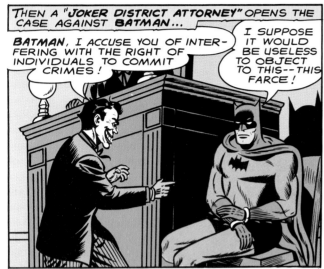

THEN A "JOKER DISTRICT ATTORNEY" OPENS THE CASE AGAINST BATMAN...

BATMAN, I ACCUSE YOU OF INTERFERING WITH THE RIGHT OF INDIVIDUALS TO COMMIT CRIMES!

I SUPPOSE IT WOULD BE USELESS TO OBJECT TO THIS--THIS FARCE!

IT WOULD! OBJECTION OVERRULED! PERSONALLY, I AGREE WITH EVERYTHING THE DISTRICT ATTORNEY HAS SAID!

THIS-- THIS IS INSANE! IT'S LIKE A SCENE OUT OF "ALICE IN WONDERLAND"!

I SHOW YOU EXHIBIT A-- THIS PHOTOGRAPH OF BATMAN INTERFERING WITH THE JOKER ON A PAST CASE!

TSK-TSK! TERRIBLE -- JUST TERRIBLE!

AND SO THE MAD "TRIAL" DRAGS ON AS MORE "EVIDENCE" IS BROUGHT IN AGAINST BATMAN.

YOUR HONOR, THAT CLOSES MY CASE AGAINST THE ACCUSED!

NOW, BATMAN--YOU MAY ACT AS YOUR DEFENSE COUNSEL SO THAT THE JURY MAY HEAR YOU!

GENTLEMEN OF THE JURY, I...

THAT'S ENOUGH! THE JURY HEARD YOU! AND THAT'S ALL I PROMISED YOU!

GENTLEMEN OF THE JURY--HOW DO YOU FIND THE PRISONER?

YOUR HONOR, WE FIND THE PRISONER GUILTY!

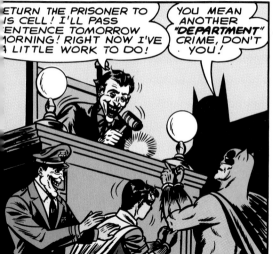

RETURN THE PRISONER TO HIS CELL! I'LL PASS SENTENCE TOMORROW MORNING! RIGHT NOW I'VE A LITTLE WORK TO DO!

YOU MEAN ANOTHER "DEPARTMENT" CRIME, DON'T YOU!

TRUE, BATMAN--TRUE! THIS JOB IS GOING TO BE GOOD FOR MY HEALTH! IT'LL BE A PRIZE JOB, BATMAN -- AND I'LL COMMIT THE CRIME RIGHT UNDER YOUR VERY NOSE! HA, HA!

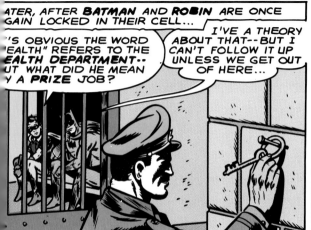

LATER, AFTER BATMAN AND ROBIN ARE ONCE AGAIN LOCKED IN THEIR CELL...

IT'S OBVIOUS THE WORD "HEALTH" REFERS TO THE HEALTH DEPARTMENT-- BUT WHAT DID HE MEAN BY A PRIZE JOB?

I'VE A THEORY ABOUT THAT--BUT I CAN'T FOLLOW IT UP UNLESS WE GET OUT OF HERE...

SAY, GUARD--IT'S THE CUSTOM FOR THE CONDEMNED PRISONER TO REQUEST WHAT HE WANTS FOR DINNER -- SO HOW ABOUT SOME TOMATO SOUP, STEAK, AND ICE CREAM!

SURE-- WHY NOT?

SHORTLY, AFTER THE GUARD BRINGS THE DINNER...

UHH... I--I FEEL AWFUL...

GUARD-- ROBIN'S ILL!

HE--HE'S COVERED WITH RED SPOTS!

IT CAN'T BE THE MEASLES OR CHICKEN POX-- BECAUSE I'VE ALREADY HAD THEM...

SMALL POX! IT'S SMALL POX! I'M GETTIN' OUTA HERE!

10

BUT WHAT ABOUT THE MONEY? ONE OF US HAS TO GUARD IT!

THE CONTAINER IS SEALED, ISN'T IT? THERE'S NO DANGER OF IT BEING STOLEN WHILE WE'RE HERE! NOW, WILL YOU PLEASE JOIN THE OTHERS?

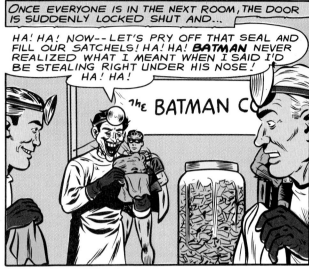

ONCE EVERYONE IS IN THE NEXT ROOM, THE DOOR IS SUDDENLY LOCKED SHUT AND...

HA! HA! NOW-- LET'S PRY OFF THAT SEAL AND FILL OUR SATCHELS! HA! HA! BATMAN NEVER REALIZED WHAT I MEANT WHEN I SAID I'D BE STEALING RIGHT UNDER HIS NOSE! HA! HA!

THE BATMAN CO

YOU'RE WRONG, JOKER-- I DID GUESS! THAT'S WHAT MADE ME FIGURE YOUR "PRIZE" CRIME REFERRED TO THE "BATMAN PRIZE CONTEST"!

WE MIGHT AS WELL GET AN ASSIST FROM OUR STAND-INS, EH, ROBIN?

UNEXPECTEDLY, THE JOKER AND A HIRELING SWITCH ON SPECIAL REFLECTORS, AND LEVEL THEM AT THE MANHUNTERS...

UHH-- BLINDING LIGHT-- CAN'T SEE!

THEY'RE HELPLESS NOW, MEN -- TAKE THEM!

HALF-BLINDED, BATMAN GROPES FOR AN ELECTRIC SWITCH...

THE MODELS OF BATPLANES AND BATMOBILES-- THEY ALL CONTAIN TINY MOTORS THAT CAN BE ACTIVATED BY THIS MASTER CONTROL SWITCH...

12

THEN, AS CRIMINALS CLOSE IN -- THEY ARE REPELLED BY A MINIATURE ARMADA...

YIIII!

OW!

THAT MOMENT OF RESPITE GIVES *BATMAN* AND *ROBIN* A CHANCE TO GET BACK TO NORMAL AND...

I'VE MANAGED TO STAY IN BUSINESS THIS LONG BECAUSE I'VE KNOWN WHEN TO RETREAT -- AND THIS IS ONE OF THOSE TIMES!

BUT AS THE *JOKER* STARTS FOR THE EXIT...

WHAT...?! TINY *BATMOBILES* -- UNDERFOOT!

HA! HA! EVEN THE BIGGEST PLANS CAN BE TRIPPED UP BY LITTLE THINGS!

13

AFTERWARD...

YOU NEED CORRECTING, *JOKER* -- SO IT'S FITTING THAT YOU SHOULD WIND UP IN THE *DEPARTMENT OF CORRECTIONS!*

END

Writer: E. Nelson Bridwell / Artists: Carmine Infantino and Murphy Anderson
Colorist: Shelley Eiber

WHEN THE POLICE ARRIVE...

I WON'T SIGN A COMPLAINT! I GOT A *MILLION* DOLLARS WORTH OF LAUGHS OUT OF THAT "CHAUFFEUR-DRIVEN" POGO STICK!

WHA-A-AT?

LATER, IN A NIGHT CLUB CALLED THE DUDE RANCH...

YOU ORDERED *STEER STEAK?* HERE'S THE STEER, SIR! WHICH CUT OF MEAT DO YOU WANT?

LOOK! HE BROUGHT THE ORDER *ON THE HOOF!* HA, HA!

SUDDENLY THE WAITER JABS THE STEER WITH A PIN AND THE ANIMAL *STAMPEDES!*

HA, HA, HA!

EEEEK!

THAT GUY'S NO WAITER! I'LL TAKE HIM TO THE BOSS!

BUT ONCE INSIDE THE CLUB OWNER'S OFFICE, THE FALSE WAITER UNMASKS!

THANKS FOR BRINGING ME HERE! NOW, *OPEN THAT SAFE*, MR. WESTON!

THE *JOKER!*

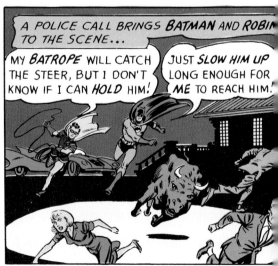

A POLICE CALL BRINGS *BATMAN* AND *ROBIN* TO THE SCENE...

MY *BATROPE* WILL CATCH THE STEER, BUT I DON'T KNOW IF I CAN *HOLD* HIM!

JUST *SLOW HIM UP* LONG ENOUGH FOR ME TO REACH HIM!

GOT HIM!

GREAT BULLDOGGING, BATMAN!

WHEN THEY QUESTION NIGHTCLUB OWNER NICK WESTON--

U MEAN YOU DON'T ARE ABOUT THE 5,000 THE **JOKER** TOLE FROM YOU?

NO! THE PUBLICITY IS **WORTH** IT! IMAGINE! A **STEER STEAK**--AND HE BRINGS IN A **LIVE STEER!** HAW! HAW!

NEXT DAY, IN THE STATELY MANOR OF BRUCE (**BATMAN**) WAYNE AND HIS WARD, DICK (**ROBIN**) GRAYSON...

IT'S **CRAZY!** THOSE PEOPLE ACTUALLY THINK IT'S **FUN** TO BE ROBBED BY THE **JOKER!**

WHO KNOWS? PERHAPS **I'D** ENJOY BEING ROBBED BY THE JOKER!

THE FOLLOWING NIGHT, ALFRED, THE WAYNE BUTLER, HANGS A PAINTING!...

LIKE IT, ALFRED?

YES, SIR! IF IT'S FRANZ HALS' **ORIGINAL** "LAUGHING CAVALIER," IT'S WORTH A **FORTUNE!**

JUST THEN, A BIZARRE FIGURE APPEARS...

BEHOLD THE **JOKER**...ARTIST OF **CRIME!** DOES MY COMICAL **PALETTE** TICKLE YOUR **PALATE?** HA, HA!

UFF! HA-HA!

SWIFTLY, HE CUTS THE PAINTING FROM ITS FRAME, AND...

TOODLE-OO! NOW *I* HAVE THE *CAVALIER*...AND ALL *YOU* HAVE LEFT IS... THE *LAUGH!*

OH, THAT PAINT GAG WAS *PRICE-LESS!* HA, HA!

QUICKLY, SIR! SWITCH TO *BATMAN* AND STOP HIM!

HA, HA! LET HIM GO! THAT'S THE FUNNIEST ACT I EVER SAW! THE *JOKER* CERTAINLY MAKES *ROBBERY* A *PLEASURE!*

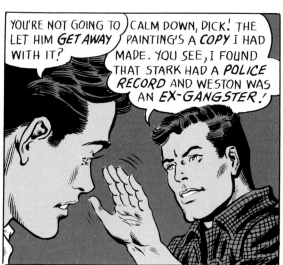

YOU'RE NOT GOING TO LET HIM *GET AWAY* WITH IT?

CALM DOWN, DICK! THE PAINTING'S A *COPY* I HAD MADE. YOU SEE, I FOUND THAT STARK HAD A *POLICE RECORD* AND WESTON WAS AN *EX-GANGSTER!*

"THAT NIGHT, I DISGUISED MYSELF AS A THUG AN' MIXED WITH SOME GABBY HOODS IN A DIVE..."

YEAH...WAYNE PAID $15,000 FOR A PAINTING SOME GUY *STOLE* FROM A MUSEUM!

GOOD THING FOR WAYNE THE *COPS* DON'T KNOW!

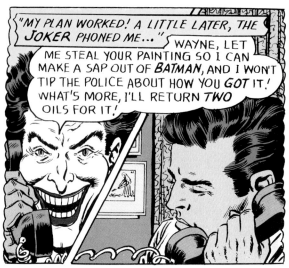

"MY PLAN WORKED! A LITTLE LATER, THE *JOKER* PHONED ME..."

WAYNE, LET ME STEAL YOUR PAINTING SO I CAN MAKE A SAP OUT OF *BATMAN*, AND I WON'T TIP THE POLICE ABOUT HOW YOU *GOT* IT! WHAT'S MORE, I'LL RETURN *TWO* OILS FOR IT!

SO THAT'S THE *JOKER'S* ANGLE-- *BLACK-MAIL* AND GREED! I'LL PLAY ALONG TO FIND OUT HIS *NEXT* MOVE!

IT'S A DEAL!

FINE! HAVE YOUR WARD AND BUTLER AS WITNESSES AND *LAUGH* AT ME!

THE NEXT DAY, AT STARK'S SHOP...

THE *JOKER* JUST LEFT! HE RETURNED *TWO* COLLECTIONS OF *STAMPS*, AS HE PROMISED-- BUT THEY'RE *RUBBER* STAMPS!

AND IN WESTON'S OFFICE, AT THE *DUDE RANCH...*

THAT RAT PROMISED TO GIVE ME *$10,000* FOR THE *$5,000* HE STOLE--BUT HE LEFT *STAGE MONEY!*

THEN... *I'M NEXT!*

THE *CLOWN OF CRIME* IS ALREADY PREPARING TO PAY BACK *BRUCE WAYNE...*

WAYNE DOUBLE-CROSSED ME WITH A *FAKE* MASTERPIECE! SO I'LL RETURN *TWO OILS--TWO DISPLAY TUBES* OF *OIL PAINT!* THE WHEELS OF MY *JOKERMOBILE* WILL SPLATTER *WAYNE MANOR* WITH THE STUFF!

BUT AS THE BIZARRE VEHICLE STARTS, A DARK JUGGERNAUT THUNDERS ONTO THE DRIVE, EXPERTLY INTERCEPTING THE *JOKERMOBILE!*

YIII! THE *BATMOBILE!*

THE *HARLEQUIN OF HATE* FLEES, BUT...

I'VE GOT THE TUBES AIMED RIGHT, *BATMAN!* LET 'ER RIP!

163

Inked by Dick Giordano / Colorist: Tom Ziuko

IT IS NEARING **ELEVEN O'CLOCK** WHEN POLICE COMMISSIONER GORDON ANSWERS A SUMMONS TO A LONELY SPOT ON THE OUTSKIRTS OF THE CITY... AND GAZES AT A HUDDLED FORM SPRAWLED IN THE RAIN-SOAKED MUD...

I'VE SEEN A LOT OF **DEAD MEN** BEFORE, COMMISSIONER -- BUT NONE LIKE **HIM!** LOOK AT THE **FACE**--

YES! TWISTED IN A **HIDEOUS GRIN**--! GHASTLY!

I WISH **THE BATMAN** WOULD ARRIVE!

I'M **HERE,** COMMISSIONER BEEN HERE FOR **TEN** MINUTES!

BLAST IT, BATMAN! MUST YOU CONSTANTLY **STARTLE** ME--?

SORRY, SIR! I WANTED TO EXAMINE THE SCENE **UNDISTURBED**

WELL, WHAT DO YOU **MAKE** OF IT?

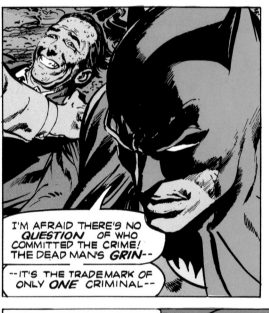

I'M AFRAID THERE'S NO **QUESTION** OF WHO COMMITTED THE CRIME! THE DEAD MAN'S **GRIN**--

--IT'S THE TRADEMARK OF ONLY **ONE** CRIMINAL--

...AND TO CLINCH IT, I FOUND THIS NEARBY!

A JOKER!

I'LL DETAIL A SQUAD OF MY **BEST DETECTIVES** IMMEDIATELY AND...

GO AHEAD COMMISSIONER -- IF IT'LL MAKE YOU **FEEL** BETTER BUT I HAVE AN IDEA **OFFICIAL** METHODS WILL BE TOO **SLOW** TO PREVENT FURTHER KILLINGS--

SO I'LL BE INVESTIGATING ON MY OWN

EVER SINCE I HEARD THE **JOKER** ESCAPED FROM THE STATE HOSPITAL FOR THE CRIMINALLY **INSANE,** I'VE BEEN EXPECTING HIM TO SHOW UP--

--BUT THERE WAS NO **WAY** TO SEARCH FOR HIM IN A CITY OF **EIGHT MILLION** UNTIL HE MADE A **MOVE**--

--WHICH HE **HAS!** AND I'VE GOT A **VERY GOOD IDEA** WHAT HE'LL TRY **NEXT!**

I'VE KEPT A CLOSE **WATCH** ON THE **MEM-BERS** OF HIS FORMER **GANG** --

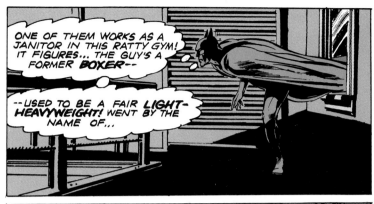

ONE OF THEM WORKS AS A **JANITOR** IN THIS RATTY GYM! IT FIGURES... THE GUY'S A FORMER **BOXER**--

--USED TO BE A FAIR **LIGHT-HEAVYWEIGHT!** WENT BY THE NAME OF...

--**PACKY WHITE!**

TH' **BATMAN!** HEY, FELLA, GOOD TA SEE YA!

C'MON... LET'S JAW WHILE I WORK OUT!

STILL PRACTICING THE OLD SKILLS, EH, **PACKY?**

YEAH... FELLA MY AGE'S GOTTA KEEP IN SHAPE!

NOW... WHAT'S ON THAT SHARP **MIND,** HUH?

AS YOU **KNOW,** THE **JOKER'S** RATTLING AROUND LOOSE! I HAVE REASON TO BELIEVE HE SNUFFED A **FRIEND** OF YOURS---

WE FOUND **PHILLY JACK BARTON** DEAD... AND HE WAS WEARING A **BIG SMILE!**

SOUNDS LIKE THE **BOSS'S STYLE,** FOR SURE!

OOPS! SORRY... MISSED THE **BAG!**

PERFECTLY ALL **RIGHT!**

SO WHAT'S POOR OL' **PHILLY** GOTTA DO WIT' ME?

OOPS!--MISSED **AGAIN!**

THINK NOTHING OF IT!

TO ANSWER YOUR **QUESTION** -- ONE OF THE **JOKER'S** THUGS ...I MEAN, **EMPLOYEES,** BETRAYED HIM!

3

WHEN WE FINALLY **NAILED** HIM, HE SWORE HE'D KILL YOU **ALL** -- REMEMBER?

CHECK! YA FIGURE HE'LL COME AFTER OL' **PACKY**?

CORRECT! I'M GUESSING HE'LL SYSTEMATICALLY MURDER EVERY **ONE** OF YOU! -- UNLESS YOU PLACE YOURSELF UNDER **POLICE PROTECTION!**

GO TO JAIL WITHOUT BEIN' **DRAGGED?** NOT **THIS** PUG--!

I CAN'T **FORCE** YOU TO COOPERATE, **PACKY**--

--HOWEVER, YOU JUST **MIGHT** HAVE A SLIGHT **ACCIDENT** -- A **FIST**-TYPE ACCIDENT--

--AND IT JUST MIGHT PUT YOU IN THE **HOSPITAL**--

--WHERE OFFICERS COULD **GUARD** YOU UNTIL THE **JOKER** IS **CAUGHT!**

YOU CAN **SURRENDER** YOURSELF -- OR WE CAN CONTINUE **PLAYING!**

YOUR CHOICE **PACKY**-- MAKE IT!

SEEIN' AS HOW YA PUT IT LIKE **THAT** ...JAIL AIN'T SUCH A BAD JOINT! I GOT A LOTTA **PALS** IN THE SLAMMER!--'ONG AS I DON'T HAVETA STAY IN THERE **LONG**! I BEEN GOIN' **STRAIGHT!**

BE WIT'CHA IN A **SECOND** --! GOTTA TAKE A DRINK O' WATER... TAKE THE TASTE OF YOUR **KNUCKLES** OUTA MY MOUTH!

THE MANLY ART OF **PUGILISM** LOST A **CHAMP** WHEN YA PUT ON YOUR MASK, FELLA!

YA KNOW, IT'S KINDA **FUNNY!** YOU-- **THE BATMAN** --WORRYIN' ABOUT A STRONG-ARM ARTIST LIKE OL' **PACKY!**

YEAH-- **HA-HA-REAL** FUNNY--

SO... **FUNNY**...HA-HA...IT **HURTS**--

AAAA-GHH--

TOO **LATE**! HE'S BEEN POISONED! --WITH THE **NERVE-TOXIN** THE **JOKER** DEVELOPED--

--THE STUFF THAT CAUSES A PERSON TO LAUGH HIMSELF TO **DEATH!**

ROUND ONE GOES TO THE JOKER!

5

169

AND, UNKNOWN TO **THE BATMAN**, HIS FOE IS ABOUT TO TAKE THE **SECOND** ROUND, ALSO! FOR, IN A SLEAZY HOTEL ROOM...

I'M S'PRISED TO **SEE** YA IN **GOTHAM**! I FIGGERED YA'D WANNA STAY CLEAR OF **THE BATMAN**!

COSY HOTEL

OH, DEAR ME, **NO**--

-- I FULLY **EXPECT** HIM TO FIND ME, **REGARDLESS** OF WHERE I HIDE! I DON'T KNOW **HOW**... OR **WHEN**...

...BUT THE **CAPED CRUSADER** WILL LOCATE ME! HE **ALWAYS** DOES! HOWEVER, I INTEND TO BE **READY** FOR HIM!

BY THE WAY, WERE **YOU** THE ONE WHO BETRAYED ME, **ALBY**?

M-ME? AW, **JOKER**, ...I'M YER **PAL**!

THEN HAVE A **CIGAR**... PAL!

TRY IT! YOU'LL **LIKE** IT!

THANKS! MMM ...NOT A BAD **SMOKE**!

HEY... I BET YOU'RE PULLIN' A **GAG** ON ME, RIGHT? I BET THIS'S AN **EXPLODING** CIGAR, RIGHT?

SAME OLD **JOKER**... ALWAYS WITH THE **GAGS**! WELL...I CAN GO ALONG WITH A LAUGH! I MEAN, WHAT **HARM** CAN A LITTLE EXPLODING CIGAR DO, RIGHT?

6

YOU!-- BIGGER MELVIN! WAIT!

NO CHANCE, LAWMAN!

THE BATMAN'S FASTER'N ME ...BUT I KNOW EVERY INCH OF THE DOCKS LIKE THE PALM OF MY HAND!

HE'LL NEVER CATCH ME!

I'LL DUCK 'ROUND THESE CRATES...

GO OVER THE WAREHOUSE WALL!

PROBABLY LOST HIM... BUT TO MAKE SURE, I'LL SLIP UNDER THE DOCKS...

...COME OUT A GOOD MILE FROM MY JOINT! YEAH, I FOXED THE BATMAN, AN' NO KIDDIN'! NO WAY FOR HIM TO GRAB ME NOW...

DIVE INTO THE SEWER PIPE...

...CRAWL A COUPLE OF BLOCKS UNDERGROUND...

AS I WAS *SAYING,* BIGGER...

GAKK!

...YOUR FORMER LEADER HAS DONE IN *THREE* OF YOUR ASSOCIATES, AND I HAVE REASON TO BELIEVE YOU'RE *NEXT* ON HIS LIST OF VICTIMS!

I'M ASKING YOU TO PUT YOUR-SELF IN *PROTEC-TIVE CUSTODY!*

S-SURE...

...ANYTHING YOU *SAY!* ONLY HOW'S ABOUT WE STOP BY MY SCOW SO'S I CAN GET MY *TOOTHBRUSH?*

A REASON-ABLE RE-QUEST! LEAD *ON!*

HEY...WELL, I DON'T WANNA SEEM *CHICKEN* OR NOTHIN'... BUT YOU MIND GOIN' IN *AHEAD* OF ME?

ANOTHER REASONABLE RE-QUEST! OKAY... FOLLOW ME!

OKAY, *BIGGER!* COAST IS *CLEAR!*

UNNGH!

BONK

173

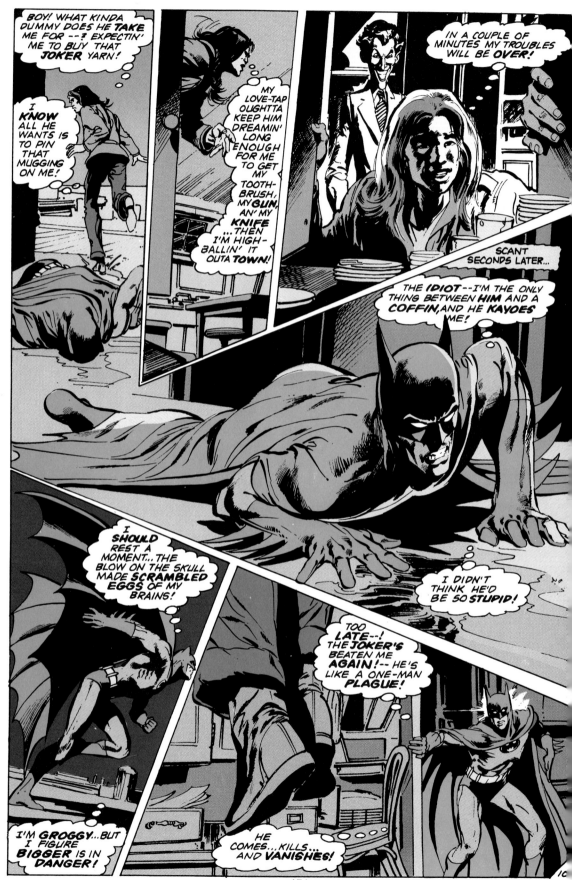

174

CONTAMINATED BEACH! KEEP OUT

YESTERDAY, A **SHIP** --A **TANKER**--RAN AGROUND JUST OFF **GOTHAM ISLAND** ...DUMPING HUNDREDS OF THOUSANDS OF GALLONS OF CRUDE OIL INTO THE SEA!

THIS **STORM** HAS PREVENTED ANY **CLEAN-UP** EFFORT--

...AND THE WIND HAS BEEN PUSHING THE FOULED WATER TOWARD THE **MAIN-LAND**!

WHICH MEANS THE **BEACHES** ARE **FULL** OF IT... AND ANY-ONE **WALKING** ON THE BEACH WOULD HAVE **SAND** AND **OIL** ON HIS SHOES!-- AS THE **JOKER** DID!

LOGICALLY, HE'D HIDE **HERE** ...IN THE **AQUARIUM BUILDING** THE GOVERNMENT CLOSED LAST MONTH!

I HAVE A **TINGLING** AT THE BASE OF MY NECK...A FEELING OF **DANGER**!

--EXACTLY WHAT I **WANT**!

YES, YES...**YES**! ALL THE WHILE I WAS BEHIND BARS, I **MISSED** OUR CLASHES!

I **DREAMED** OF... **HUMILIATING** YOU-- IN A SPECIALLY **HUMOROUS** WAY!

WITH NO EFFORT AT **STEALTH**, THE **BATMAN** BOLDLY ENTERS THE BUILDING...AND IS GREETED BY A PIERCINGLY CHILLING VOICE...

OH, **BATMAN**! YOU **FOUND** ME! I WAS **CERTAIN** YOU WOULD...AND I'M **GLAD**!

ANY PARTICULAR **REASON**, JOKER?

HOW DOES A SHARK EAT IF HE LOSES HIS TEETH? A SHARK CANNOT LOSE HIS TEETH BECAUSE TEETH ARE BROKEN NEW ONES ROTATE AND GROW

CARE TO **BEGIN**?

178

I'VE **NEVER** HAD TO FIGHT SO **UN-PREPARED!** I'VE NEVER MET A **SEA PREDATOR** IN HIS OWN ELEMENT!

STILL, THERE **MAY BE** A **WORK-ABLE MANEUVER**--

...USE THE CHAIN-LINKS TO PUT ITS **TEETH** OUT OF COMMISSION AND--

--HEAVE! HEAVE!! ...MAYBE SNAP ITS **SPINE**...OR SOMETHING!

BREAK, BLAST YOU!-- **BREAK!!**

BUT...WITHIN *YARDS* OF *FREEDOM*, THE FLEE-ING MADMAN *SLIPS*...

...*FALLS!*

FRANTIC, HE *RISES*...TO BE CON-FRONTED BY A PILLAR OF GREY *RAGE*--

IT'S *OVER, JOKER!*--*FINISHED!*

THEY'RE GOING TO PUT YOU PRECISELY WHERE YOU *BELONG*--IN A PADDED *CELL!* AND I HOPE THEY LOSE THE *KEY!*

N-NOT *FAIR!* I WAS SO *CLOSE*--UH!

YOU *WOULD'VE* ES-CAPED, ALL RIGHT--EXCEPT FOR THE *OIL SLIME* ON THE BEACH!

YOU *SLIPPE* ON IT...AND YOU'LL GO ON SLIPPING--TO THAT *CELL!*

186

YES, AWESOME IS *THE MASKED MANHUNTER'S* ANGER, AND SWIFT HAS ALWAYS BEEN HIS VENGEANCE AGAINST THE LAWLESS...

SOMEWHERE IN THE CITY *THE JOKER'S* LURKING... LAUGHING AT ALL THAT'S SACRED AND GOOD!

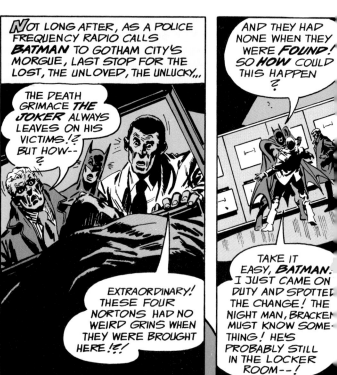

*N*OT LONG AFTER, AS A POLICE FREQUENCY RADIO CALLS *BATMAN* TO GOTHAM CITY'S MORGUE, LAST STOP FOR THE LOST, THE UNLOVED, THE UNLUCKY...

THE DEATH GRIMACE *THE JOKER* ALWAYS LEAVES ON HIS VICTIMS!? BUT HOW--?

EXTRAORDINARY! THESE FOUR NORTONS HAD NO WEIRD GRINS WHEN THEY WERE BROUGHT HERE!?!

AND THEY HAD NONE WHEN THEY WERE *FOUND!* SO *HOW* COULD THIS HAPPEN?

TAKE IT EASY, *BATMAN!* I JUST CAME ON DUTY AND SPOTTED THE CHANGE! THE NIGHT MAN, BRACKEN MUST KNOW SOMETHING! HE'S PROBABLY STILL IN THE LOCKER ROOM--!

HE'D BETTER TALK FAST AND STRAIGHT WHEN I GET MY GAUNTLETS...

EMPLOYEES' LOCKER ROOM

...ON HIM!

UNNNNN!

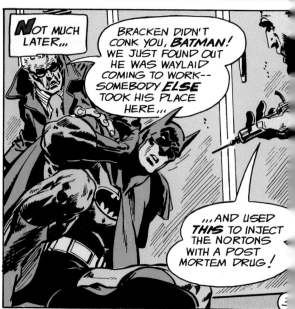

*N*OT MUCH LATER...

BRACKEN DIDN'T CONK YOU, *BATMAN!* WE JUST FOUND OUT HE WAS WAYLAID COMING TO WORK-- SOMEBODY *ELSE* TOOK HIS PLACE HERE...

...AND USED *THIS* TO INJECT THE NORTONS WITH A POST MORTEM DRUG!

THE *JOKER'S* USUAL GIMMICK-- LEAVING THE VICTIM'S FACE WITH A HORRIBLE GRIMACE! BUT WHY DIDN'T HE DO IT BACK AT THE MURDER SCENE?

MAYBE THERE WASN'T TIME-- OR HE JUST FORGOT!

HE USUALLY *DOESN'T*, COMMISSIONER! ANYWAY, HE CAUGHT ME FLAT-FOOTED AND GOT CLEAN AWAY! BUT I MUST PICK UP HIS TRAIL--*I MUST!*

*I*N THE NEXT FEW DAYS, THE *MASKED MANHUNTER* LISTENS...

HE TALKS...

HE PERSUADES...

HE BARGAINS...

POLICE

*A*ND HE COMES UP WITH...

NOTHING! NOT A SINGLE CLUE TO THE *JOKER'S* WHEREABOUTS!

4

DAWN BREAKS, AND THE HOURS MELT INTO LATE MORNING, THEN...

ON THE *BAT HOT-LINE...* THE BIG SYNDICATE BOSS HIMSELF, *RIZZO!*

RIZZO!? THAT WAS ONE GUY I COULDN'T THREATEN WITHOUT STIRRING UP A LEGAL HORNETS' NEST!

OKAY, RIZZO, WHAT'S THE BOSS OF BOSSES WANT WITH ME - ?

I GOT A DEAL FOR YOU, *BATMAN!* YOU'VE BEEN PUTTING SO MUCH HEAT ON MY STREET SOLDIERS LOOKING FOR *THE JOKER,* OUR OPERATIONS HAVE BEEN CUT IN HALF!

SO, BEING A PUBLIC-SPIRITED CITIZEN, I'M GIVING YOU A TIP ON *THE JOKER* -- SO YOU'LL LAY OFF!

GO CHECK OUT THE *GOTHAM GRAVEL COMPANY'S* MARINE DIVISION! THAT'S ALL! GOODBYE!

CAN YOU TRUST THE CITY'S BIGGEST RACKETS KING?

SOMETHING TELLS ME IT'S LEGIT! *JOKER'S* GETTING THE BACKLASH OF INGRATITUDE FROM THE VERY UNDERWORLD HE SOUGHT TO PROTECT!

IT'S MY FIRST LEAD ON THAT IN-HUMAN CREEP!

SHORTLY, GOTHAM'S WATERFRONT...

THAT OLD BARGE *HAS* TO BE THE "MARINE DIVISION"! BUT IS IT *THE JOKER'S* LAIR?

AMIDST THE STENCH OF ROTTING TIMBERS AND POLLUTED TIDES, *THE BATMAN* SLIPS ONTO THE OLD BARGE...

DESERTED! WHAT'S THAT ON THE TABLE? A DECK OF CARDS--?

ALL OF THEM *JOKERS!* HE WAS HERE! AND FROM THE LOOK OF THOSE FOOD TINS... VERY RECENTLY!

THEN, AS SOMETHING ELSE CATCHES HIS EYE...

AN AD, CIRCLED, AND THE NAME SLADE, WRITTEN! *SLADE?* SOUNDS FAMILIAR...

ONE HOUR LATER, THE STEAMY ATMOSPHERE OF THE GOTHAM TURKISH BATHS...

CAN HARDLY SEE IN THIS PLACE... BUT MY BAT-SENSE TELLS ME SOMETHING'S ABOUT TO HAPPEN!

YOU'RE SO RIGHT, *BATMAN,* FOR SUDDENLY APPEARING IN THE MIST, LIKE SOME HORRIBLY GRINNING GHOST...

THE *JOKER?!* WITH A GUN... STALKING SOMEBODY?!

WHO IS THE INTENDED VICTIM OF THE MAN-WHO-SMILES-WITHOUT-MIRTH, THE AWESOME, GHASTLY *JOKER?* STALK ON--TO *PART 2* ON NEXT PAGE FOLLOWING...

PART 2 "THE UNHOLY ALLIES"

IN THE SUFFOCATING STEAM, A KILLER GLIDES TOWARD A HUMAN TARGET-- AND STALKING THE WOULD-BE ASSASSIN-- THE BATMAN...

HE'S AIMING AT-- MY GOD! I *RECOGNIZE* HIM!

THE NEXT INSTANT...

?

YOU'RE NOT CLAIMING ANOTHER VICTIM, *JOKER!*

YOU FOOL, *BATMAN!* YOU KNOW NOT WHAT YOU DO!

I--I'M HIT!!

AND AS *THE MASKED MANHUNTER* SLUMPS TO THE TORRID TILES...

HUH--? COPS... AFTER THE JOKER?!

194

SHORTLY...

JOKER AND HIS PIGEON GOT AWAY! LUCKY FOR YOU IT'S ONLY A FLESH WOUND, AND I PUT A TAIL ON YOU SO WE ARRIVED IN TIME!

BLAST IT, GORDON--I DON'T WANT YOUR BOYS IN BLUE GETTING IN MY WAY!

NOW, YOU LISTEN! I'M NOT LETTING YOU CARRY ON A PRIVATE VENDETTA!

GOOD THING YOU'RE HURT... IT'LL KEEP YOU HERE WHILE MY DEPARTMENT BRINGS THAT KILLER TO JUSTICE-- LEGAL AND PROPER!

DON'T LET BATMAN STIR OUT OF THIS ROOM!

SOMETHING ODD ABOUT ALL THIS... I RECOGNIZED JOKER'S TARGET AS BURT SLADE, ONE OF THE UNDERWORLD'S TOP KILLERS!

BUT WHY WAS JOKER AFTER HIM? AND WHAT DID HE MEAN BY THOSE WORDS... "BATMAN, YOU KNOW NOT WHAT YOU DO!"?

GOT TO GET OUT OF HERE-- !!

DONNING HIS COSTUME, THE BATMAN WEAKLY MOVES TOWARD THE WINDOW...

AN EASY LEAP FOR ME, NORMALLY--BUT NOW... WITH THIS HOLE IN ME, I'M NOT SURE! GOT TO TRY IT, ANYWAY!

THE NEXT MOMENT...

NOT GOING TO MAKE IT-- !

8

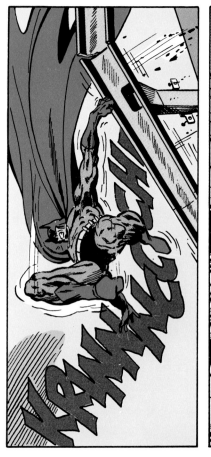

SOON, THE OFFICE OF GOTHAM CITY'S HARBORMASTER...

GOTHAM GRAVEL BARGE NUMBER 3, *BATMAN*... WHY, IT WAS A HUNDRED MILES UPRIVER LAST WEDNESDAY NIGHT!

BLAZES! AND FROM THE COMPANY RECORDS, IT'S CLEAR *JOKER* WAS ABOARD, DISGUISED AS A *BARGE TENDER!*

SOON,....

HAVE YOU FLIPPED YOUR COWL? HOW CAN YOU SAY *THE JOKER* DIDN'T KILL THE NORTONS??

WE WERE BLIND TO IT BEFORE! IT ALL ADDS UP! FIRST, *JOKER* WASN'T EVEN *IN* GOTHAM CITY THAT NIGHT!

SO HE COULD'VE HAD IT DONE BY A *HENCHMAN!*

NO, HE'S ALWAYS DONE HIS *OWN* KILL-ING-- AND HE NEVER SLIPPED UP LEAVING THE TELLTALE JOKER DEATH GRIN ON HIS VICTIMS-! RIGHT?

BUT SOMEBODY INFILTRATED THE MORGUE LATER TO GIVE THE BODIES THEIR DEATH GRIMACES IN A BETTER-LATE-THAN-NEVER TRY TO MAKE SURE WE'D LAY THE CRIME AT *THE JOKER'S* DOOR!

HMMM, YOU'VE GOT A POINT...

NOW ADD THAT TO THE FACT *THE JOKER'S* STALKING A KNOWN, VICIOUS KILLER, BURT SLADE... AND I'LL BET MY CAPE *SLADE* MASSACRED THE NORTONS AND PINNED IT ON *THE JOKER!*

AND *JOKER'S* GETTING *EVEN*? BUT WHY DIDN'T HE COME FORWARD IF HE'S *INNOCENT*?

THE JOKER CLAIMING INNOCENCE? WHO'D EVER BELIEVE SUCH A FANTASTIC THING? WOULD **YOU**? WOULD **I**?

I SEE WHAT YOU MEAN! THEN, WE'VE ALL BEEN DUPED... GOTHAM CITY'S SEEKING VENGEANCE AGAINST **THE WRONG MAN**!

YES, AND IT'S SO IMPORTANT TO GET SLADE, I'M GOING TO DO SOMETHING I NEVER DREAMED WAS POSSIBLE--MAKE A DEAL WITH MY OLDEST ENEMY... **THE JOKER**!

WHAT? YOU'RE NOT SERIOUS!

BUT **BATMAN** IS SERIOUS, FOR SHORTLY...

Joker! I KNOW THE TRUTH! LET'S TALK DEAL! BATMAN

MAN, IT'S WILD, **BATMAN** LAID REAL BREAD ON US TO COVER THE CITY WITH THIS MESSAGE!

NEARBY...

USING THE **GRAFFITI GANG** THIS WAY IS A BIT **FAR** OUT--BUT I **MUST** CONTACT HIM--AND **FAST**!

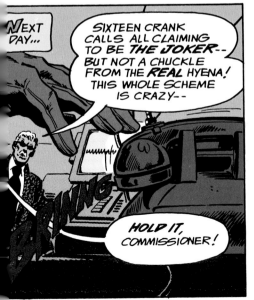

NEXT DAY...

SIXTEEN CRANK CALLS ALL CLAIMING TO BE **THE JOKER**-- BUT NOT A CHUCKLE FROM THE **REAL** HYENA! THIS WHOLE SCHEME IS CRAZY--

HOLD IT, COMMISSIONER!

HA! HA!! **JOKER** HERE, **BATMAN**! NOW WHAT'S THIS DEAL YOU'VE GOT UNDER YOUR COWL? **HA! HA! HA!**

VOICE-PRINT CHECKS EXACTLY! IT'S **HIM**, ALL RIGHT!

I'D KNOW THAT BONE-CHILLING LAUGH **ANYWHERE**!

JOKER, I KNOW YOU'RE INNOCENT AND THAT BURT SLADE KILLED THE NORTONS.

I'M OFFERING TO WORK WITH YOU TO GET HIM-- A TRUCE BE- TWEEN US UNTIL THAT PUNK'S BE- HIND BARS!

HA! HA! WELL, WELL, BATMAN, YOU'RE FINALLY DEVELOPING BRAINS!

I ACCEPT YOUR OFFER--BUT NO TRICKS! AND NO POLICE! I HAVE A LEAD ON SLADE'S MOVEMENTS!

GO TO A PHONE BOOTH AT 179th STREET AND GOTHAM BOULEVARD!

I WILL CALL THERE EXACTLY AT 3 O'CLOCK! BE TALKING TO YOU, "PAL"! HA! HA! HA!

IT'S BEGUN! WE'RE NOW A TEAM! I'M OFF TO ESTABLISH FURTHER CONTACT-- BUT IF YOU PUT A TAIL ON ME, GORDON--

OKAY, OKAY-- BUT I NEVER DREAMED I'D LIVE TO SEE THIS DAY-- YOU WORKING WITH,... THE JOKER!

GOT TO, OLD FRIEND! HE SEEMS TO HAVE INSIDE KNOWLEDGE OF SLADE AND HIS CRIMINAL HABITS!

AND AS THE MASKED MANHUNTER HURTLES TO HIS STRANGE RENDEZVOUS,...

HATED TO FIB TO BATMAN, BUT I DID PUT A "TAIL" ON HIM... NOT THE KIND HE'D SPOT!

THE BAT-PHONE RECEIVER WAS COATED WITH IN- VISIBLE CHEMICAL PARTICLES, SO HIS ONE GAUNTLET WILL ACT AS A TRACKING LOCATOR!

BATMAN MAY NEED PROTECTION-- AND I'M NOT LOSING A CHANCE TO BAG *THE JOKER!*

HE MAY BE INNOCENT OF THE NORTON SLAY- INGS, BUT HE'S GUILTY OF PLENTY OF OTHERS!

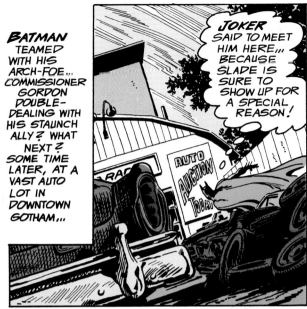

BATMAN TEAMED WITH HIS ARCH-FOE... COMMISSIONER GORDON DOUBLE- DEALING WITH HIS STAUNCH ALLY? WHAT NEXT? SOME TIME LATER, AT A VAST AUTO LOT IN DOWNTOWN GOTHAM...

JOKER SAID TO MEET HIM HERE,,, BECAUSE SLADE IS SURE TO SHOW UP FOR A SPECIAL REASON!

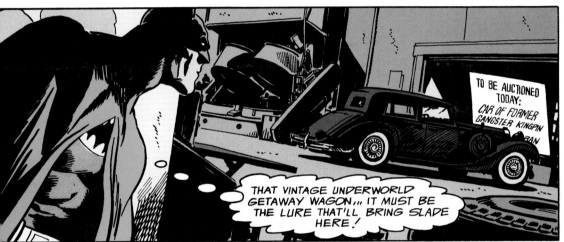

TO BE AUCTIONED TODAY: CAR OF FORMER GANGSTER KINGPIN

THAT VINTAGE UNDERWORLD GETAWAY WAGON,,, IT MUST BE THE LURE THAT'LL BRING SLADE HERE!

AND AS THE BIDDING BEGINS...

$10,500!

THAT'S *SLADE* UP FRONT! BUT WHERE'S *THE JOKER?*

SOLD!

SLADE BOUGHT THE CAR! IF I TACKLE HIM HERE, SOMEONE'S LIABLE TO GET HURT! HE'S *ARMED* AND *DEADLY!*

12

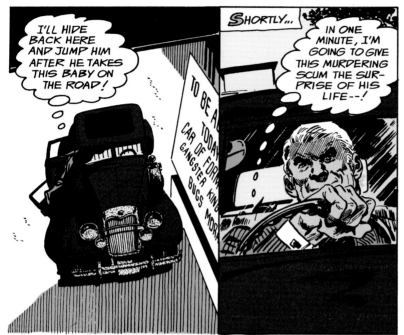

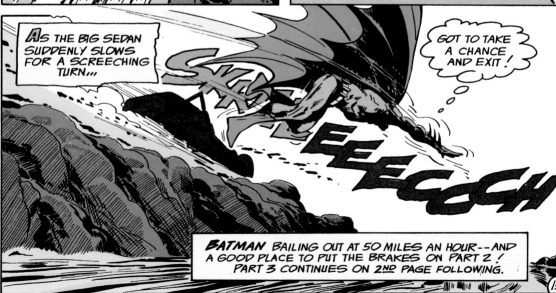

A CULVERT'S A HANDY THING. IT CARRIES AWAY DRAINAGE WATER--OR IT BREAKS A *BATMAN'S* FALL...

THE POLICE WILL NEVER CATCH THAT SOUPED-UP SPECIAL! GORDON *LIED*--THEY WERE TAILING ME! MUST MAKE CONTACT WITH *THE JOKER* AGAIN!

SOON, AS A BEDRAGGLED *BATMAN* ANSWERS THE RINGING IN A LONELY PHONE BOOTH...

YOU *BUMBLER!* I HID IN THE GARAGE AND SAW EVERYTHING. NOW SLADE'S GOTTEN AWAY AGAIN!

SORRY, *JOKER!* CAN'T FIGURE *HOW* HE GUESSED I WAS IN THE CAR!

NOW, LISTEN, GREAT CRIME-FIGHTER, IF YOUR POLICE PALS SHOW UP AGAIN, OUR DEAL'S *OFF!*

BELIEVE ME, IT WAS A COMPLETE SURPRISE! GORDON DOUBLECROSSED ME! IT WON'T HAPPEN AGAIN!

IT BETTER *NOT!* SLADE'S PRETTY SPOOKED--I'LL BET HE'S LEFT GOTHAM! I'VE A HUNCH TO WHERE HE'S GONE!

STAND BY FOR FURTHER INSTRUCTIONS, *BAT-SAP!* HA! HA! HA! HA!

CLICK!

MUCH AS I HATE IT, I'VE GOT TO TAKE THAT LAUGHING GOON'S INSULTS-- CATCHING SLADE'S MORE IMPORTANT THAN PRIDE!

14

SOME TIME LATER, POLICE HEADQUARTERS...

BLAST! I'M NOT GETTING A TRACKING BLIP ON BATMAN! WHAT COULD HAVE GONE WRONG?

WHAT WENT WRONG, COMMISSIONER? WELL, AS A SLEEK CAR HEADS NORTH FROM GOTHAM...

JOKER SAYS SLADE'S MOST LIKELY GONE TO AN OLD HIDEOUT NEAR CANALVILLE... MILES UPSTATE!

...ONE OF BATMAN'S GAUNTLETS GRIPPING THE CAR'S WHEEL HAD BEEN WASHED CLEAN OF THE TRACKING CHEMICALS BY WATER IN THE CULVERT...

AND AS HE STREAKS TOWARDS HIS RENDEZVOUS...

WHEREVER HE IS, BATMAN'S ON HIS OWN! I CAN'T HELP HIM!

GOOD LUCK, OLD FRIEND. I'LL BE PRAYING FOR YOU--!

TWO HOURS LATER...

HERE IT IS-- CANALVILLE, A SLEEPY SMALL TOWN THAT'S BEEN RUNNING DOWNHILL SINCE THE CANAL WAS ABANDONED DECADES AGO!

THIS IS IT-- THE MESSAGE *JOKER* SAID HE'D LEAVE ON THE CIVIL WAR MONUMENT!

COME to old LOCK 39 OUTSIDE TOWN! J.

SHORTLY...

SOME STRETCHES OF THE OLD CANAL STILL CONTAIN WATER!

NO ONE HERE! WHAT'S THAT ON THE LOCK BOTTOM?

BATMAN'S KEEN EYES FOCUS ON THE SMALL OBJECT SOME 40 FEET DOWN IN THE OLD STONE LOCK...

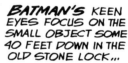

A PLAYING CARD! MUST BE *JOKER'S* NEXT MESSAGE!

16

THE JOKE'S ON YOU, BATSAP!

HA! HA! HA! HA!

JOKER !?

YES, "PAL," AND YOU FELL NEATLY INTO MY TRAP-- FOR, MY MIGHTY, BRILLIANT *CAPED CRUSADER,* 'TWAS A TRAP ALL ALONG! HA! HA! HA!

DON'T MOVE, *BATMAN,* OR YOU'RE *DEAD!*

BURT SLADE --?

MY PARTNER IN DELICIOUS CRIME! OF COURSE, I KILLED THE NORTONS MYSELF -- AND THEN THREW SUSPICION ONTO SLADE BY FALSE CLUES!

PUTTING DEATH GRIMACES ON THE CORPSES, DOCTORING THE HARBORMASTER'S RECORDS, PRETENDING TO STALK SLADE... EVEN HAVING RIZZO GIVE YOU A PHONY TIP ON MY HIDEOUT...

...ALL WERE DESIGNED TO MAKE YOU DOUBT YOUR ORIGINAL CON- CLUSION THAT I, *THE JOKER,* HAD DONE WHAT I REALLY *DID* DO! HA! HA! HA!

I PICKED SLADE BECAUSE HE HATED YOU AS MUCH AS I-- AND BECAUSE YOU'D BELIEVE HE'S COLD- BLOODED ENOUGH...

...TO HAVE WIPED OUT THE NORTONS FOR THE SAME REASON THAT I REALLY DID THEM IN!

17

205

HA! HA! HA! AT LAST-- I'VE TASTED THE *ULTIMATE* TRIUMPH! *BATMAN* IS NO MORE!

BUT UNSEEN BELOW, IN A SUPREME EFFORT FOR SURVIVAL, A MAN CLINGS TO A BIG, RUSTY OLD MOORING RING...

THOUGHT MY ARMS WOULD BE TORN OFF... BUT I HUNG ON!

SUDDENLY...

HUH? HE'S ALIVE?!-- UNNNGH!!

KA-POW!

ALIVE AND KICKING, SLADE!

HE GOT SLADE... NOW HE'S COMING FOR *ME*!

BATMAN'S OWN CAR!

HA-HA-HA! I'LL STEAL IT... AND LEAVE HIM IN MY DUST!!

WHY WON'T IT START? WHY?

IT MUST START! IT MUST!

THE NEXT INSTANT...

YAAAAHH! PLEASE... MERCY...

YOU MURDEROUS SWINE--I SHOULD END YOUR FOUL LIFE WITH MY OWN HANDS...

BUT THAT WOULD GIVE YOU A FINAL VICTORY, MAKING ME INTO A KILLER LIKE YOURSELF!

THE CAR... WOULDN'T START... I COULD HAVE ESCAPED...

NO WAY, YOU GHASTLY CLOWN!

THE IGNITION'S CONTROLLED BY THIS PHONY RADIO WHICH IS REALLY A KEY PUNCH SAFETY DEVICE -- BUT YOU HAVE TO KNOW THE CODE... JUST 6 LITTLE LETTERS! LIKE SO!

BATMAN

GUESS THE LAST LAUGH'S ON YOU, JOKER! HA! HA! HA!

THE END

207

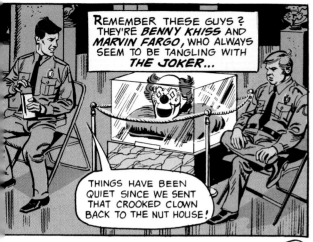

REMEMBER THESE GUYS? THEY'RE *BENNY KHISS* AND *MARVIN FARGO*, WHO ALWAYS SEEM TO BE TANGLING WITH *THE JOKER*...

THINGS HAVE BEEN QUIET SINCE WE SENT THAT CROOKED CLOWN BACK TO THE NUT HOUSE!

WE LOST THE JOB WE HAD THEN...

...BUT WE LUCKED INTO *THIS* JOB... GUARDING A SILLY *MASK*!

GIMME A CUPPA *COFFEE*, BENNY!

HEY... SOME KINDA *MIST* IS COMIN' FROM MY JUG... HA HA HA HA HA...

NOT... *MIST*... AH-HA-HA--

BONK TONK

--LAUGHING GAS... OWWW!

AT THAT MOMENT, THE *CURATOR* OF THIS PRIVATE MUSEUM ENTERS AND SHOUTS--

WHAT'S GOING *ON*?

HA HA HA HA HA HA

KLUMB

HA HA HA

LATER...THE HAPLESS CURATOR IS INTERVIEWED BY *JACK RYDER* OF *WHAM-TV*...

...HE STOLE A RARE *JEWELED COMEDY MASK* BELIEVED TO BE THE WORK OF *CELLINI!*

ANY IDEA OF THE THIEF'S *IDENTITY?*

WE KNOW...

QUIET, DUMMY!

YES, MISTER RYDER, *I KNOW* WHO IT WAS!

I GLIMPSED *GREEN HAIR*... AND HEARD A *MANIACAL LAUGH*--

--WHICH ADD UP TO JUST *ONE MAN*...AN *OUTLAW—THE CREEPER!*

NOW...*EXCUSE* ME! I MUST SEE OUR *INSURANCE AGENT!*

THE... *CREEPER?*

YOU GUYS LOOK LIKE YOU'VE JUST GOTTEN A *PARKING TICKET*... AND YOU DON'T OWN A *CAR!*--WHY?

HE SAID *THE CREEPER* SWIPED THE THINGUS! *MAYBE* HE'S *RIGHT*--

--ONLY *WE* WOULD'VE SWORN IT WAS *THE JOKER!*

SO THE CURATOR THINKS KHISS AND FARGO ARE DOPES, EH? WELL, *THEY* CAN GIVE HIM LESSONS IN CRIMINAL IDENTIFICATION*!*

THAT THIEF *COULDN'T* HAVE BEEN *THE CREEPER*--

--BECAUSE *I'M THE CREEPER...AND I* POSITIVELY *DIDN'T* SWIPE THE MASK!

SO I'M *DOUBLE-DARNED* IF I'LL TAKE THE LOUSY *RAP!*

--WHICH IS THE CUE FOR OLD *FUNNY FACE* TO GET INTO THE *ACTION!*

IT'S NOT LONG SINCE I HELPED *THE BATMAN* TAKE *RÂS-AL-GHÛL*... AND NOW I'LL BE TACKLING ANOTHER OF HIS FOES!

JACK RYDER TOUCHES A TINY *ACTIVATOR* ATTACHED TO HIS *WATCHBAND*--

--AND AN *ASTONISHING* TRANSFORMATION OCCURS*!*...

I'VE A *VERY* GOOD IDEA WHERE *THE JOKER* WILL STRIKE *NEXT!* IT'S A *CRIME*--

--HE WON'T BE ABLE TO *RESIST!*

HAHA!

4

MEANWHILE, ACROSS TOWN...

STEP ON IT, JOE! WE GOTTA GET THIS BOOK TO THE LIBRARY BEFORE CLOSING!

IT'S A PRICELESS COPY OF THE WORLD'S VERY FIRST JOKE BOOK... PRINTED IN LATIN!

THEY'RE GONNA DISPLAY IT, AND...

HEY... ALL OF A SUDDEN, WE'RE NOT MOVING!

AN' EITHER WE'RE FLYING... OR SOMEBODY'S PULLING THE STREET AWAY!

HA-HA-HA-

YOU... IN THE CAR! YOU HAVE A CHOICE...

YOU CAN HAND UP THOSE PAGES OF RIB-TICKLERS— OR I SWITCH OFF THE MAGNET HOLDING YOU!

THE FALL WON'T HURT--

--BUT THE STOP WILL BE SIMPLY SMASHING! HA HA HA!

OKAY... OKAY! WE GET THE POINT!

WE OUGHT TO! THAT JOKE IS OLDER THAN THE BLASTED BOOK!

AS I FIGURED... THE JOKER AMBUSHED THE ANCIENT GUISEPPE PENNERINI VOLUME OF MIRTH!--HIS KIND OF CAPER!

HE'LL PROBABLY HEAD FOR THE JOKERMOBILE I SPOTTED!

THE SCREWBALL DOESN'T *REALIZE* IT YET--

--BUT HE'S ABOUT TO BE *INTERCEPTED*--

--BY A *CHUCKLESOME CREEPER!*

HA HA HA

HA HA HA

S MAAASH!

THAT *LAUGH...* YOU?--THE *CREEPER!*

IN PERSON!

TELL YOU WHAT, PASTY-FACE--WE CAN HAVE A *LAUGHING CONTEST...* *FISTS* AT CLOSE QUARTERS ...

...OR YOU CAN *SURRENDER!*

YOU OPT FOR THE *FIST-*ROUTE, HEY?

I DIDN'T THINK YOU *WENT* FOR THE OLD HAND-TO-HAND!

BUT I'M *GLAD* YOU DO! NEXT TO *ICE CREAM SODAS,* BIFFING BADDIES IS MY FAVORITE *RECREATION!*

SWING, WON'T YOU?

IT'S NO *FUN...*

...IF YOU JUST STAND AND GET *BIFFED!*

213

6

SPLITTING ALREADY? JOKER, YOU *ARE* A DISAPPOINTMENT! I AT *LEAST* EXPECTED YOU TO TRADE *REPARTEE* WITH ME!

YOU KNOW... GAGS... SNAPPY PATTER--

--SIDE-SPLITTERS ...EVEN HA-HA-HA'S?

MERCY! I AM *DEFEATED*... *CRUSHED*... *WRECKED*!

HE'S *DAZED*... HE CAN'T TELL WHERE I *AM*!

OKAY, *JOKER*-- ON YOUR *FEET*!

THEN... ACTIVATED BY A *THREAD* IN THE *JOKER'S LAPEL*, THE LEAD-WEIGHTED TAILS OF HIS COAT SLAM INTO *THE CREEPER*...

--ONE THAT'S *BOUND* TO LEAVE YOU *CHOKED UP*! HA HA HA!

THERE'S GOING TO BE A *SURPRISE ENDING* TO THIS TALE--

ADMIT IT! I'M NOT ONLY *HILARIOUS*, I LEAVE YOU *BREATHLESS!*

UNKNOWN TO *EITHER* ANTAGONIST, *THE CREEPER'S ACTIVATOR* SLIPS FROM HIS WRIST AND DROPS INTO *THE JOKER'S POCKET--!*

ENOUGH CHIT-CHAT!

BESIDES, YOU'RE WRINKLING MY *SUIT!*

HE'S *UNCONSCIOUS*... *ALIVE*, BUT *SNOOZING!*

WELL! AS LONG AS I'VE INHERITED A PRIME *SUPER-HERO*, I SHOULD TAKE *ADVANTAGE* OF THE SITUATION!

AH-*HA!* GOT IT!

THAT NIGHT, IN *THE JOKER'S HA-HACIENDA*...

MMMM...THE KNOCK ON *THE CREEPER'S CRANIUM* WAS HARDER THAN I *THOUGHT!* HE'S *STILL* COUNTING SHEEP!

WHILE I WAIT, I'LL CONSULT THE *PAPER* FOR *IDEAS!*

8

CASHEWS By Sandy Saturn

--THAT IS, I'LL LOOK FOR IDEAS *AFTER* I CONSULT MY FAVORITE SECTION--THE *COMICS!*

SANDY SATURN'S A *GENIUS...* "CASHEWS" HAS MADE HIM RICH!

WHAT'S YOUR NAME, KID?

CHARLIE CASHEW!

CHARLIE *WHAT?*

CASHEW!

GESUNDHEIT!

DICK STAR

RICH ,,, YES, *RICH!*

OH, *GOOD!* I *HAVE* MY IDEA! --FOUND IN THE *FUNNIES!* HA-HA-HA

UNNGH

AH,,,MY CAPRICIOUS CAPTIVE *AWAKENS!*

W-WHERE *AM I? WHO* AM I?

HE DOESN'T *REMEMBER!* HE HAS *AMNESIA!*

THE GODS OF *NASTY* ARE *GRINNING* AT ME TONIGHT!

WHY AM I *BOUND?*

A *B-AAAD* MAN TIED YOU... THE SLIMY SLOB WHO DRAWS A *COMIC STRIP!* WHAT'S WORSE,,, HE'S ACCUSING *YOU* OF *CRIMES* THAT *HE* COMMITTED!

HE'S *ROTTEN* TO THE *CORE--*

--WHILE *I'M* YOUR *BUDDY!*

TELL YOU *WHAT--* YOU *CATCH* HIM,,, BRING HIM TO *ME!*--

--AND I'LL *FORCE* HIM TO *ADMIT* HIS LIES AND YOU'LL BE *CLEARED!* A *DEAL--?*

SURE,,, WHY NOT?

So, the next morning, in the studio of cartoonist *Sandy Saturn...*

Listen, you **moronic** bodyguards... get your bods **outside** and make sure I'm not **disturbed!**

Yessir!

We work for him for **ten years** and he don't even call us by our **names!**

He lost his temper long ago... and it's **never** been found!

They think I'm **rotten...** guess I **am!**

I used to be a real **sweetheart...**

...but drawing this **cutesy** trash gets on my nerves!

Turns my **stomach...** meeting **deadlines...** being **whimsical** seven days a week!

I shoulda been a **stockbroker...** plumber...hobo... **anything!** --but no...I hadda be **creative!**

C-RA-AASH

You got a **nerve,** dropping in...disturbing me! Whaddya **want?**

You!

Y-you're the... C-C-C-**reeper!** **Hellp!**

10

217

S-S-STAY BACK, OR--

--OR WHAT--

--LITTLE MAN?

OR--I WON'T GIVE YOU MY AU-AU-AUTOGRAPH!

HA-HA-HA-HA-

HA-HA-HA-HA

-HA-HA-HA-HA-

A-HA-HA-HA-HA

HERE'S THE INK-SLINGER!

LEAVE HIM TO ME! I'LL PERSUADE HIM TO COOPERATE!

YOU CAN GO INTO THE NEXT ROOM AND WATCH TV!

AND...

GOOD EVENING! WELCOME TO THE WHAM-TV NEWS!

I'M WILLIAM BATSON, SUBSTI-TUTING FOR...ER-- JACK RYDER!

RYDER... SOMETHING FAMILIAR ABOUT THAT NAME!

12

AT THE TOP OF THE NEWS... POLICE ARE STILL SEARCHING FOR THE *CREEPER*, BELIEVED TO HAVE STOLEN THE *CELLINI MASK*...

WHAM TV NEWS

IT'S *TRUE!* I *AM* AN OUTLAW... *HUNTED!*

I HADN'T REALLY *BELIEVED* IT... TILL *NOW!*

SOMETHING *NAGGING* AT MY MEMORY... BUT IT WON'T *COME--*

--CAN'T *REMEMBER*...

...*CAN'T!*

MEANWHILE...

SATURN, YOU CAN PLY YOUR *INKY TRADE* WHILE I EXPLAIN WHY I'VE HAD YOU *BROUGHT* TO ME!

YOU'RE ALL *HEART!*

YOU WILL INSTRUCT YOUR *AGENT* TO WITHDRAW *ONE MILLION DOLLARS* FROM WHEREVER YOU STASH YOUR LOOT, AND DELIVER SAME TO *ME!*

UPON *RECEIPT*, I SHALL *RELEASE* YOU!

LIKE I SAID... ALL *HEART!*

SATURN HAS CONFESSED TO *FRAMING* ME?

EVEN *BETTER!* HE'S GIVEN ME *PROOF* OF YOUR INNOCENCE!

THE EVIDENCE IS IN THIS *BAG!*

I'LL PHONE THE *MAYOR,* THE *DISTRICT ATTORNEY* AND THE *POLICE CHIEF* TO MEET US AT *HEADQUARTERS!*

THEY'LL GET A *BANG* OUT OF SEEING YOU! HA HA HA!

I AM *DISGUSTINGLY* CLEVER! WITH THE MAYOR, THE D.A., THE HEAD *FUZZ*-- AND *THE CREEPER* DEAD, THE TOWN WILL BE MY *OYSTER!*

WITHIN THE HOUR...

YOUR MOMENT OF *TRIUMPH* HAS ARRIVED, *CREEPY!*

GO ON *IN!* I'LL *WAIT* HERE!

...WAIT UNTIL I HEAR THE BOMB'S *BOOM!*

OH, I'M SO SMART I FEEL LIKE *HUGGING* MYSELF!

IN FACT... I *WILL!*

SUDDENLY, AN *EXPLOSION* WRACKS THE BUILDING--!

KA-WOOOM

POLICE PRECINCT 13

HAVING STOPPED TO *CELEBRATE*, THE JOKER ARRIVES AT HIS *HA-HACIENDA* HIDEAWAY AT *MIDNIGHT*, AND...

STILL BUSY, *SATURN*?

--BUSY *WAITING*, JOKER--

--FOR *YOU*!

YOU DON'T *RECOGNIZE* ME--BUT WE'VE MET!

I WON'T OFFER YOU MY *HAND*... I'M A TRIFLE *CHOOSY*!

WILL YOU SETTLE FOR MY *FIST*?

I'LL GIFT YOU WITH ANOTHER *LOVE*-TAP AND DELIVER YOU TO THE *HEAT*!

READY--?

NOT *QUITE*--!

BLACK INK

MY *EYES*--!

OUR POSITIONS ARE *REVERSED*! *MY* TURN TO BE A ROUGHNECK! HA-HA-HA!

MY VISION'S CLEARED... WON'T DO ME ANY *GOOD*, THOUGH!

EVEN *THE CREEPER'S* TERRIFIC STRENGTH CAN'T BREAK FREE OF THE GRIP OF A *HOMICIDAL MANIAC*!

AT THIS FATEFUL INSTANT, A TINY *DEVICE* DROPS ONTO THE TABLE...

MY *ACTIVATOR!* IT MUST'VE SLIPPED INTO *THE JOKER'S* POCKET WHEN WE WERE FIGHTING IN THE *JUNKYARD!*

HE MUST HAVE ACCIDENTALLY *PRESSED* IT AT THE POLICE STATION... *TRANSFORMING* ME!

INCREDIBLE LUCK... BUT IT WON'T *HELP* ME UNLESS I CAN REACH IT WITH MY *CHIN!*

CONTACT!

A RAW SURGE OF *POWER* AND *JACK RYDER* AGAIN BECOMES --

--*THE CREEPER!?!*

MY CHANGE CAUGHT HIM BY SURPRISE... HE'S LOST HIS *ADVANTAGE!*

I'M TOO *WEARY* TO TRADE FURTHER *WITTICISMS* --

--I PREFER JUST TO *FINISH* YOU! HA HA HA!

HA HA HA

CAN'T WE ᵇHEH-HEHᵇ *TALK* THIS OVER--?

SOCCK

HA-HA-HA-HA

The End.

225

Colorist: Petra Scotese

READ THE STORY BY: STEVE ENGLEHART

...AND *THEN*...

UNHEARD AND UNSEEN, *THE BATMAN* REMAINS *STILL* FOR SEVERAL MOMENTS, *WEIGHING* IT ALL AGAIN IN HIS MIND...

NOK NOK~

WHA--

OH MY GOD!

SILVER ST. CLOUD...

...MAY I *COME IN?*

*T*IME *SUSPENDS* ITSELF, AS THEY STARE INTO *EACH OTHER'S* EYES-- HERS *WIDENED*, HIS *BLANK*...

SHE *KNOWS* WHO I AM, BENEATH THIS MASK! SHE *CALLED* TO ME-- *STARED* LIKE SHE'S STARING *NOW!**

FOR *YEARS*, I'VE KEPT MY AFFAIRS *SHORT*, FEARING THIS *VERY THING*--A WOMAN WHO KNEW THE MAN BEHIND THE *MASK!* THIS TIME, I LET MYSELF *INDULGE!*

I KNOW HER *TOO WELL* TO MISS THE *SHOCK* RUNNING THROUGH HER-- JUST AS *SHE* KNOWS *ME!* WE'VE BEEN *TOO CLOSE*, SHARED *TOO MUCH*, FOR *TOO LONG!*

SHE *KNOWS!*

*LAST ISH-- *JULIE*

MS. ST. CLOUD...I THOUGHT YOU HAD SOMETHING TO *TELL* ME LAST NIGHT....!

DID I....?

NO! NO, I-- DON'T THINK SO!

WHA--?

②

WHAT--WHAT COULD *I* KNOW ABOUT-- *ANYTHING?*

I'D NEVER SEEN THAT *DEADSHOT* GUY BEFORE--!

THAT'S *NOT* WHAT I *MEANT!*

WELL, I DON'T KNOW WHAT ELSE TO *TELL YOU,* BATMAN!

REALLY! I'M AFRAID YOU'VE MADE A *MISTAKE!*

LOOK AT HER *HAND* SHAKE! SHE'S *HIDING* SOMETHING--

--BUT *WHY?*

SHOULD I JUST *TAKE OFF* MY MASK--*FORCE* THIS GAME TO AN *END?*

UT IN THE WORLD OF *THE BATMAN,* THERE ARE *MANY SHADOWS....!*

NO! IF SHE *DOESN'T* KNOW --...

--IF IT WAS *SOMETHING ELSE* THAT SHOCKED HER-- I'D BE A *FOOL!*

I CAME HERE THINKING SHE *KNEW,* TO SEE WHERE WE WENT FROM *THERE*--PREPARED TO DEAL WITH *ANYTHING*--

--EXCEPT *THIS!*

WOULD YOU *SAY* SOMETHING, PLEASE? I HAVE A *DATE* COMING TO PICK ME UP SOON --

--*BRUCE WAYNE!* PERHAPS YOU *KNOW* EACH OTHER?

WHATEVER'S GOING ON, SHE'S QUICK TO *RECOVER!*

MAYBE I *HAVE* MADE A MISTAKE, MS. ST, CLOUD!

IF THAT SHOULD PROVE TO BE THE *CASE,* I *APOLOGIZE!*

UNTIL WE MEET *AGAIN!*

OH, GOD...

HE *KNOWS!*

BUT WHAT ELSE COULD I *DO?*

THAT WAS *THE BATMAN!*

A *LIVING LEGEND!*

HE'S KEPT HIS *TRUE* IDENTITY SECRET FOR *YEARS!*

HOW COULD I LOOK IN THOSE *PALE SLITS* AND SAY, "*I'VE* FIGURED OUT YOUR *SECRET!"*? EVEN IF IT WERE *TRUE*--?

"*YOU'RE* REALLY MY *BOY FRIEND, BATMAN!* I CAN SEE WHAT *OTHERS* WOULD *NEVER* NOTICE--

--BECAUSE *I'VE* SPENT SO MANY EVENINGS STUDYING YOUR *JAW!"*

WHAT COULD I *SAY*-- AND WHAT WOULD *HE* SAY *THEN?* I *LOVE* BRUCE WAYNE!

--I *DON'T* WANT TO *LOSE*--

RING RING

H-HELLO--

SILVER! THIS IS *BRUCE*--

I JUST WANTED YOU TO *KNOW*-- I'LL BE A *LITTLE LATE!* I-- HAVE TO WORK A FEW THINGS *OUT* YET--

THAT'S-- OKAY BRUCE! I HAVE A *HEADACHE* ANYWAY! WHY DON'T WE JUST *POSTPONE* TONIGHT?

JUST PUT IT OFF FOR A *BETTER TIME?*

THAT SOUNDS-- SENSIBLE--

I'VE GOT TO GET *OUT* OF HERE!

I NEED TIME TO *THINK*-- WHERE HE WON'T *FIND* ME--!

CLICK

THERE'S A *LOT* OF THINKING GOING ON TONIGHT... VERY *SERIOUS* THINKING...

...BUT *DON'T DESPAIR,* ACTION-LOVERS! *YOUR* DAY IS DAWNING *SOON!*

THEY SAY *THE BATMAN* CAN SOLVE *ANYTHING*--

--BUT HE'S *UP A STUMP* ON *THIS* ONE! "*DOES* SHE OR *DOESN'T* SHE?"--

--AND WHAT IF SHE *DOES?*

I'VE GONE TO *GREAT LENGTHS* TO KEEP MY IDENTITY SECRET, FOR THE *BEST* OF REASONS!

--BRUCE WAYNE *MUST* REMAIN A *SAFE RETREAT!*

I CRIED *NO TEARS* WHEN *MAGDA* BECAME A MONSTER!*

*SHE AND HUGO STRANGE LEARNED THE SECRET IN *'TEC* #471-472! -- *JULIE*

BUT I DON'T WANT *SILVER* TO GO THAT ROUTE--

--I JUST *WANT HER*--

--*PERIOD!*

--MY WORLD GOES *CRAZY* SOMETIMES!

--I'M *IN LOVE* WITH THAT GIRL-- THE *REAL ME,* UNDERNEATH ALL THE MASKS!

AND *STILL,* THE MAN BENEATH THE MASK CAN'T BE *CARELESSLY REVEALED!* MY *SECRETS* ARE MY PROTECTION FROM *DEATH!*

EVER SINCE *JOE CHILL* STEPPED OUT OF THE DARK TO GUN MY *PARENTS* DOWN--

HELP! HELP, POLICE!

230

BATMAN! OUR FISH! OUR FISH!

GET A GRIP ON YOURSELF, MAN! WHAT ARE YOU YELLING ABOUT?

LOOK!

WHAT THE--! ALL OF THEM -- WITH THE JOKER'S FACE?!?

ALL OF 'EM! AND IT'S THE SAME FOR EVERYBODY ELSE!

OUR WHOLE CATCH IS CONTAMINATED WITH THAT LUNATIC GRIN! HERRING-- COD--! ALL OF 'EM LAUGHING AT US!

IT SCARES THE BRITCHES OFF ME!

SEE THE INKOLOGY OF TERRY AUSTIN!

IT'S SUPPOSED TO! FEAR CLOUDS YOUR MIND, AND THAT'S THE JOKER'S STRONGEST WEAPON!

BUT WHAT DOES HE WANT? WHY WOULD HE MAKE THE FISH LOOK LIKE HIM?

THAT I DON'T KNOW! WITH ORDINARY MEN, YOU MIGHT FIGURE SOME MOTIVE--

--BUT THE JOKER'S MIND IS CLOUDED IN MADNESS! HIS MOTIVES MAKE SENSE TO HIM ALONE!

6

IN THE HOURS THAT *FOLLOW*, THE STRANGE PHENOMENON PROVES TO BE *LESS* THAN AN *ISOLATED EVENT!*

ALL ALONG THE *EASTERN SEABOARD...*

...AND UP AND DOWN THE *WESTERN*, AS *WELL...*

... THE *JOKER-FISH* ARE SUDDENLY *EVERYWHERE!*

WHEN AMERICA AWAKES TO ITS *MORNING MEDIA...*

...IT IS THE *ONLY* TOPIC OF *NOTE!*

--BUT AS YET, THERE HAS BEEN *NO FURTHER MOVE* FROM THE MACABRE MASTER OF MIRTH!

HIGH NOON, IN *GOTHAM CITY--*

COPYRIGHT COMMISSION
GOTHAM CITY DIV.

KRA

EEEEE

BUTTON IT, LADY! NO NOISE FROM *NOBODY!*

HANDS BEHIND YOUR HEADS! YOU'VE GOT A *VISITOR!*

COPYRIGHT FORM 2SH7A3
1. MAKE SURE ALL 6 CARBON SHEETS ARE STRAIGHT.
2. FILL OUT ALL PERTINENT DATA.
3. SUBMIT TO SUPERVISOR.
4. PERUSE THE PENCILOGRAPHY OF MARSHALL ROGERS.

7

GOOD LORD!

WHERE?

OH, HAHAHAHAA, I *SEE!* IT WAS JUST AN *EXPRESSION--*

--OF *ENDEARMENT*, EH, MR. FRANCIS? COME ON, YOU CAN TELL *ME!* YOU'VE ALWAYS SECRETLY *ADMIRED* ME, *HAVEN'T* YOU?

J-JOKER-- I--

NEVER MIND! WE'VE NO TIME FOR *PLEASANTRIES*, YOU AND I!

THIS IS *SERIOUS BUSINESS!* I'VE MADE CERTAIN THAT WE WON'T BE *INTERRUPTED*, SO THAT WE CAN MAKE ARRANGEMENTS LIKE *MEN OF LEISURE!*

⑧

WH-**WHAT** ARRANGEMENTS?

FOR MY **FISH**, OF COURSE!

I MIGHT AS WELL **TELL** YOU, FRANCIS--THIS HAS ALL BEEN WORKED OUT **FAR IN ADVANCE!** YOU ARE, FINALLY, JUST A **COG**, SO DON'T SPEAK TO ME **AGAIN!**

NOW--WHAT IS EVERYBODY IN THE COUNTRY **TALKING** ABOUT?

UH... YOUR **FISH**...?

I **TOLD** YOU NOT TO **TALK!** I DON'T **NEED** YOU TO ANSWER MY QUESTIONS! **I** CAN ANSWER MY QUESTIONS **MYSELF!**

I **ALWAYS** ANSWER MY QUESTIONS MYSELF!

HURUMPH... AS I WAS **SAYING...**

...EVERYBODY'S TALKING ABOUT MY **JOKER-FISH!** THEY **ALL** RECOGNIZE THE **FACE**--IT'S MY **FORTUNE,** EVEN ON A **FLOUNDER'S FIZZ**-- AND SINCE I PLAN TO **CONTINUE** SECRETLY DUMPING THE **CHEMICAL** THAT GIVES THE FISH MY FACE, THE LITTLE **FINNIES** ARE **PERMANENTLY** IDENTIFIED WITH ME! NO MATTER **WHAT** THEY **ONCE** WERE, THEY'RE JUST **JOKER-FISH NOW!**

SOOO...

...ONCE WE FILL OUT ALL YOUR TEDIOUS **COPYRIGHT FORMS**--

-- I'LL GET A **CUT** OF EVERY **FISH-SALE** IN **AMERICA!**

A **NICKEL** PER FISH-SANDWICH--FIFTY CENTS FOR **FILET OF SOLE!** **MILLIONS OF DOLLARS** A **DAY,** TO FINANCE MY FRANKLY HEDONISTIC **LIFE-STYLE!** AND ALL SO **SIMPLE!** WHAT A **JOKE!** HA HA HA HA HAHA

JOKER, IT--IT'S **IMPOSSIBLE!**

WHAT? **IMPOSSIBLE,** YOU SAY? NO --

--**NOBODY** CAN COPYRIGHT **FISH**--OR EVEN **FISH FACES!** THEY'RE A **NATURAL RESOURCE!**

I *WARN* YOU, FRANCIS... DON'T CAUSE ME TO BECOME *ANGRY!*

I-I CAN'T *HELP* IT! IT'S THE *LAW!*

BUT THE FISH SHARE MY *UNIQUE FACE!* IF COLONEL *WHAT'S-HIS-NAME* CAN HAVE *CHICKENS,* WHEN THEY DON'T EVEN HAVE *MUSTACHES--!*

--AND YOU *DENY* THIS TO ME! YOU *SEE* WHY I AM *FORCED* TO CRIME!

YOU HAVE UNTIL *MIDNIGHT* TO *CHANGE YOUR MIND,* FRANCIS! IF YOU *DON'T,* YOU'LL BE THE *POOREST FISH* OF ALL--

--AND *DEAD* AS A *MACKEREL!* HAHAHAHAHA

HE'S--HE'S *INSANE!*

HAHA

()UTSIDE--

GET BACK TO YOUR *DUMPING,* BOYS-- AND ALERT THE *OTHER* CREWS! I HAVE *JUST BEGUN* TO FIGHT!

TRY TO CHEAT *THE JOKER,* WILL HE? WE'LL SEE WHO *LAUGHS LAST!*

WHAT ARE *YOU* GOING TO DO, BOSS?

I? I HAVE *ANOTHER* MATTER TO ATTEND TO, BLUE-EYES!

AND BY THE *WAY--*

10

MIND YOUR OWN BUSINESS!

HONK

SKREECH

WHA--?!

HAHAHAHAH

THREE-THIRTY, AT THE ELEGANT *TOBACCONISTS'* *CLUB*, WHERE THE *GOTHAM ELITE* MEET AND GREET...

RUPERT--?

UH--!

CRIPES, RUPE! WHAT ARE YOU SO *JUMPY*, FOR?

MARKO!

WELL, *O'COURSE!* WHO *ELSE*, RUPE?

ARE YOU TAKIN' THOSE *DIET PILLS* AGAIN? YOU DON'T *LOOK* GOOD!

I'M *FINE*, PAISAN'! *FINE!* TOUGH AS *NAILS!*

WHATEVER YOU *SAY!* YOU'RE THE *BOSS!*

C'MON-- THE *COUNCIL MEETIN'S* ABOUT TO START! THE BOYS ARE *WAITIN'* FOR YA!

THEY WANNA KNOW ABOUT YOUR *BIG PLAN* FOR *THE BATMAN*, RUPE! WE AIN'T HEARD WHAT YOU *WORKED UP* FOR 'IM YET, AN' THE BIT ABOUT DECLARIN' 'IM *OFF LIMITS* AIN'T *COMIN' OFF* TOO WELL!

PEOPLE JUST DON'T *LISTEN* TO US LIKE THEY *USED* TO! THE LOUSY *MEDIA*---

UH-- LISTEN-- MARKO-- I'VE GOT TO *WASH UP* FIRST!

I'LL MEET YOU *INSIDE!*

236

JEEZ! I THOUGHT *MARKO* WAS THE *GHOST!**

*THREE ISSUES AGO, BOSS THORNE HAD *HUGO STRANGE* KILLED! THE LAST *TWO ISSUES*, HUGO HAS *REAPPEARED*, THREATENING *REVENGE...!* --JULIE

I'VE KNOWN MARKO FOR *FORTY-FIVE YEARS!* BLAST IT--I'M THE *MOST POWERFUL MAN IN GOTHAM CITY!* HOW COULD I LET--

AAAAAAA

SCREEEEEE

WHAT'S THE *MATTER* WITH YOU, THORNE?

GET UP! THIS IS *SERIOUS BUSINESS,* AND I'M A *BUSY MAN!*

YOU --YOU'RE NOT--?

ARE YOU INSINUATING YOU COULD *MISTAKE* ME FOR *SOMEONE ELSE?* THORNE, YOU'RE LUCKY I DON'T WANT *YOU* DEAD!

HEED MY *WORDS,* FAT MAN: I *KNOW* YOU BID FOR *THE BATMAN'S* IDENTITY, ALONGSIDE *THE PENGUIN* AND *MYSELF!* I SUSPECT YOU'RE BEHIND *PROF. STRANGE'S DISAPPEARANCE!*

BUT *OBVIOUSLY,* YOU DIDN'T *LEARN THE BATMAN'S* IDENTITY, AND *THAT'S* WHY YOU YET *LIVE!* I DON'T *WANT* THAT SECRET *PENETRATED-- EVER--*

--SINCE IT WOULD TAKE AWAY MY *FUN* -- THE *THRILL* OF THE *JOUST* WITH MY *PERFECT OPPONENT!*

YOU? YOU'RE PROTECTING-- HIM?

LIKE *HUGO STRANGE!!*

THE *JOKER MUST HAVE THE BATMAN!* NAY, THE JOKER *DESERVES* THE BATMAN!

WHAT *FUN* WOULD THERE BE IN HUMBLING *MERE POLICEMEN?*

I AM THE *GREATEST CRIMINAL EVER KNOWN! HA HA HA HA!*

AND FOR *ANYONE ELSE* TO DESTROY *THE BATMAN* WOULD BE *UNWORTHY* OF *ME!*

12

WHEN YOU LIGHT THAT *BEACON-* COMMISSIONER--

--I'LL *COME!* THAT'S THE WAY IT'S *ALWAYS* BEEN, AND THE WAY IT'LL *ALWAYS BE!*

BUT WON'T THIS GET YOU IN *DUTCH* AT *CITY HALL?*

LET THEM WRITE ME A *REPRIMAND!*

I'VE GOT A *PROBLEM* YOU'LL WANT TO SOLVE!

LET'S GET TO *WORK*, COMMISSIONER!

THIS MAN--

HAHAHAHA! WE INTERRUPT OUR REGULARLY-SCHEDULED *RE-RUNS* TO BRING YOU THE FOLLOWING *FIRESIDE CHAT!*

GOOD EVENING, MY FELLOW *AMERICANS!* TONIGHT, AT PRECISELY *TWELVE O'CLOCK,* I WILL KILL *G. CARL FRANCIS!*

THE *JOKER* HAS *SPOKEN!*

*T*HE MINUTES DRAG INTO THE *EVENING*, PILING UP INTO *HOURS* OF PAINS-TAKING *PREPARATIONS! THE BATMAN* TAKES *TOTAL CHARGE*--AND THE POLICE *ACCEPT* HIM *ABSOLUTELY*, AS ONE OF *THEM!*

TICK TOCK TICK

TICK TOCK

*B*UT *SOME* OF THEM HAVE TRIED TO BLOCK *THE JOKER* AT *OTHER TIMES,* AND NOW THE *RANGE* OF HIS *MAD GENIUS!*

*T*HE MOOD IS *MORE* THAN *GRIM!*

11:55! FRANCIS IS *CORDONED OFF* HERE, AND THE HOUSE IS *SURROUNDED OUTSIDE!* HE'S *EATEN* NOTHING SINCE THE THREAT--ALL *WATER'S* BROUGHT IN FROM THE *POLICE LAB--!*

WHAT HAVEN'T I *COVERED?*

TICK TOCK TICK TOCK TICK TOCK

14

239

I WISH THE *STORM* WOULD BREAK--CLEAR THE *AIR* SOMEHOW! YOU CAN CUT THE *ELECTRICITY* WITH A *KNIFE!*

I WISH *SILVER* WOULD ANSWER THE *PHONE* WHEN I CALL! SHE'S BEEN GONE *ALL DAY!*

I WISH *HUGO STRANGE* WOULD TURN UP!

COME ON, JOKER-- MOVE!

BATMAN--?

BATMAN, *TELL* ME-- I'VE HEARD THAT *THE PENGUIN, THE SCARECROW, THE RIDDLER* KILL PEOPLE WHO GET IN THEIR *WAY* SOMETIMES! BUT *THIS*--!

I'M JUST A *PAPER-PUSHER!* I DON'T *MAKE THE LAWS!* WHY *ME??*

IF NOT *YOU,* THEN *SOMEONE ELSE,* MR. FRANCIS! *THE JOKER'S* A *TIME-BOMB*-- AND *EVERY SO OFTEN,* HE JUST *HAS TO EXPLODE!*

WHA--? GAS--COMING IN THROUGH THE *HEATING DUCTS!*

GOFF

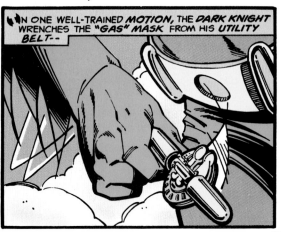

IN ONE WELL-TRAINED *MOTION,* THE *DARK KNIGHT* WRENCHES THE "*GAS*" MASK FROM HIS *UTILITY BELT*--

--AND CLAPS IT ACROSS THE *TARGET'S FACE*

I CAN *HOLD MY BREATH* LONG ENOUGH TO ESCAPE--

--BUT I DOUBT *YOU* CAN, FRANCIS!

HOWEVER...

BONG BONG

AGGHH!

BONG
BONG BONG

BONG
BONG BONG

BONG
BONG
BONG

BONG

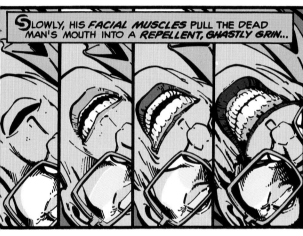

SLOWLY, HIS *FACIAL MUSCLES* PULL THE DEAD MAN'S MOUTH INTO A *REPELLENT, GHASTLY GRIN...*

...THE SIGN OF *THE JOKER!*

I DON'T *UNDERSTAND!* SOME OF *US* DIDN'T HAVE MASKS-- *WE* BREATHED THE GAS!

WHY DIDN'T *WE DIE?*

HE DIDN'T WANT YOU! HE WANTED *FRANCIS--* ALONE!

NOW THAT I'VE BREATHED THE GAS *MYSELF,* I *RECOGNIZE* IT! IT'S ONE PART OF A *BINARY COMPOUND--*

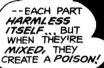

--EACH PART *HARMLESS* ITSELF... BUT WHEN THEY'RE *MIXED,* THEY CREATE A *POISON!*

THE JOKER MUST HAVE SECRETLY SPRAYED HIM WITH THE *OTHER* GAS WHEN HE THREATENED HIM AT *NOON!*

SO ONLY HE, IN A *ROOMFUL OF PEOPLE,* WOULD *REACT!* IT'S *DIABOLICAL!*

HELLO, LATE-SHOW LOVERS -- AND LOVERS OF THE *LATE-SHOW!* G. CARL FRANCIS IS *DEAD,* AS I *VOWED!*

16

BUT I *STILL* DON'T HAVE WHAT I *REQUIRE*--A *LEGAL CLAIM* TO YOUR NEW--*IMPROVED*--*JOKER-FISH!* IF THAT DOESN'T CHANGE BY 3 A.M., THE *NUMBER-TWO BUREAUCRAT* WILL FEEL MY WRATH!

THE *JOKER* HAS *SPOKEN!*

*T*HE *BATMAN* MAKES *NO REPLY!*

*M*EANWHILE, SOME *THREE HUNDRED* MILES TO THE *WEST...*

HUH? IT'S A *GIRL*--!

HI! I'M SURE GLAD YOU *STOPPED!* SOMETHING'S WRONG WITH MY *CAR!*

HEY! AREN'T YOU--

--*RUPERT THORNE?*

UH--*YEAH!* WE MET AT *BRUCE WAYNE'S* PARTY, DIDN'T WE? WAS IT--

--*SILVER?*

IT *WAS!*

CAN YOU GIVE ME A *LIFT?*

WELL--I'M IN A *HURRY*--

GREAT! SO AM *I!*

IT SURE WAS LUCKY MEETING YOU HERE!

*T*HE CAR ROLLS AWAY, AND QUICKLY *DISAPPEARS* IN THE *DARK!* HIGH *OVERHEAD*, A BLAST OF *THUNDER* MARKS ITS *PASSAGE!*

*W*ITH A *SHRIEK* AND A *SHIVER*, THE *STORM BEGINS...*

242

AN ALMOST LEGENDARY FIGURE, THE COWLED SHADOW OF *THE BATMAN* PROWLS THROUGH THE NIGHT, PREYING UPON CRIMINAL *PARASITES* LIKE THE *WINGED CREATURE* WHOSE NAME HE HAS ADOPTED!

BUT THIS NIGHT, A *PARASITE* HAS REMAINED *MADDENINGLY ELUSIVE!* *THE JOKER,* ARCH-CRIMINAL TO THE *WORLD,* HAS THREATENED *DEATH* FOR MEN WHOSE ONLY *OFFENSE* WAS FAILING TO FOLLOW THE *CRIME-CLOWN'S* LUNATIC LOGIC!

BATMAN
CREATED BY BOB KANE

STEVE ENGLEHART: *WRITER* ✶ MARSHALL ROGERS: *PENCILLER* ✶ TERRY AUSTIN: *INKER*
MILTON SNAPINN: *LETTERER* ✶ JULIUS SCHWARTZ: *EDITOR*

HE CLAIMS A *PERCENTAGE* OF ALL *FISH-SALES* IN THE COUNTRY, BECAUSE HE CAUSED THE *FISHES'* FACES TO RESEMBLE HIS *OWN!* YOU SEE--*YOU* DON'T UNDERSTAND THAT ANY BETTER THAN THE *COPYRIGHT COMMISSION* DID! BUT ONE OF THEM HAS *ALREADY DIED* THIS NIGHT--

--AND THE NIGHT IS *FAR FROM FINISHED!*

THREE A.M., IN A *BLINDING RAINSTORM!* I DON'T LIKE THE *FEEL* OF IT, O'HARA!

IT'S *JOKER WEATHER!*

TRUE, COMMISSIONER... BUT IT'S ALSO *TAILOR-MADE--*

--FOR *HIM!*

"SIGN OF THE JOKER!"

Colorist: Petra Scotese

WELL, OUR PREPARATIONS ARE *COMPLETE* -- BUT THEY WERE BEFORE THAT DARNED *JACKANAPES* KILLED *G. CARL FRANCIS* AT *MIDNIGHT!* ✳

IT AIN'T *OUR* FAULT THE DEATH-PENALTY DON'T APPLY TO *CRAZIES!*

BESIDES, YE DON'T WANT TO BE SCARIN' THE LAD WE'RE HERE TO *PROTECT!*

I DON'T KNOW... MAYBE I'M GETTING *TOO OLD* FOR THIS *JOB!* I CAN'T SHAKE THE FEELING THAT NO MATTER *WHAT WE DO...*

CLICK

MR. JACKSON'S HOLDIN' UP QUITE *WELL...CONSIDERIN'!*

NOW, COMMISSIONER, DON'T BE TALKIN' LIKE THAT! YE'VE ALWAYS PUT *THE JOKER* BEHIND BARS IN THE *END!*

✳*LAST ISSUE!*--JULIE

I GUESS YOU'RE *RIGHT...*

WHAT WAS *THAT?*

GREAK

THAT'S AS MAY BE, JACKSON -- BUT LOOK WHAT HE'S GOT IN HIS *MOUTH!*

THERE'S SOMETHING *WRONG!*

THE FISH HAS *AFFECTED* HIM!

MY GOD! A JOKER-*FISH!*

...BUT WE'LL FIND OUT SOON ENOUGH!

IT'S ALMOST *THREE!*

OH, IT'S JUST *ERNEST,* COMMISSIONER-- MY *CAT!* HE'S BEEN OUT *PROWLING* SINCE BEFORE YOU *ARRIVED!*

HE'S *HARMLESS!*

ERNEST! *OUTSIDE!*

MEERROWWW

MEEH

②

244

GOOD LORD!

RRRAWWWR

MEERAWWW

UNNGH!

=UHF!=

T.UNK

SAINTS PRESERVE US! THE *SIGN OF THE JOKER* -- THAT *HIDEOUS GRIN!*

THE FIEND *GOT HIM!* DESPITE *ALL OUR PRECAUTIONS* --

-- HE GOT *JACKSON!*

EVEN *MADDENED,* THE CAT KNEW HIS *MASTER!* IT WAS THE ONE THING I OVER-LOOKED WHEN I PROPOSED OUR *TRADING FACES!*

THE *JOKER* ALWAYS HAS AN *ANGLE...*

...*BATMAN!*

HELLO THERE, *BATMAN!* THOMAS JACKSON IS DEAD, AS I VOWED!

BUT I *STILL* DON'T HAVE MY LEGAL CLAIM TO MY *JOKER-FISH!*

IF THAT DOESN'T CHANGE BY DAWN, THE NEXT COMMISSION MEMBER WILL FEEL MY WRATH!

3

THE JOKER HAS SPOKEN! HAHAHAHA

AND FROM SOMEWHERE NEARBY, TOO! NO TV STATION IS BROADCASTING AT THIS HOUR, SO HE MUST BE JAMMING THE FREQUENCY ON *HIS OWN* TRANSMITTER!

I'LL BE IN TOUCH!

THE JOKER'S LAUGH HAS BEEN LIKENED TO RAINING *ICE-CUBES*...AND THAT'S *JUST WHAT* THE DANK DECEMBER DELUGE FEELS LIKE AS *THE BATMAN* SWINGS INTO *ACTION!*

FREED, NOW, OF HIS BINDING DISGUISE, HIS BLOOD SINGING IN HIS VEINS, *THE BATMAN* RETURNS TO HIS *ELEMENT!*

AND THEN--

EH? THAT SHIMMERING FORM--!

IT LOOKS LIKE--

--HUGO STRANGE!

BUT WHEN SIX POUNDING STRIDES CARRY HIM INTO THE *WOODS*--

GONE!

OR--WAS HE *EVER HERE?* HE'S BEEN MISSING SO LONG, I WAS ALMOST SURE HE'D *BOUGHT IT!**

*AND INDEED, STRANGE IS DEAD-- BUT HIS MURDER AT RUPERT THORNE'S ORDERS HAS SO FAR ESCAPED DETECTION!
-- JULIE

NO *FOOTPRINTS!* THE GRASS ISN'T EVEN *BENT*--

WAIT A MINUTE!

WHAT'S THIS?

VAPOR ANALYSIS METER

BEYOND ANY DOUBT, HE KNOWS THIS WAS LEFT HERE FOR HIM--BUT WHO LEFT IT? HOW? AND WHY?

HIS OWN WORDS, ONLY HOURS OLD, COME BACK TO HIM NOW--

--CARRIED ON THE RISING WIND THAT PLASTERS HIS COWL ACROSS HIS CORDED NECK--

"--MY WORLD GOES CRAZY SOMETIMES...!"

AND IN ANOTHER PART OF THAT WORLD..., IN THE CRIME CLOWN'S NEW HA-HACIENDA...

LAUGH, CLOWN, LAUGH-- AND LAUGH AGAIN!

THE POLICE ARE COMPLETELY AT BAY! THE BATMAN IS BAYING AT THE MOON! NO ONE CAN BEAT THE JOKER!

SOON, NOW-- SOON, THEY'LL SEE IT MY WAY! THEY'LL KNOW I MEAN WHAT I SAY! TODAY THE AMERICAN FISH--

--AND TOMORROW, ALL THE FISH IN THE WORLD!

BUT--WHAT IF EVERYBODY STOPS EATING FISH? I HADN'T THOUGHT OF THAT!

WHAT IF THEY ALL CONSPIRE AGAINST ME--

--LEAVE MY JOKER-FISH IN THE SEA?

BUT NO--THAT WOULD NEVER WORK!

THE VEGETARIANS WOULDN'T GO ALONG!

AND ANYWAY--

--I COULD USE MY CHEMICALS ON THE CATTLE!

JOKER-BURGERS!

OUTRAGEOUS!

A MAN THAT MAD IS WORTH MORE SPACE... BUT WE HAVE OTHER MEN TO MEET BEFORE DAWN!

SO IT IS THAT WE TURN...

5

...TO *RUPERT THORNE*, POLITICAL BOSS OF *GOTHAM CITY*...

...AND HIS HITCH-HIKING PASSENGER, *SILVER ST. CLOUD!*

WE MUST BE CLOSE TO *AKRON!* WE'VE BEEN DRIVING NEARLY *FOUR HOURS* SINCE HE PICKED ME UP!

I GUESS I *SHOULD* HAVE GOTTEN OUT AT THE FIRST *GAS STATION*-- GONE BACK TO *FIX MY CAR!* BUT--I DON'T *NEED* MY CAR!

I NEED *TIME TO THINK*-- ABOUT *BRUCE* AND ME! WHO *CARES* WHERE I AM, IF IT'S NOT *GOTHAM?*

WHAT AM I GOING TO *DO?* I'M *SURE* BRUCE IS *THE BATMAN*-- AND I *SHOULD* SUMMON UP THE NERVE, LIKE I ALWAYS HAVE *BEFORE*, AND DEAL WITH *WHATEVER HAPPENS!*

BUT I *CAN'T!*

IT'S LIKE LEARNING HE'S SECRETLY *ROBERT REDFORD!* IF HE --HE'S *REALLY* THE *BATMAN*, AND HE HASN'T WANTED TO *TELL* ME, HE MUST HAVE A *GOOD REASON*--!

THANK GOD THIS SKIRT DOESN'T *TALK* MUCH!

I NEED THE *COMPANY*, BUT I AIN'T IN *SHAPE* TO KEEP UP A *CONVERSATION!*

IT WAS A *MISTAKE* TO TAKE THE CAR *MYSELF* AND LEAVE *SGT. STARK* BEHIND! BUT WHEN THE *GHOST*--

--THREATENED *ME*--

--WELL, I'M *TOUGH!*

I'VE ALWAYS BEEN TOUGH! BUT--I PUT MY HAND RIGHT *THROUGH* HIS BODY--!

HE SAID THE *NEXT* TIME HE APPEARED, I'D--I'D--!

BUT HE *WON'T* SHOW--NOT IF THE *DAME* WOULD GET IT *WITH* ME! HE HAD SOME KIND OF CRAZY *CODE OF HONOR!* YEAH--

IT'S FOUR O'CLOCK-- HEAR NOW THE *NEWS!*

--SHE'S MY *PROTECTION!*

GOOD MORNING! THE JOKER IS BACK IN THE HEADLINES! GOTHAM CITY WAS ROCKED OVERNIGHT BY TWO SENSATIONAL MURDERS, BOTH ALLEGEDLY THE HANDI-WORK OF THE *ACE OF KNAVES!* IN EACH CASE, POLICE AND THE *BATMAN* WERE WARNED IN ADVANCE, BUT--

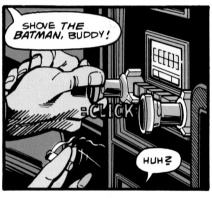

SHOVE *THE BATMAN,* BUDDY!

CLICK

HUH?

LET ME *TELL* YOU SOMETHING, YOUNG LADY! (HARUMPH!...) AS THE *PRESIDENT* OF THE *GOTHAM CITY COUNCIL,* I DARE SAY YOUR TOWN WOULD BE A LOT BETTER OFF WITHOUT *THE BATMAN!*

THAT *ONE MAN* IS THE CAUSE OF ALL THE CITY'S PROBLEMS!

NOW, JUST A *MINUTE--!*

YOU'RE NOT SUPPOSED TO BE SO LILY-WHITE YOURSELF--"*BOSS*"!

THE WAY I HEAR IT, YOU AND YOUR "*COUNCIL*" HAVE BEEN GRAFTING OFF *GOTHAM* FOR *YEARS!* YOU'VE GOT A WHOLE *POLITICAL MACHINE* TO KEEP YOU *ELECTED* BY HOOK OR BY CROOK--!

I DON'T HAVE TO *STAND* FOR THIS!

YOUNG LADY, I'M *DUE SOME RESPECT!* I'M THE *PRESIDENT* OF THE--

NOBODY WHO PUTS *THE BATMAN* DOWN IS DUE ANYTHING! I BET *YOU'RE* BEHIND THE CAMPAIGN TO HAVE HIM *THROWN OUT OF TOWN!*

THORNE, THAT ONE MAN HAS GIVEN HIS *LIFE* TO GOTHAM --THE *CITY,* THE *PEOPLE*--HE'S OUR *AVENGING ANGEL!*

THEY SAY *NOBODY CARES* ABOUT THE CITY ANY MORE, BUT *HE DOES!* HE--

7

249

GET OUT! GET OUT, YOU DUMB BROAD! I DON'T NEED THIS AGGRAVATION! TAKE YOUR BLEEDING HEART AND GET OUT!

COOL YOUR ENGINES, THORNE! I'M GETTING!

WELL... WHAT NOW, SILVER?

GUESS I'LL CHECK OUT THAT GLOW OVER THERE!

WHAT LUCK! THERE'S SOMEONE UP AT THIS HOUR!

WHAT'S THE TROUBLE, LADY?

MISTER, CAN I CHARTER YOUR PLANE?

WO HOURS *LATER*, BACK IN *GOTHAM CITY*-- JUST BEFORE A WINTRY EAST-COAST *DAWN*...

DID YOU GET ANY *SLEEP*, COMMISSIONER?

A *LITTLE*, THANKS! FORTY-FIVE MINUTES OR SO!

÷YAWN÷ I CAN'T PULL THESE *ALL-NIGHT TOURS* ANY MORE, LIKE *YOU*! AND WHY *SHOULD* I, WHEN THE JOKER'S AS DEPENDABLE AS *CLOCK-WORK*!

DAWN HE SAID, *DAWN* IT'LL BE!

PERHAPS! BUT HE MAKES HIS PREPARATIONS *AHEAD OF TIME*, JUST LIKE *WE* DO!

Y'KNOW I WAS DREAMING ABOUT MY DAYS ON THE *BEAT*! BOSS THORNE HAD JUST BEEN ELECTED FOR THE *FIRST TIME*, AND HE *CAME* TO ME--

YOU!

WHAT TH--?

BATMAN! HAVE YOU GONE *CRAZY?* THAT'S ONE OF OUR BOYS--!

NO, COMMISSIONER! IT ONLY *LOOKS* LIKE HIM!

LISTEN TO THE MAN, GORDON!

I *KNEW* YOU'D HAVE ALL THE *CAT-DOORS* PLUGGED THIS TIME. SO I CAME TO DO THE JOB *MYSELF!*

LIVE--AND *IN PERSON!* THE *CALIPH OF CLOWNS*-- THE *GRAND MOGUL OF MOUNTE-BANKS*--

--THE ONE AND ONLY JOKER!!

PRE-RECORDED FOR THIS *TIME-ZONE!*

HIS BADGE-- SQUIRTING SOMETHING! LOOK OUT!

252

ACID, CHIEF! A SINGLE DROP SPELLS DOOM!

IN SUCH A MANNER WOULD I HAVE STRUCK MY VICTIM DOWN, AS I PRETENDED TO PROTECT HIM!

BUT THE BATMAN HAS HIS OWN CHEMICAL GAMES! IT WAS THE GAS HUGO STRANGE SPRAYED ME WITH, WASN'T IT?* THAT'S HOW YOU KNEW!

I KNOW NOW THAT IT WAS, JOKER! UNTIL THE ANALYZER RESPONDED TO YOU, ALL I HAD WAS A HUNCH --

*AT HUGO'S AUCTION IN #472! --J.S.

--A HUNCH THAT WHOEVER LEFT IT FOR ME MEANT IT TO BE OF HELP!

BLOK

WHAT'S THE MATTER?

BAT GOT YOUR TONGUE?

YOU'RE ALWAYS A PARTY-POOP--

--JUST WHEN I'M BEGINNING TO HAVE FUN!

ONTO THE RAIN-SLICK FIRE-ESCAPE SCRAMBLES THE JOKER, NARROWLY AVOIDING THE BATMAN'S CLUTCHING ARMS!

CATCH ME IF YOU CAN!

AND EVEN AS THE DARK KNIGHT TAKES THE DARE--

OH, MY GOD!

TAXI

253

NICE WEATHER FOR *FISH*, DON'T YOU THINK?

I'M *SO* IN TUNE WITH THE *TIMES!*

NEXT WEEK I'M *LICENSING* THIS FACE TO *ROCK BANDS!*

LAUGH *NOW*-- CRY *LATER*, JOKER!

I'LL LAUGH UNTIL YOU *HIT BOTTOM!* HOW'S *THAT?*

CL UP

BATMAN-- HANG *ON!*

THE CABBIE KNEW WHERE TO *FIND* HIM--THE *JOKER* ANNOUNCED IT TO THE *WORLD*--BUT I NEVER EXPECTED *THIS!*

ONE POTATO-- *TWO* POTATO-- *THREE* POTATO-- *FOUR!*

AND *ALL MASHED!*

HAVE I COME BACK TO *GOTHAM*-- JUST TO SEE BRUCE *DIE?*

DON'T COUNT YOUR POTATOES BEFORE THEY'RE *HATCHED*, MADMAN!

⊤HE FIRE ESCAPE *SHUDDERS* UNDER THE IMPACT OF *THE BATMAN'S* BLOW...

⊤HE JOKER STAGGERS TOWARD THE EDGE OF *ETERNITY*--

--AND THEN, WITH HIS PHENOMENAL *CAT-LIKE GRACE*, HE HOLDS *ON!*

YOU CAN'T BEAT *THE JOKER*, FOOL --

--THE JOKER IS *TRUMP!*

IN THE *OLD DAYS*, COURT JESTERS WERE HELD IN HIGH *ESTEEM!*

EVEN THE *KINGS* ENVIED THEIR FREEDOM TO DO WHATEVER CAME INTO THEIR *HEADS!*

EVERY- THING GOES TO *POT!*

HE'S LOOKING FOR *MORE SECURE FOOTING!* IN SOME WAYS, HE'S AS SANE AS *ANYBODY!*

--EXCEPT *ME* FOR GOING AFTER HIM!

254

THE STORM BROODED FOR *DAYS* BEFORE BREAKING, BUT *NOW* THERE'S NO HOLDING IT *BACK!*

GREAT *SHEETS* OF WATER POUND DOWN LIKE CRASHING *OCEAN WAVES* --

-- *SMEARING* THE SIGHT OF *SILVER ST. CLOUD* AS SHE FIGHTS TO PEER UPWARD INTO THE STORM'S *FULL FURY* --

SMEARING HER SIGHT -- BUT NEVER *COMPLETELY OBLITERATING* WHAT SHE SEES --

JOKER! YOU *LUNATIC* -- THERE'S NO PLACE YOU CAN *GO* FROM HERE!

I CAN GO OVER YOUR *DEAD BODY,* BATMAN!

LOVELY WEATHER FOR *FISH,* ISN'T IT? OR DID I *SAY* THAT?

I WANT YOU TO HEAR ALL MY *BEST LINES* BEFORE YOU DO YOUR DIVE INTO THE *DAMP SPONGE!*

HIS *BADGE!* THE *ACID* --

13

SUDDEN, DESPERATE LUNGE --

AND THEN ALL AT ONCE --

ONG MOMENTS LATER...

NO SIGN OF ANYONE CRAWLING OUT OF THE *RIVER* ANYWHERE ALONG HERE! CAN HE REALLY BE *GONE*, AT LONG *LAST*?

I'VE THOUGHT THAT *BEFORE*, AND BEEN *WRONG*!

WELL HE'S FINISHED FOR *NOW*!

BATMAN--!

SILVER!

MAYBE I *KNOW* WHAT YOU *WANTED* ME TO SAY THE *OTHER NIGHT*--

--ABOUT WHAT I'VE *LEARNED* OF YOU!

MAYBE I CAME *BACK* HERE--TO *TELL* YOU!

MAYBE I --

--I EVEN LOVE YOU!

BATMAN--PLEASE! DON'T SAY *ANYTHING*! I HAVE SOMETHING TO SAY TO *YOU*!

SILVER--

UT JUST *NOW*, I SAW THE BATMAN IN ACTION! NOT AS A NEWS ITEM ON *TV*-- NOT AS A *MYSTERIOUS HERO* I'VE ALWAYS *ADMIRED*--!

SAW YOU--THE MAN INSIDE! THE MAN I *LOVE*!

SAW YOU *FIGHTING WITH* A MADMAN, STRADDLING A GIRDER IN THE BLINDING LIGHTNING STORM!

I LOVE YOU--BUT I COULDN'T *LIVE* WITH *THAT*! NEVER KNOWING WHAT *EACH NIGHT* WOULD BRING!

VER KNOWING HEN YOUR *LUCK* LL *RUN OUT*!

SILVER--

NO! IT'S *OVER*! I CAN'T LET IT GO ON ANY *LONGER*!

WE HAVE TO *STOP* BEFORE WE *CAN'T* STOP-- BEFORE WE CAN'T--

--HELP--

--OURSELVES!

15

SINCE 1899, *GOTHAM POLICE HEADQUARTERS* HAS STOOD AT THE JUNCTION OF THE AREA CALLED *FIVE POINTS*, ON THE LOWER EAST SIDE OF THE CITY...

IN THE PAST 17 YEARS, *COMMISSIONER JAMES W. GORDON* HAS COME TO KNOW THE MARBLED CORRIDORS OF THIS PROUD OLD BUILDING *WELL;* IT HAS BECOME A *SECOND HOME* TO HIM--

--BUT *TONIGHT,* AS THE LEGENDARY *BAT-SIGNAL* SLASHES ACROSS A STORM-SWEPT SKY, IT MAY ALSO BECOME HIS *TOMB!*

BAT MAN

CREATED BY BOB KANE

COMMISSIONER *GORDON!* I THINK THIS IS FOR *YOU,* SIR!

DREADFUL BIRTHDAY, DEAR JOKER...!

LEN **WEIN** WRITER

WALT **SIMONSON** & DICK **GIORDANO** ARTISTS

BEN **ODA** LETTERER

PAUL **LEVITZ** EDITOR

Colorist: Julianna Ferriter

IN THE GLORIOUS PALE WHITE *FLESH*!

CONSIDERING YOUR *CONDITION*, GENTLEMEN, YOU NEEDN'T *STAND*-- BUT I *WOULD* APPRECIATE A ROUSING ROUND OF *APPLAUSE*!

AND WHATEVER THE *JOKER* WANTS, HE ALMOST INVARIABLY *GETS*!

HA HA HA HA HA

THAT UNHOLY *LAUGHTER*-- AND THAT *OUTRAGEOUS CAR*!

IT DOESN'T TAKE MUCH *EFFORT* TO FIGURE OUT WHY GORDON *SUMMONED* ME!

THE JOKER MAY BE A *HOMICIDAL MANIAC* OF THE HIGHEST ORDER-- BUT HE'S CERTAINLY NOT *SHY*!

AND HE'S AS *CRAFTY* AS THEY COME!

JUDGING FROM THE *UNCONTROLLED HYSTERIA* I HEAR, HE'S SOMEHOW FILLED THE BUILDING WITH *LAUGHING GAS*--

--BUT BEFORE I'M *DONE* WITH HIM, HE'LL BE LAUGHING OUT OF THE *OTHER* SIDE OF HIS TWISTED CRIMSON *MOUTH*!

THEN, *GAS FILTER* CLENCHED TIGHTLY IN HIS TEETH, THE DARK KNIGHT *ENTERS* THE BESIEGED BUILDING--

--IN SINGULARLY *SPECTACULAR* FASHION!

SKRASH!

AH -- *THE BATMAN!* WHAT AN *EXPECTED* SURPRISE! AND WHAT A *WASTE* OF A PERFECTLY GOOD *WINDOW!*

COULDN'T YOU HAVE USED THE *DOOR?*

BUT THE BATMAN DOES NOT *REPLY*--

UNNFF!!

--AT LEAST, NOT IN SO MANY *WORDS!*

LORD, HE'S AS *CRAZY* AS THE *BOSS!*

THAT'S *ANOTHER* THING ABOUT THE JOKER THAT HASN'T *CHANGED*--!

HIS *HIRED MUSCLE* IS STILL AS *INEPT* AS EVER!

BUT *WHY* HAS THAT GRINNING GARGOYLE RISKED *INVADING* POLICE--

--EH?

THE JOKER IS *GONE!*

AND SO IS COMMISSIONER GORDON!

NO! I'M TOO LATE!

AND WITHOUT THE *BATMOBILE*, I HAVEN'T GOT A PRAYER OF *CATCHING* THEM!

TOODLE-*OO*, SUCKER! DON'T FORGET TO *WRITE* NOW, HEAR?

WRRROOM!

LUNATIC!

CRIPES! WHAT'S THAT MANIAC *UP TO?*

HE GOT THE COMMISSIONER *TOO?*

WHAT DO YOU MEAN --"*TOO*"?

GEEZ, YOU DON'T *KNOW?* THAT'S WHY WE *CALLED* YOU.

WE JUST GOT A RE-PORT FROM *UPSTATE*-- FROM *NEW CARTHAGE!*

"SEEMS YOUR PAL *ROBIN* STOPPED TO HELP A '*DAMSEL IN DISTRESS*' EARLIER TONIGHT..."

"HE VOLUNTEERED TO HELP HER FIX A *FLAT TIRE* ..."

"ONLY THAT *SPARE* WASN'T NO *TIRE* ..."

HUH? IT'S SOME KIND OF SUPER-STICKY *TAFFY!?!*

I'M *STUCK!!*

"AND THAT '*DAMSEL*' WASN'T NO *LADY!*"

HA HA HA

THE COMMISSIONER WANTED TO BE SURE YOU *KNEW!*

AND NOW *HE'S* DISAPPEARED AS WELL --BUT *WHY?*

HOW DO YOU SECOND-GUESS A *MADMAN?*

SHORTLY, AT BRUCE WAYNE'S PENTHOUSE APARTMENT ATOP THE *WAYNE FOUNDATION* BUILDING, AS AN ODD BLACK SHAPE *ECLIPSES* THE COOL FULL MOON...

THANK YOU FOR THE *ASPIRIN*, ALFRED. THEY SEEM TO *HELP*... A *LITTLE*.

YOUR *HEADACHES* APPEAR TO BE GROWING MORE *FREQUENT*, MISS KYLE.

MIGHT I SUGGEST YOU SEE A *DOCTOR--?*

ACTUALLY, I HAVE AN APPOINTMENT WITH BRUCE'S *DR. DUNDEE* IN -- *EH?*

OH, *EXCUSE* ME-- I DIDN'T KNOW BRUCE HAD *COMPANY*, SELINA.

THAT'S *OKAY*, LUCIUS-- BRUCE CAN ONLY HAVE *COMPANY* IF HE'S *HERE!*

BRUCE IS *OUT?* BUT HE ASKED ME TO COME OVER TO DISCUSS THESE *ARBITRAGE DEALS--!?*

HE GOT *CALLED AWAY*... ON SUDDEN *BUSINESS*.

I'D HAVE THOUGHT *YOU* OF ALL PEOPLE WOULD BE *USED* TO THAT, MR. FOX.

EH? FOOTSTEPS ON THE ROOF--?!? MASTER BRUCE MUST BE *RETURNING!*

I'D BEST *DISTRACT* MASTER FOX AND MISS KYLE WHILE--

BUT THOUGH ALFRED'S CONCERN IS NOT *UNFOUNDED--*

KWA-WHOOM!

--HIS PLANNED *DISTRACTION* WILL HARDLY BE *NECESSARY!*

MY, MY-- IT'S AMAZING HOW *FAR* A LITTLE *DYNAMITE* WILL GO THESE DAYS, ISN'T IT?

LOOKS LIKE THEY'RE ALL STILL *BREATHIN',* BOSS-- BUT THEY AIN'T GONNA BE *MOVIN'* FOR A WHILE!

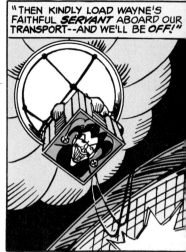

"THEN KINDLY LOAD WAYNE'S FAITHFUL *SERVANT* ABOARD OUR TRANSPORT-- AND WE'LL BE *OFF!"*

YOU'VE BEEN *OFF* FOR AS LONG AS I'VE *KNOWN* YOU, JOKER!

WHAT--? COULD IT *BE?*

SELINA KYLE-- THE SULTRY *CATWOMAN--HERE?!?*

IT NOT ONLY *COULD* BE, SMILEY--

--IT VERY DEFINITELY *IS!*

CHOK

NOW, WHY DON'T YOU AND YOUR TRAINED GORILLAS TAKE A *HIKE,* JOKER--

--WHILE YOU STILL *CAN!*

MY DEAR SELINA-- *PLEASE!*

I PROFUSELY *APOLOGIZE* IF I'VE ACCIDENTALLY INTERRUPTED A *CAPER* OF YOUR OWN!

ACCEPT THESE *ROSES* AS A TOKEN OF MY *SINCERITY!*

I *WARN* YOU, JOKER-- IF YOU'RE *TRYING* ANYTHING--!

OH, I *ASSURE* YOU, MY DEAR--

--I MOST CERTAINLY *AM!*

UUNNFFF!!

POW!

266

AND WHEN SELINA KYLE AT LAST REGAINS *CONSCIOUSNESS*...

WH-WHAT HAPPENED--?!?

I WAS HOPING *YOU* COULD TELL *ME* THAT--

--THOUGH I THINK I ALREADY *KNOW!*

HELLO... BATMAN!

HELLO, SELINA--THE JOKER NEVER MAKES IT *EASY*, DOES HE?

WHILE, IN THE CRIME CLOWN'S HIDDEN HA-HACIENDA...

IMPRESSIVE, ISN'T IT? I CALL IT MY *VICTIM-GO-ROUND!*

JUST WHAT DO YOU *WANT* FROM US, JOKER?

WHY--*VENGEANCE*, OF COURSE! WHAT *ELSE?*

TOMORROW IS MY BIRTHDAY...

...AND BY WAY OF CELEBRATION...

...I INTEND TO *ELIMINATE* ALL YOU WHO'VE *CROSSED* ME...

...WHILE ALL OF GOTHAM CITY *WATCHES!*

IT'S NOT EXACTLY THE CATCHER'S MITT I REALLY WANTED--

--BUT IT'S A PRETTY FAIR *SECOND PLACE!*

HAHAHAHA

SHEESH.

8

AND LIKE LEMMINGS, THEY *COME*, LURED BY THE PROMISE OF SOMETHING FOR *NOTHING*--

--PEOPLE WHO'VE CHOSEN TO *IGNORE* THAT WISE OLD *ADAGE*:

"THERE'S NO SUCH THING AS A *FREE LUNCH!*"

THE COLISEUM IS COMPLETELY *FILLED* LONG BEFORE THE DESIGNATED HOUR...

AND AT PRECISELY 9:00PM, THE BUILDING'S HEAVY STEEL DOORS CLICK *SHUT*--

--*OMINOUSLY!*

FOR SEVERAL LONG MINUTES, THE CROWD BEHAVES AS CROWDS ARE WONT TO *DO*--

--SOME *SILENT*, SOME *FIDGETING*--

--SOME ALREADY STAMPING THEIR FEET WITH *IMPATIENCE*--

--AND THEN, ABRUPTLY, THEIR LONG WAIT IS *OVER!*

HEY, *WHAT*--?!?

IT'S SOME KIND'A *GAS*--

--COMIN' FROM THE *AIR-VENTS!*

THE PARALYZING FUMES SPREAD *SWIFTLY*, AND WITHIN SECONDS, THERE IS NO *MOVEMENT* WITHIN THE SPRAWLING HALL--

--SAVE THE FRENZIED *BEATING* OF SEVERAL THOUSAND FRIGHTENED *HEARTS!*

SUDDENLY, THE HOUSE-LIGHTS BEGIN TO FLICKER AND *DIM*--

--AND THERE IS *DARKNESS!*

270

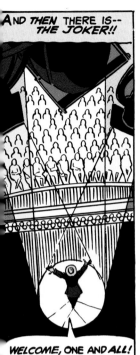

AND *THEN* THERE IS-- *THE JOKER!!*

WELCOME, ONE AND *ALL!*

AND THANK YOU FOR COMING TO MY *PARTY!*

I THINK I CAN ASSURE YOU *SURPRISES GALORE--*

-- COMMENCING *NOW!*

THE INVITATION PROMISED *REFRESHMENTS* AFTER ALL--

KWA-VOOMP!

--AND *THE JOKER* ALWAYS *DELIVERS!*

PRESENTING, FOR THE FIRST TIME ON ANY *STAGE,* LIVE AND IN *COLOR,* THE CAKE TO *END* ALL CAKES--

--EVEN AS IT ENDS THE *LIVES* OF MY GREATEST *ENEMIES!!*

PLEASE SAVE ALL YOUR *APPLAUSE* UNTIL THE *FINALE!*

12

I GUARANTEE IT WILL BE WELL WORTH THE *WAIT!*

ONE PUSH OF THIS HANDY LITTLE *DETONATOR* WILL IGNITE THE *INCENDIARY CANDLES* CROWNING MY *CAKE*--

--AND WHEN THEY'RE BURNING *BRIGHTLY,* I'LL MAKE A *WISH* AND BLOW THEM *OUT!*

WON'T THAT BE *FUN?*

NOT FOR THOSE OF US *TIED* TO THESE CANDLES, JOKER!

OH, DON'T BE SUCH A *PARTY-POOP!*

THAT'S *ENOUGH,* MADMAN!

THE PARTY IS *OVER!*

I WAS WONDERING WHERE *YOU* WERE HIDING, BATMAN!

YOU KNEW I'D *BE* HERE, JOKER!

I'D HAVE BEEN *HEART-BROKEN* IF YOU WEREN'T!

THEN YOU *ALSO* KNOW I WON'T LET YOU *CREMATE* YOUR *CAPTIVES!*

THAT'S ENTIRELY UP TO *YOU* SPORT! IF YOU *SURRENDER*--

--I'LL GLADLY LET THE REST OF THEM *GO!*

ALL RIGHT, JOKER-- YOU *WIN!*

DON'T I *ALWAYS?*

YOU SHOULD BE *FLATTERED,* BATMAN-- I SAVED YOU THE *GUEST OF HONOR* SPOT!

EXACTLY WHAT I *EXPECTED!*

BATMAN-- *NO!* YOU CAN'T *TRUST* HIM!

13

OUT OF THE MOUTHS OF *BABES* AND ALL THAT!

ROBIN'S *RIGHT*, YOU KNOW!

JOKER, WHAT ABOUT OUR *DEAL*? YOU SAID YOU'D *FREE* THEM!

OH, *COME* NOW, SILLY BOY-- YOU DIDN'T HONESTLY *BELIEVE* ME, DID YOU?

FRANKLY, JOKER--

--NO!

K-K-K.

AT THE PRESS OF A CONCEALED *BUTTON*, THE DARKNIGHT DETECTIVE'S CANDLE SUDDENLY BEGINS TO *SIZZLE*--

--THEN ROCKETS SKYWARD LIKE A GIANT *FIREWORKS* ON THE *FOURTH* OF JULY!

KWAVAVOOM

YOU MAY HAVE SAVED *YOURSELF*, BATMAN--

--BUT YOU'LL NEVER SAVE YOUR *FRIENDS*!

SLAM!

14

273

SNIK   SNIK   SNIK

HE *DID* IT!

HIS *BATARANGS* *SEVERED* THE CANDLES' *FUSES!*

BATMAN *SAVED* US!

DID YOU EVER DOUBT HE *WOULD,* SIR?

AND HIS FINAL *BATARANG* CUT THE *ROPES* HOLDING ME--

SLASH

--SO *I* CAN FINALLY *CUT LOOSE!*

I OWE YOU CREEPS SOME *BRUISES!*

WATCH OUT FOR THE *JOKER,* ROBIN!

ME? I THOUGHT *YOU* WERE WATCHING OUT FOR HIM!

THE JOKER WATCHES OUT FOR *HIMSELF,* FOOLS!

'BYE NOW!

THERE! HE'S HEADED FOR THE *DOCKS!*

SHOULD'VE KNOWN HE'D HAVE PLANNED HIS *GETAWAY!*

I MAY BE *CRAZY,* BATMAN --BUT I'M NOT *STUPID!*

HE WHO FAILS AND *RUNS AWAY,* LIVES TO *WIN* ANOTHER DAY!

VROOM!

BLAST HIM--

16

275

--HE NEVER MAKES IT *EASY!*

BUT HE HASN'T *SPOTTED* ME YET--WHICH *HELPS!*

JUST A *LITTLE CLOSER,* THEN--

AH, IT'S *YOU* AGAIN! NEVER *GIVE UP,* DO YOU?

NOPE! BUT IF YOU'RE *SMART,* JOKER--

--*YOU WILL!*

I'VE HAD JUST ABOUT *ENOUGH* OF YOU FOR ONE NIGHT--

OH-- *REALLY?*

SQUIRSH!

--AND NO *ACID-SQUIRTING* FLOWERS OR *ELECTRIFIED JOY-BUZZERS* OR ANYTHING *ELSE* YOU CAN MUSTER IS GOING TO *SAVE* YOU FROM ME!

MY, WE ARE IN A *SNIT,* AREN'T WE?

UUNNFF!!

WOK!

BUT THE JOKER IS *NOTHING* IF NOT *WELL-HEELED!*

EH? THE BOAT'S *OUT OF CONTROL!*

WE'RE HEADING STRAIGHT FOR THOSE *SHOALS!*

277

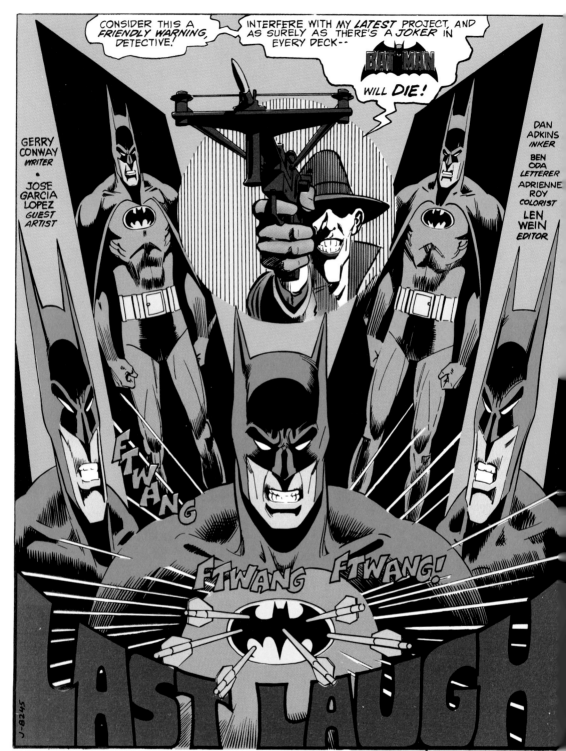

I-I DON'T KNOW WHAT YOU'RE *TALKING* ABOUT--!

THE *DOCTORED PHOTOS* THAT *"REVEALED"* MY SECRET IDENTITY AS A *GOTHAM GANG BOSS!*

WHO GAVE THEM TO YOU?

THORNE!

"BOSS" RUPERT THORNE!

CLICK

IN GOD WE TRUST

THERE.

THAT WASN'T SO HARD, NOW *WAS* IT?

COMMISSIONER *GORDON--* Y-YOU WERE *HERE?* YOU *HEARD?*

IT'S *EX-COMMISSIONER,* REEVES. JUST PLAIN *JAMES GORDON.*

YES, I HEARD. YOU *SICKEN* ME.

BUT, *JIM*--I JUST DID WHAT I *HAD* TO--!

IT WAS *POLITICS!*

ROBIN... GET HIM OUT OF HERE.

SO, WE GUESSED *RIGHT.*

THORNE HAS WORMED HIS WAY BACK INTO GOTHAM POLITICS.

HIS *DIRTY TRICKS* COST REEVES THE *ELECTION--*

--AND SINCE *RUPERT THORNE* NEVER DOES ANYTHING WITHOUT A *REASON--*

-- THAT MEANS HE WAS BACKING *HAMILTON HILL* FOR MAYOR ALL ALONG.

BUT HOW DO WE *PROVE* IT?

JIM... THAT'S *MY* JOB.

CUT TO:

6

MORNING, THE NEXT DAY...

--THIS IS *OLIVIA ORTEGA* FOR SPOTLIGHT NEWS.

WE'RE AT *GOTHAM CENTRAL STATION,* AN HISTORIC *LANDMARK*-- SHORTLY TO BE *TORN DOWN* IN THE NAME OF *PROGRESS.*

FOR MORE *DETAILS,* LET'S--

VICKI ASKED ME TO MEET HER HERE THIS MORNING-- SHE'S *PHOTOGRAPHING* ALL THIS FOR *PICTURE NEWS MAGAZINE--*

--BUT EVEN THOUGH SHE'S PUTTING UP A *BOLD FRONT,* SHE SEEMS *MOODY, WITHDRAWN!*

SOMETHING'S REALLY *DISTURBING* HER-- BUT *WHAT?*

IF *BRUCE WAYNE* COULD SHARE *VICKI VALE'S* THOUGHTS, HE'D *KNOW...*

...FOR EVEN AS SHE STANDS *SMILING,* SHE'S RELIVING A *NIGHTMARE:*

BANG

REMEMBERING, IN AWFUL *VIVID DETAIL,* HOW SHE WITNESSED A *LATE-NIGHT* CONFRONTATION BETWEEN *RUPERT THORNE* AND HER PUBLISHER *MORTON MONROE...*

...A CONFRONTATION THAT *CLIMAXED* IN *MONROE'S SUICIDE!*

...YES, MS. ORTEGA, WE'RE TRYING TO *PRESERVE* THE STATION'S LANDMARK *FACADE...*

...SO WE'VE DEVELOPED A SPECIAL *COMPUTER-CONTROLLED FUSE.*

EACH *EXPLOSIVE CHARGE* FIXED TO THE FACADE WILL BE ACTIVATED IN *SEQUENCE* FROM THIS COMMAND POST...

7

...A SEQUENCE *PROGRAMMED* BY THE COMPUTER.

IT'S DESIGNED TO *POP* THE FACADE ONTO WAITING AIR MATTRESSES WITHOUT *DAMAGING* IT.

NOW, IF YOU'LL ALL *STEP BACK*...

...WE'LL *PROCEED.*

NOTHING.

NOT EVEN A *FIZZLE.*

CAN'T *UNDERSTAND* IT!

THE COMPUTER'S *NEVER* MAL-FUNCTIONED BE-- *GOOD LORD!*

THE *COMPUTER'S GONE!*

SIR, LOOK AT THE *MONITOR!*

WHERE IN HEAVEN DID *THAT* COME FROM?

NOT FROM *HEAVEN,* FRIEND!

THAT'S THE *SIGN OF THE JOKER!*

WAYNE MANOR, FIFTY MINUTES LATER...

WHY WEREN'T YOU *NOTIFIED,* SIR?

WHEN *THE JOKER* ESCAPES *ARKHAM ASYLUM,* THE POLICE ALWAYS-- OH.

EXACTLY, ALFRED!

WITH *COMMISSIONER PETER PAULING* NOW IN CHARGE--

-- THE BATMAN IS ON THE *OUTS.*

IF *COMMISSIONER PAULING* AND *MAYOR HILL* ARE INDEED PAWNS OF *"BOSS" THORNE*--

-- THEN NOT ONLY *YOU,* BUT ALL *GOTHAM,* IS IN TERRIBLE *DANGER!*

8

285

--ATTACHED TO A RADIO-CONTROLLED FUSE.

IT ALL FITS.

A SOUND.

HE SPINS ABOUT, AS LIGHT PINS HIM--

--BUT EVEN AS HE TURNS, THE DRUGGED ARROW STRIKES--

HAHAHA

--THROWING HIM BACKWARD INTO DARKNESS AND SILENCE.

RISE AND SHINE, DETECTIVE.

IT'S TIME TO WAKE UP, YOU SLEEPY-HEAD.

HA HA HA

HA HA

WE WOULDN'T WANT YOU TO MISS YOUR OWN EXECUTION.

288

CRACKLING WITH GLEE, THE JOKER TURNS AWAY--

THIS COMPUTER IS A *MARVELOUS* DEVICE, BATMAN.

BY FIRING THE *EXPLOSIVES* ALONG THIS CLIFF-EDGE AT JUST THE *RIGHT* INTERVALS--

--AND THE BATMAN ACTS.

--IT'LL CUT THE ROCK AS SKILLFULLY AS A *SCULPTOR'S KNIFE!*

THIS *COMPUTER SIMULATION* SHOWS THE PREDICTED *RESULT.*

LOVELY, JUST *LOVELY!*

ROPE FRAYS-- AND BREAKS.

IMAGINE HOW GOTHAM WILL *REACT*--

--WHEN ITS CITIZENS RISE TO SEE *MY* IMAGE WATCHING OVER THEM.

IT'LL BE *GLORIOUS!*

ONLY ONE HAND IS FREE--

--BUT ONE HAND IS ALL HE NEEDS.

CLIK

HMMM

12

-- EVEN **THE BATMAN** CAN BE LEFT **SPEECHLESS.**

IT WORKED...

IT **WORKED!**

I'VE **WON,** BATMAN! DO WHAT YOU WANT-- **I'VE WON!**

LOOK **AGAIN,** JOKER.

OHHH, NO!

MY BEAUTIFUL **MONUMENT--**

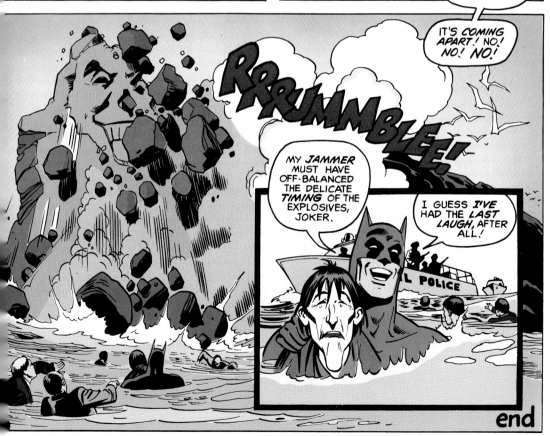

IT'S **COMING APART!** NO! NO! **NO!**

RRRUMMBLEE!

MY **JAMMER** MUST HAVE OFF-BALANCED THE DELICATE **TIMING** OF THE EXPLOSIVES, JOKER.

I GUESS **I'VE** HAD THE **LAST LAUGH,** AFTER ALL!

L POLICE

end

293

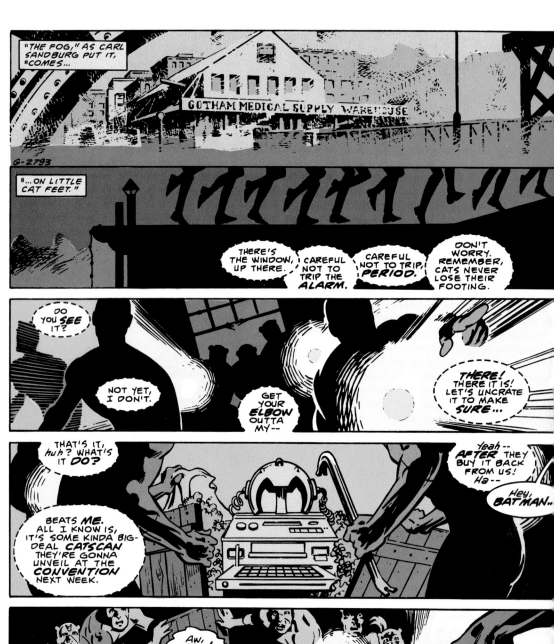

"THE FOG," AS CARL SANDBURG PUT IT, "COMES...

GOTHAM MEDICAL SUPPLY WAREHOUSE

G-2793

"...ON LITTLE CAT FEET."

THERE'S THE WINDOW, UP THERE.

CAREFUL NOT TO TRIP THE ALARM.

CAREFUL NOT TO TRIP. *PERIOD.*

DON'T WORRY. REMEMBER, CATS NEVER LOSE THEIR FOOTING.

DO YOU *SEE* IT?

NOT YET, I DON'T.

GET YOUR *ELBOW* OUTTA MY--

THERE! THERE IT IS! LET'S UNCRATE IT TO MAKE *SURE*...

THAT'S IT, *huh?* WHAT'S IT *DO?*

BEATS *ME.* ALL I KNOW IS, IT'S SOME KINDA BIG-DEAL *CATSCAN* THEY'RE GONNA UNVEIL AT THE *CONVENTION* NEXT WEEK.

Yeah-- *AFTER* THEY BUY IT BACK FROM US! Ha--

Hey, *BATMAN*...

AW, *NO*...!

...WHAT DO YOU CALL NINE *CAT BURGLARS* DOING 10-TO-25 FOR *ARMED ROBBERY?*

1

294

... THEN I'D BETTER START ACTING.

"TO BRUISE, OR NOT TO BRUISE... THAT IS THE QUESTION..."

UNFFF!

YOUR PIECE, MAN -- USE IT!

I WOULDN'T...

AGGGH!

... BUT IF YOU INSIST...

... I'LL MAKE SURE IT DOES SOME GOOD.

ANESTHETIC GAS

BANG

BRA TANN

SSSST

HOW'D HE FIND OUT? HOW'D HE KNOW?

DOESN'T MATTER. WHAT MATTERS IS, WE TAKE 'EM DOWN...

3

...SOUNDS LIKE YOU'VE FORGOTTEN OUR *ACE-IN-THE-HOLE.*

SLOW AND *EASY,* OLD-TIMER, AND WE'LL BE--

RRROWRRRR

WHAT'S THAT-- *NO!*

HSSSST

I TREATED YOU *WELL,* CRANDALL ...GAVE YOU A DECENT *STAKE* TO START OVER AGAIN WHEN I BROKE UP MY *GANG*...AND *THIS* IS HOW YOU PAY ME BACK...!

C-CAT-WOMAN... NO... PLEASE...

AT LEAST *PRETEND* YOU'RE A *MAN,* CRANDALL...

...NOT A *MOUSE.*

AND THANK GOD I'M NOT *HUNGRY.*

CRAKKKT

AND SOON...

NOW DO YOU BELIEVE ME, DARLING? I TURNED IN MY OWN GANG AFTER I HEARD RUMORS THEY MIGHT TRY THIS ROBBERY... DOESN'T THAT PROVE I'M ON YOUR SIDE?

THAT WAS NEVER THE ISSUE, SELINA...

...THE ISSUE IS WHETHER OR NOT WE CAN HAVE ANY KIND OF RELATIONSHIP IN OUR LINE OF WORK.

WHY DON'T YOU AND I DISCUSS THAT, BRUCE ... AT MY PLACE ... ALONE.

PLEASE, SELINA... NOT IN FRONT OF THE BOY.

Oh, BROTHER.

HAVE IT YOUR WAY, BRUCE... FOR NOW. JUST REMEMBER, A GIRL CAN'T WAIT FOREVER... AND THERE ARE LOTS OF FISH IN THE SEA.

I DON'T BLAME YOU FOR TAKING IT SLOW WITH HER, BATMAN ... SHE'S QUITE A HANDFUL...

IT'S NOT THAT, ROBIN...

...IT'S ME. IT SEEMS LIKE EVERY TIME I GET INVOLVED WITH A WOMAN, SOMETHING COMES BETWEEN US... TO RUIN IT. I DON'T KNOW WHY...

...BUT ONE THING'S CERTAIN--IT'S NOTHING I'LL SOLVE TONIGHT. COME ON...

"...LET'S GO HOME."

AND HERE'S A GOLDEN OLDIE COMIN' AT YOU FROM *WOON* AND YOURS TRULY, *BARRY DARK.* IT'S A LITTLE THING *GLENN FREY* CALLS "YOU BELONG TO THE CITY..."

♪ *...YOU BELONG TO THE NIGHT.*

ELSEWHERE...

WHAT ARE WE GONNA *DO...?*

...THE BOSS AIN'T PULLED A JOB IN *MONTHS...* OUR *CASH FLOW* SITUATION IS *DETERIORATIN' RAPIDLY!*

YOU KNOW THAT *I* KNOW THAT...

...BUT SOMEBODY'S GOTTA TELL *HIM...*

"...AND IT SURE AIN'T GONNA BE ME!"

RRRIP!

BAH! ALL IS *WORMWOOD* AND *BITTER VETCH!* MY GENIUS HAS *FLOWN...* MY INSPIRATION IS *GONE!*

7

THAM GAZETT

"DYNAMIC TRIO" NABS GANG

THE BATMAN, ROBIN, AND CATWOMAN JOIN FORCES

--YOUR...

GOOD WORK, STRAIGHT LINE!

JUST DOING MY *JOB*...!

LET'S TRY IT *AGAIN,* JAY...

...AND FORGET THIS IS A *PRACTICE SESSION.*

YOU'RE IN AN *ALLEY,* ON GOTHAM'S *LOWER EAST SIDE,* TRACING DOWN A *LEAD...*

9

...WHEN SUDDENLY, YOU'RE *DISCOVERED.* A WHOLE *GANG* ATTACKS YOU-- AND THEY'RE *ARMED.*

NO *PROBLEM,* BRUCE...

...A FEW CAPSULES OF *TEAR GAS'LL* --HUH?

WRONG, JAY...

...THE UTILITY BELT IS A *TOOL*--NOT A *CURE-ALL!* YOU HAVE TO LEARN TO SOLVE PROBLEMS *WITHOUT* IT! NOW LET'S TRY THAT *DEFENSIVE STANCE* AGAIN--

BEG PARDON, SIRS... BUT DINNER IS *SERVED.*

Oh, boy, POT ROAST! MY *FAVORITE*--

ALFRED, WHAT'S THE *BIG IDEA?*

KLAKT

I'M *SORRY,* MASTER JAY, BUT YOU ARE AS FAMILIAR WITH MASTER BRUCE'S RULE AS I--

"...*BUSINESS* BEFORE *PLEASURE.*"

10

303

GOOD TO *SEE* YOU, BATMAN--NOW I CAN TURN THIS THING OFF BEFORE THE DEPUTY MAYOR BREAKS ME DOWN TO *SERGEANT.*

BEEN GIVING YOU A LOT OF *HEAT,* GORDON?

NOTHING I CAN'T *HANDLE,* BATMAN --SOME DAYS, I THINK I WAS BORN IN A *KITCHEN.* NO, IT'S--

HEY...

...WHAT'S *SHE* DOING HERE?

PURRRR

SHE SAID SHE WAS MEETING *YOU.* YOU *HAVE* BEEN WORKING TOGETHER, SO I ASSUMED--

IT'S ALL RIGHT, CAPTAIN. WHY HAVE YOU *CALLED* US, SIR?

IT'S *THE JOKER,* BATMAN. HE'S *BACK.*

WELL, O-*KAY.*

THIS CARD WAS DROPPED OFF AT ONE OF THE *PRE-CINCTS,* A FEW MINUTES AGO; THE MESSENGER WAS GONE BEFORE THEY KNEW WHAT IT *WAS.* IT BEARS NO *FINGERPRINTS,* NO MARK OF ANY *KIND...*

...EXCEPT, OF COURSE, FOR THE WRITING ON THE *BACK*.

Milling around for a clue, old foe? You'll never get the score. -The Joker

"GET THE *SCORE*?" HE'S UNDER*SCORED* THE WORD "MILLING"! HE'S GONNA ROB THE *GOTHAM FLOUR COMPANY* --MILL!

"MILLING" ALSO REFERS TO THE CORRUGATING ON THE EDGE OF A *COIN*...

A "MILLER'S THUMB" IS A SMALL *FISH*... THEY'RE *DELICIOUS*.

E ALSO NDER-CORED HE FIRST WO ETTERS OF HIS AME-- *J-O* OR *-O-E*...

...AND THE *GOTHAM PUBLIC LIBRARY* IS EXHIBIT-ING A RARE FIRST EDITION OF "*JOE MILLER'S JOKE BOOK*" ALL THIS WEEK!

HOLY GUTENBERG! LET'S GO!

NOT SO *FAST*, ROBIN.

HUH--?

...*NEVER* DO THAT AGAIN!

...OKAY, BATMAN.

?

12

305

PLACES, EVERYONE...

HA HA HA HA HA HA HA HA

...IT WON'T BE LONG BEFORE OUR *STAR PLAYERS* ENTER, STAGE RIGHT, AND THE *CURTAIN* SHALL RISE! BUT *FIRST...*

JOE MILLER'S JOKE BOOK

TINK

KRASSSH

HA HA HA HA AT LAST...!

THEY'RE HEEEEERE...!

NOT A *MIRROR*, JOKER--BUT IT'LL COST YOU AT LEAST *SEVEN YEARS*--OF *HARD TIME!*

...BUT Y'CAN'T BE TOO *CAREFUL* WITH THAT GUY...

...I MEAN, HE COULD BE *ANY-WHERE*...

OR ANY-*THING!*

NOOOOOOOOOO...

JOINED THE *OPPOSITION* HAVE WE, MY DEAR? TRYING TO CHANGE OUR *SPOTS?*

YES! AND WHAT *ABOUT* IT?

I'M TRYING TO DO SOMETHING *DECENT* WITH MY LIFE -- AND THAT'S MORE THAN *YOU'LL* EVER DO!

I *QUITE* AGREE, DEAR TABBY...

...THE THOUGHT OF DOING ANY-THING DECENT POSITIVELY TURNS MY *STOMACH*... AND SOON, I THINK, *YOURS!*

AGGGGH!

15

309

WELL, DEAR SELINA ISN'T BEING VERY **TALK-ATIVE** TONIGHT... MAYBE THE **CAT'S** GOT HER TONGUE, hahaha!

HOHO HOHO

BUT **SERIOUSLY**, FOLKS, LET ME INTRO-DUCE MY **NEXT** GUEST...

...A BRILLIANT SCIENTIST, A FORMER NOBEL PRIZE NOMINEE, AND A **REAL** PARTY ANIMAL, **DR. MOON!** DOC, TELL US WHAT NUMBER YOU'RE GOING TO PERFORM HERE TONIGHT.

Er...**THANK** YOU, MR. JOKER...

CLAP CLAP CLAP

...IT IS MY FIRM **BELIEF** --AS YOU MAY BE AWARE-- THAT MAN IS NOTHING MORE THAN AN **ANIMAL**, AN UTTER **SLAVE** TO THE DEMANDS OF HIS CARNAL **CAGE**.

YOU HAVE HEARD SOME ESPOUSE THE FALLACY OF **FREE WILL**...

...I TELL YOU, FREE WILL IS A **MYTH**. THE MIND IS **CLAY**, SHAPED AND MOLDED AS THE **BODY** REQUIRES. YOU HAVE HEARD IT SAID THE WAY TO A MAN'S **HEART** IS THROUGH HIS **STOMACH**...?

I SAY THE WAY TO A MAN'S **MIND** IS THROUGH HIS **BODY**. I SHALL **PROVE** THIS, TONIGHT.

NICE JOB, DOC. CARE FOR A **CIGAR**?

I DO NOT OFTEN **INDULGE**, BUT PERHAPS THIS **ONCE**...

BANG

HA HA HA HA HA HA HA HA

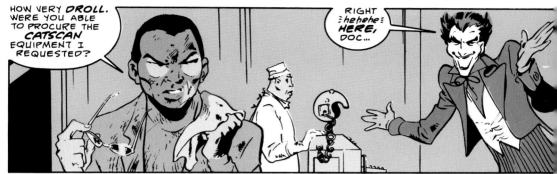

HOW VERY **DROLL.** WERE YOU ABLE TO PROCURE THE **CATSCAN** EQUIPMENT I REQUESTED?

RIGHT ≡hehehe≡ **HERE,** DOC...

Ah, **SPLENOID.** AS YOU DOUBTLESS KNOW, THE NORMAL USE OF THE CATSCAN EQUIPMENT IS TO MONITOR THE PATIENT'S BRAIN CELLS FOR **ACTIVITY...**

WELL, OF **COURSE...**

... MY LATEST RESEARCHES INDICATE THAT, PROPERLY ALTERED, A CATSCAN MAY ALSO ENABLE ONE TO "REPROGRAM" A PATIENT'S MIND, IF YOU WILL, AS THOUGH IT WERE A COMPUTER.

THIS HELPS TO CONFIRM MY THEORY OF FREE WILL, YOU WILL NOTE.

I WAS JUST ABOUT TO **MENTION** THAT...

YES. WELL, NOW I AM **READY.**

SO? WHAT'S THE **DELAY?**

MY RESEARCHES ALSO INDICATE THE PROCESS IS ACCOMPANIED BY NO LITTLE **PAIN.** I SHOULD LIKE TO WAIT UNTIL THE SUBJECT IS **CONSCIOUS** TO MEASURE THE **LEVEL.**

DOC...

...YOU'RE **MY** KIND OF GUY!

TH-**THANK** YOU, MR. JOKER...

...WOULD YOU CARE FOR A **CIGAR?**

19

HAHAHAHH

ROBIN? ROBIN!

HE'S OUT. THAT'S FOR THE BEST...

...BUT HE'S STILL LIABLE TO *STRANGLE* HIMSELF IF HE EVEN *STIRS*--WHICH LEAVES IT *UP* TO *ME*.

AS I *RECALL*, THE ONLY WAY TO ESCAPE THESE CHINESE PUZZLES IS BY *RELAXING* ...NOT *RESISTING* THEM.

GOT TO *RELAX* EVERY MUSCLE IN MY *BODY*... GO *AGAINST* EVERY INSTINCT TO *STRUGGLE*, TO *FIGHT*...

...FOR A *QUARTER-CENTURY* I'VE TRAINED MY MIND TO BE THE MASTER OF MY BODY...TIME TO PUT IT TO THE *TEST*.

HE FOCUSES HIS *MIND*, HIS *SELF*, HIS VERY *ESSENCE* ON A POINT OUTSIDE HIMSELF...

...HE THINKS OF A *SUMMER BREEZE*, A RUNNING *BROOK*, A WAVING FIELD OF *WHEAT*...

...HE ENVISIONS ROCK-HARD MUSCLES BECOMING *PLIANT*...

...*FLUID*...

...*YIELDING*...

...HIS MIND IS A DOOR THAT SHUTS OUT THE WORLD... INCLUDING THE FADING GASP OF THE BOY WHO IS LIKE A *SON* TO HIM...

BRUCE...

20

OKER, LET ME
UT OF HERE!
HEN I GET
REE, I'LL--
SSSSSST

OH, I
INK *NOT*,
Y DEAR...

...YOU SEE, BY THE TIME
MY ADVERSARY ESCAPES
THE *TRAP* I SET FOR HIM
--AND HE ALWAYS *DOES*--
YOU'LL BE ONLY TOO GLAD
TO HELP ME *HUMILIATE*
HIM--THE BAD *DOCTOR*
WILL SEE TO THAT.

WHY ARE
YOU *DOING*
THIS? WHY CAN'T
YOU LEAVE ME
ALONE?

I'M ONLY
DOING THIS FOR
YOUR OWN *GOOD!*
WE THIEVES HAVE
TO STICK
TOGETHER,
MY DEAR...

...EVEN IF I HAVE TO
TEAR YOUR MIND TO
PIECES TO *DO*
IT!

ON

HAHA HAHA HAH

NEXT:
"THE *LAST*
LAUGH!"

315

316

I ALLUS **SAID** YOU SHOULD DROP IN MORE **OFTEN**, BATMAN! LIKE A **TABLE**?

YOU **KNOW** WHAT I WANT, McSURLEY--

--WHERE'S **PROFILE**?

Uh... HE AIN'T **IN** T'NIGHT, BATMAN, HE--

CHUKKT

I'LL SEE FOR **MYSELF**, THANKS.

HIYA, BATS.

NOT **HARDLY**.

HELLO, RHONDA. STAYING OUT OF **TROUBLE**?

I WON'T BE LONG. YOU MIND THE STORE, CHUM.

Gulp O-OKAY, BATMAN!

WHAT'LL IT **BE**, KID? WE'RE **OUTTA** BIRD SEED!

MILK.

MILK?

MAKE IT **TWO**.

TELL YOUR BOSS HE'S GOT **COMPANY**, MOOSE.

HE AIN'T SEEIN' **NO ONE**, BATMAN --'SPECIALLY **YOU**. AN' I GOT ORDERS t'**KEEP** IT THAT WAY.

I **SEE**.

MOOSE, YOUR SHOELACE IS UNTIED.

NO, IT AIN'T. THAT WORKED **LAST** TIME...

...BUT NOT **NOW**. I'M TOO **SMART** FOR YA.

sigh I SUPPOSE YOU'RE **RIGHT**.

MOOSE, **MY** SHOELACE IS UNTIED.

IS IT? LEMME --

SEE?

I CAN GET THE **BEANS**, BUT THEY'LL **COST** YOU --

SOMETHING JUST CAME **UP**, FRISCO. I'LL GET **BACK** TO YOU.

BATMAN, THIS IS QUITE **UNEXPECTED** ... OF COURSE, IT ALWAYS **IS**, ISN'T IT?

WOULD YOU **LIKE** SOMETHING? SOME **SHERRY**, PERHAPS A CUP OF **TEA**? PLEASE, SIT DOWN...

4

OH, VERY *WELL*. WHAT IS IT YOU *WANT*?

THE *JOKER*.

THE *JOKER*? BATMAN, I WON'T BOTHER TO DENY THAT I KNOW WHERE HE *IS*, BUT I CAN'T *TELL* YOU. IT WOULD *RUIN* ME AS AN *INFORMATION BROKER*.

MY *CLIENTELE* WOULD *DESERT* ME IN *DROVES*. NO, I'M AFRAID IT'S QUITE *UNTHINKABLE*.

THEN HERE'S THE *DRILL*, PROFILE...

...TELL ME WHAT YOU *KNOW* ABOUT THE ROBBERY AT THE *KROFT DIAMOND EXCHANGE*.

THE KROFT DIAMOND -- THERE HASN'T *BEEN* ANY ROBBERY AT THE KROFT DIAMOND EXCHANGE!

NOT *YET*...

...BUT THERE *MIGHT* BE... AND GORDON'S *COPS* MIGHT FIND YOUR *PRINTS* ON THE *SCENE*... AND YOU MIGHT GO TO *PRISON*.

EVER BEEN *INSIDE*, PROFILE?

N-NO.

YOU'D BE REAL *POPULAR* UP THERE, PROFILE...

...IF YOU *CATCH* MY DRIFT.

TH-THE ABANDONED *JESTER NOVELTIES* FACTORY! HE'S *THERE*!

...THE WOMAN'S MIND IS, ACCORDING TO MY *CALCULATIONS*, FULLY-- er--RECALIBRATED. SHE SHOULD FEEL YOU ARE HER *ALLY*.

EXCELLENT, DR. *MOON!* NOW, DEAR *SELINA*, HERE'S THE *MILLION-DOLLAR QUESTION*...

WHO IS *BATMAN?* WHAT'S HIS *SECRET IDENTITY?*

I MUST *PROTEST*, MR. JOKER!

IF YOU TRY TO *FORCE* INFORMATION FROM HER, SO SOON AFTER THE *TREATMENT*, IT MAY BE *JUMBLED*... OR WORSE, *LOST*.

THE RESULTING MENTAL DISRUPTION WOULD BE *INTERESTING*, BUT NOT WITHOUT A *CONTROL*-- *MRFFF!*

TAKE TWO ASPIRINS AND CALL M IN THE *MORNING* DOC! NOW SELINA...

...YOU *KNOW* ME, DON'T YOU? AND YOU *TRUST* ME...

Y-YES...

THEN *TELL* ME... WHO IS *BATMAN?*

HE'S... HE'S...

...ROBERT BENSON...

HA HA HA HA

HE'S IN THERE, ALL RIGHT! SOUNDS LIKE *GRADUATION DAY* AT THE *LAUGHING ACADEMY!*

YOU KNOW THE *PLAN*, CHUM...

...BUT IF YOU WANT TO *BOW OUT*, I'LL *UNDERSTAND!* THE JOKER'S GOONS CAN BE PRETTY *ROUGH CUSTOMERS!*

SAVE YOUR SYMPATHY FOR *THEM*, BATMAN--ESPECIALLY *STRAIGHT LINE!*

GOOD BOY! YOU'VE GOT *TWO* MINUTES!

THAT *LONG?* HECK, I MAY STOP FOR *LUNCH* ON THE WAY!

...Yeah, IT'S GOOD TO SEE THE BOSS BACK IN *FORM* AGAIN, BUT I STILL AIN'T SEEN ANY *MOOLAH!*

DON'T *WORRY!* TO THE *JOKER*, CASH IS JUST A *BY-PRODUCT!* HE'LL COME *THROUGH!*

YOU MEAN-- "HE *IS* THROUGH*!*" AND SO ARE *YOU!*

HUH? WHAT TH--?

YOU *DOPES!* YOUR MOTHER ROBS *PARKING METERS!* YOUR FATHER'S ON *PAROLE!*

HOW'D HE KNOW ABOUT MY *MOTHER...?*

SHADDAP AND *RUN!*

8

ROBIN'S HERE, IN THE EAST WING! EVERYBODY COME AND GIVE US A HAND!

THE BRAT? ALONE?

NO, YOU FOOLS! IT'S A DIVERSION, IT'S--

IT'S THE TRUTH, JOKER!

CRASH

YOU--!

DO SOMETHING SENSIBLE FOR ONCE, JOKER --SURRENDER!

WHAT? AND BE DRUMMED OUT OF THE UNION?

Hiiiii--YA! ME MAKEE HAMBURGER OUTTA AMELICAN CLIME-FIGHTER!

OOOF!

OUT OF HERE, SELINA! QUICKLY!

DO I KNOW HIM...?

"STRAIGHT LINE," THE JOKER CALLED HIM. ANY OTHER TIME, I'D BE GLAD TO MAKE HIM EAT THAT HEADBAND...

Hiiiii...

10

--YAAAAH!

...BUT WITH SELINA STILL THE JOKER'S *CAPTIVE*...

...I CAN'T ALLOW MYSELF THE *LUXURY!*

RRRRIP

CRIZZZ

WHOOOSHT

WHOOOSHT

THAT *SOUND*...A *PLANE* OF SOME SORT.

NO...

...A *CAR.*

11

WE'LL BE **SEEING** YOU, BATMAN-- MUCH **SOONER** THAN YOU EXPECT, eh, SELINA?

Mrowr...

SOMETIME **LATER**...

BATMAN, ARE YOU **OKAY?** YOU LOOK LIKE SOMETHING THE **CAT**-- OOPS!

WHAT'S THE **SIT**-**UATION,** ROBIN?

I ROUNDED UP MOST OF THE JOKER'S MEN-- ALL BUT **STRAIGHT LINE**-- AND LOOK WHO I FOUND TRYING TO SNEAK AWAY!

RELEASE ME, YOU YOUNG HOODLUM! I DEMAND TO CONTACT MY EMBASSY!

WHAT DID YOU DO TO THE **CATWOMAN?**

I MERELY... er..."RECALIBRATED" HER, CONFORMING TO MR. JOKER'S WISHES.

AND CAN IT BE **UNDONE?**

ONLY BY **ME,** IF AT LL... AND I WILL **OT!** WOULD YOU SK DA VINCI TO PAINT VER THE **MONA ISA?** WOULD YOU SK **MICHELANGELO** O RESCULPT--

BOY, YOU'RE THE **LOWEST!**

GREAT MEN ARE **INVARIABLY** MISUNDERSTOOD IN THEIR OWN TIME. BUT FUTURE GENERATIONS WILL RANK ME WITH **MENGELE,** WITH--

WEEEEEOO

BATMAN --?

I **HEAR** THEM, ROBIN.

14

COME **ON**, CHUM--THE COPS WILL ONLY DELAY US **MORE**, AND WE'VE GOT TO FIND SELINA BEFORE IT'S **TOO LATE!**

BUT **HOW**, BATMAN?

THE JOKER'S OBVIOUSLY TRYING TO TURN SELINA BACK TO HER **CRIMINAL WAYS!** TO DO THAT, HE'LL USE THE PATH OF **LEAST RESISTANCE--**

HE'LL SET HER UP TO COMMIT A **CAT-CRIME!**

EXACTLY! AND THERE WAS SOMETHING I SPOTTED IN THE NEWSPAPER SHE WAS READING IN **CAPTAIN GORDON'S** OFFICE...

Gotham C
Volume 237 Numb
BER 15 1986

BENSON HEIRESS STILL IN CATALEPTI TRANCE

THE SECRETARY FOR MILLIO
BENSON REPORTS NO SUCCES
ING A CURE FOR DAUGHTER

AND YOU THINK THEY'RE GOING TO THE **BENSONS**? BECAUSE OF THE **CATALEPTIC** TRANCE ANGLE?

I **DO**, AND WITH SELINA IN HER PRESENT STATE...

"...THE BENSONS ARE IN MORE DANGER THAN THEY'VE EVER **KNOWN.**"

ISN'T IT **PURR-FECT**, SELINA? A GIANT **CAT'S CRADLE**, TO CELEBRATE YOUR RETURN TO A LIFE OF **CRIME!**

I **APPROVE!**

15

SO, YOU'RE *THE BATMAN,* eh, BENSON? I NEVER WOULD HAVE *THOUGHT* IT TO LOOK AT YOU, BUT--

I DON'T KNOW WHAT YOU *MEAN!* WHAT DO YOU *WANT?*

I WANT YOU TO *ADMIT* TO DEAR SELINA THAT YOUR AFFECTION FOR HER WAS ALL A *SHAM...* OR YOUR DAUGHTER WILL BE SLEEPING A MUCH *DEEPER* SLEEP THAN CATALEPSY!

I'LL SAY *ANYTHING,* JUST LEAVE MELISSA *ALONE!*

HE *SOUNDS* LIKE HE'S TELLIN' THE *TRUTH,* BOSS!

BUT HE *IS* THE BATMAN! THE CATWOMAN *SAID* SO!

BUT WHAT IF DOC MOON WAS RIGHT, AND SHE *DID* FORGET WHO BATS IS? MAYBE SHE PICKED UP THIS BENSON'S NAME SOMEPLACE *ELSE?* THE *NEWSPAPER* STORY, MAYBE?

THEY WERE *HOME* WHEN WE GOT HERE, AND *LOOK* AT THIS GUY--HIS FACE AIN'T EVEN *SCRATCHED,* LIKE BATMAN'S SHOULD BE.

DETAILS, *DETAILS!*

ESIDES, YOU LWAYS SAID OU NEVER WANTED T'KILL BATMAN.

I *DON'T.* I DERIVE FAR MORE PLEASURE FROM OUR CONTINUAL BATTLES OF WITS THAN I WOULD FROM HIS SINGLE *DEATH...*

16

...BUT TO DESTROY HIS EFFECTIVENESS-- TO TAKE AWAY THE *ANONYMITY* HE SO LOVES--*THAT* WOULD BE A PLEASURE, *eh*, SELINA?

YES. TAKE AWAY HIS IDENTITY AS A CRIME-FIGHTER, AS HE TRIED TO TAKE AWAY *MINE*, AS A *THIEF*.

ENOUGH *BADINAGE!* BATMAN'S FAR TOO NOBLE TO SAVE HIS *OWN* HIDE, STRAIGHT LINE... BUT HIS *DAUGHTER* SHOULD BE AN-OTHER MATTER!

RIGHT, BOSS!

AND NOW I THINK IT'S TIME FOR THE *FIRST SHIFT* TO START! HA HAHA

GOTCHA, FOREMAN!

VROOOM

MELISSA! NO!

STOP THIS, JOKER! WHAT-EVER ELSE I AM, I'M *NOT* A KILLER!

THAT'S YOUR *TROUBLE*, SELINA... YOU NEVER CULTIVATE ANY NEW *INTERESTS!* JUST *WATCH*, AND--

SLASSH

I SAID "NO!"

I KNEW IT WASN'T TOO LATE, SELINA!

Y-YOU?

YEAH-- US!

BUT YOU--

BUT THEY--

BUT I--

I DON'T CARE HOW MANY OF YOU THERE ARE --I'LL KILL YOU ALL!

SMELL MY FLOWER, BRAT!

NO THANKS, JOKER...

"...YOU DON'T HAVE A PERMIT FOR THAT PISTIL!

KICK!

UNNGH!

18

IT'S NOT TOO *LATE*, SELINA! THE DAMAGE CAN BE *UNDONE*... YOU CAN BE MADE *NORMAL*...

I *AM* NORMAL, LOVER...

...AND I *LIKE* IT!

CRACKT

OWTCH!

WOW, YOU'RE *ROBIN*, AREN'T YOU? CAN I HAVE YOUR *AUTOGRAPH*?

I THINK THAT CAN BE ARRANGED...

LOOK OUT, ROBIN!

THANKS, KID...

YIIII...

...IF I EVER NEED AN *ASSISTANT*, YOU'RE *IT*!

CRZZZ

19

D-DADDY...?

MELISSA!

BAH! WHEN I'M CONTRIBUTING TO THE HAPPY ENDING, I KNOW I'M BOMBING! AND SPEAKING OF WHICH... THIS SMOKE BOMB WILL GIVE US A CLEAN GETAWAY! COMING, CHILDREN?

POUF

RIGHT WITH YOU, JOKER... MY CATGUT LADDER WILL GIVE US A LEG UP ON OUR PURSUERS!

"TOMORROW," AS A GREAT PHILOSOPHER PUT IT, "IS ANOTHER DAY!"

MAYBE SO, JOKER ...BUT THEY ALL LOOK THE SAME FROM BEHIND BARS!

NOT SO FAST, SHORTY-- I HAVEN'T PUNCHED YOUR TICKET, YET!

HURRY UP, JOKER!

DON'T BE CATTY, SELINA! IT'S--

20

335

IT'S *OVER*, JOKER! YOU'RE TAKING THE *FALL*!

THAT MAKES *TWO* OF YOU, HANDSOME!

SELINA, *DON'T--!*

PUNK

WHUMP

YOU'D BE A LOT OF *FUN*, IF YOU WEREN'T SO *STRAIGHT!* SEE YOU *AROUND.*

SELINA, THIS ISN'T *YOU* TALKING, IT'S MOON'S *TREAT-MENT*, IT--

MAYBE AN AD IN THE *LOST-AND-FOUND* WILL-- *UNGGGGH!*

GLOK

LOST YOUR LITTLE *KITTEN*, BATMAN? TOO *BAD.* HA HA *HA HA HA*

STOP *LAUGHING!* DO YOU *HEAR* ME, JOKER?

21

FOR YEARS, YOU'VE SNEERED AND LAUGHED AT EVERYTHING *DECENT*...

...BUT *NO MORE*, DO YOU *HEAR* ME?

NO MORE!

BATMAN, *STOP*...!

STOP! YOU'LL *KILL* HIM!

HE *TOOK* HER FROM ME, ROBIN... EVERY WOMAN I LOVE, SOMETHING AL- WAYS *TAKES* HER FROM ME...

YOU LOST THE CATWOMAN, *yeah*... BUT YOU CAUGHT THE JOKER... AND YOU SAVED THE *BENSONS* ...SAVED THEIR *LIVES*...

...THAT'S *SOME- THING.*

NO, ROBIN...

...THAT'S *EVERY- THING.*

COME ON, CHUM, LET'S GO *HOME.*

337

ENO

STILL CRAZY AFTER ALL THESE YEARS

I was, what, eight years old when I was first introduced to the Joker? When I re-read that first Joker story now (as told in BATMAN #1), I get no sense of why the character made such an awesome impression on me at the time. The milk-white skin? The prominent horse teeth? The ruby-red lips? The wild shock of green hair? I'm not sure. Maybe it was the things he did. Even then he was the ultimate Batman villain (probably still is), capable of the most dastardly acts. Anyway, my memories are that my lifelong addiction to reading comics began with the Joker's first appearance. I was terrified by his stark, maniacal countenance and as everyone knows, a young boy is drawn to what terrifies him. Batman's victories over the Joker were always much more dramatic and satisfying for me. Although I knew the Batman was bound to be victorious over the many villains who dotted his landscape, I always felt that when he faced the Joker, Batman came as close to meeting his match as he ever would. On some occasions, I was sure that there was no way that Batman could prevail. The Joker was *that* good! (And crazy!)

BRIAN BOLLAND

Of course, I was too young then to analyze the reasons for the Joker's success, but now in retrospect, it seems clear that there are essentially two reasons that the Joker has enjoyed a level of recognition, popularity (notoriety?) and longevity in the Batman mythos, surpassed only by Batman himself and perhaps Robin. One reason is his origin (or origins). In each of the several variations of the Joker's origins that have been offered up through the decades, one element is constant: The Joker was created in a single traumatic, mind-shattering moment when a major crisis caused him to lose his hold on his rationality… and sanity. Some say that in this respect his origin is a lot like the Batman's. We (as readers) can relate to human beings who endure unbelievable stress and pain and are altered forever by the experience.

The second reason for the Joker's long-term success is his innate adaptability. Through five decades of storytelling, in various media, readers' (and viewers') tastes have changed often. These shifts in taste invariably dictated changes in the character portrayal of the Batman. From camp to sci-fi, to grim and gritty, to just plain silly, the Joker was able to adapt and walk in lock step with the Batman. For that reason, I wasn't surprised that the Joker was one of the most popular villains on the old TV show; or that he was a major player in the ground-breaking THE DARK KNIGHT RETURNS; or that the Joker's presence in the recent Warner Bros. big-screen release BATMAN was a major factor in the film's record-breaking run.

Another measure of the Joker's value to the Batman legend is the number of writers and artists who would almost kill for the opportunity to write or draw a Batman story that features the villain you love to hate. And although each of the creators who gets the coveted assignment brings a new vision, a new spin to his or her version of the Joker, the result is always the same: a villain worthy of the Batman's considerable skills and whose villainy only feeds the Batman's heroics.

See? The Joker is THAT good! (And crazy!)

— *Dick Giordano*
VP/Editorial Director
of DC Comics and
noted Batman artist

*n*ot even in a book as big as this one can there be room for every story starring the Joker. For each tale reprinted in this volume, the editors evaluated ten stories that *didn't* make the final cut. Not that it wasn't educational — reviewing those tales provided more interesting insights into the Clown Prince of Crime. For one thing, there's the matter of his *death*, 45 years ago…

The Joker's second appearance originally was slotted for DETECTIVE COMICS #40 but was rescheduled at the last minute as the last tale in BATMAN #1. After having ranted and raved in the first story in that issue (reprinted here) that no jail could hold him, the Joker made good his boast by using a powerful explosive from chemicals hidden inside two false teeth. On a rampage, he committed all sorts of brazen thefts and murders, killing Gotham's police chief and battling Batman to a near-standstill. While brandishing a knife against his foe, however, the Joker accidentally stabbed himself. Batman and Robin then vanished quietly into the night, believing their enemy to be dead.

And he was.

Originally, anyway. After the story was completed, it dawned on Batman creator Bob Kane how wonderful a character the Joker was and how much could be done with him. At the last minute, Kane redrew the story's final panel to have an attending doctor remark that, much to everyone's surprise, the Joker was going to *live after all!*

The survival of the Joker sparked a long-running tradition surrounding the Harlequin of Hate: at his most evil, the Joker has a tendency to this day to find himself trapped in "dooms" of his own making rather than be apprehended like a common criminal. And of all Batman's foes, none has shown up hale and hearty after *certain* death in explosions,

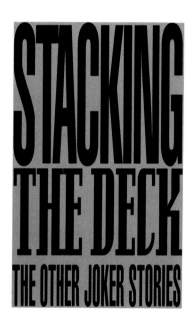

fires, cave-ins, drownings, and the like as often as he has. Batman had to learn very early on that, regardless of the circumstances, if the Joker's dead body wasn't found among the debris, then he was alive. Somehow, he was alive. And he would return.

But that hasn't kept the Batman from trying to *reform* his foe from time to time. For instance, in BATMAN #2, the Darknight Detective, upon hearing of the Joker's recovery, made plans to abduct him before he could escape on his own. The idea was to then "take him to a famous brain specialist for an operation, so that he can be cured and turned into a valuable citizen," according to the man who dresses up every night in a bat costume. But a nationwide crime syndicate beat Batman to the punch. In a show of typical Joker gratitude, the Crime Clown immediately double-crossed the syndicate and went after a cache of rare jewels. In the process, he crossed Catwoman's path and, in the resulting struggle, the Joker was left to perish inside a flaming castle.

The Joker survived (was there any real doubt?) to battle Batman over a priceless jade Buddha (DETECTIVE #45), to organize his own carnival of crime (in "The Case of the Joker's Crime Circus"), to set up an elaborate citywide burglary racket (BATMAN #5), and to stage a spectacular diamond theft (BATMAN #7). At long last, in the eighth issue of BATMAN, the Gotham Guardian — under orders from the President himself — finally managed to actually *apprehend* his foe.

Was that it for the Joker's criminal career? Had he finally been brought to justice? No such luck. The slippery felon escaped imprisonment three more times before finally being sentenced by the authorities to the electric chair in DETECTIVE #64's "The Joker Walks the Last Mile." Immediately following the execution, however, the Joker's corpse is stolen by his henchmen who inject a specially prepared serum into his veins, bringing him *back to life.*

Yes, the Joker was back... but, contrary to cliché, not "deadlier than ever." In fact, more by coincidence than by design, the Mad Jester's revivification marked an important turning point for Batman's writers for the next 31 years. It was about this time that the Batman feature began losing its dark, dangerous, *film noir* edge, and the Joker's actions were actually toned down. His felonies became less macabre and more zany, his crimes revolving around gimmicks such as committing bizarre thefts in mysterious patterns or around weird themes.

All in all, it was actually a pretty fair trade: Joker stories became less moody but, on the whole, more memorable. For example, one of the better Joker stories from this period (and one of the few drawn by Jerry Robinson) was "Slay 'Em With Flowers," in which the Ace of Knaves and his men assumed control of a flower shop that catered to Gotham City's wealthiest citizens. By secreting knockout gas pellets in specific plants, the Joker's gang robbed millionaires citywide with ease — until Batman and Robin finally doped out their foe's methods and put an end to his crimes (DETECTIVE #76).

BRIAN BOLLAND

Another tale, one that narrowly escaped inclusion in this volume, was "Rackety-Rax Racket" (BATMAN #32). Inspired by the strange initiation hazing pranks of a local college fraternity, the Joker kidnapped Batman and threatened to murder him if Robin did not perform a series of carefully outlined and highly embarrassing stunts, all of which were secretly engineered to provide a cover for the Joker's robberies. Ultimately, Batman escaped and restored order — and even helped Robin save face in Gotham.

Other notable Joker tales from the '40s? Well, there was the first Joker/Penguin team-up,

"Knights of Knavery," reprinted in THE GREATEST BATMAN STORIES; "Gamble With Doom," an excellent Bill Finger/Jim Mooney/Ray Burnley story from BATMAN #44 in which the Joker forced Batman to engage in deadly giant-sized games of chance in order to save Robin's life; and the one with our favorite title, "The Joker Follows Suit," the beautifully-drawn Jerry Robinson tale in which the Clown Prince, exasperated with his arch-nemesis and his crime-fighting equipment, opted to imitate his method of operation in a Joker-like fashion. Applying his criminal genius to the task of planning perfect crimes for all of Gotham's gangsters, the Joker constructed a Jokermobile, a Jokergyro, and special Jokersignals with which crooks could summon assistance. Batman and Robin eventually put him out of business, but not without a fierce struggle (BATMAN #37).

As Batman entered the 1950s, whatever dark mood once permeated his stories was all but completely gone. His adventures became more and more tame, and even the use of Batman's long-established Rogues Gallery — Joker, Penguin, Catwoman, and others — became sparse. For every really good Joker tale published during this period, there was at least one truly mediocre story. How many times could the Joker fool Batman with mysterious patterns that spelled out his own name ("Let's see, Robin — he's struck the Justice Building, the Orpheum House, Knight Jewelers, and Electrical Equipment Engineers... *what could he be up to?*")? The mid- to late-'50s, especially, was a slack period by any true Batman fan's evaluation.

This isn't to say that a few good stories didn't surface from time to time. In addition to those represented in this volume, other Joker tales that were considered for inclusion were stories like BATMAN #67's "The Man Who Wrote the Joker's Jokes," which showed a disconsolate Grim Jester worrying about whether he had "gone stale" in his ability to plan villainy. Concerned, he hired a team of underworld gag writers to concoct Joker-like crimes *for* him. A clever scheme, but not clever enough to outwit the Batman.

In the particularly funny "The Joker's Millions" (DETECTIVE #180), the Joker actually resigned from his career of crime when he inherited a fortune in cash from a former crime rival and began an ostentatious — though law-abiding — life of leisure. Soon after being informed by the Internal Revenue Service that he owed millions in taxes, though, the Joker discovered that his rival got the last laugh: the inheritance was counterfeit. Rather than admit that he, of all people, had been bamboozled, the Joker was forced to take up crime in order to accumulate tax money. Not yet defeated, though, he found a neat twist in committing brazen stick-ups and safecracking — decidedly un-Jokerish crimes — as secretly as possible, figuring that no one would ever suspect him of such pedestrian affairs. Though he got away with it for a while, Batman eventually sized up the situation and cleverly tricked the Joker into making a confession that led to his imprisonment.

BRIAN BOLLAND

It's not tough to ascertain a trend here. Joker stories were becoming more flat-out outrageous — which, believe it or not, was a better approach than was taken during the 1960s, as we shall see. One of the most bizarre Joker yarns of this time was "Batman — Clown of Crime." Here, the Batman pursued the Joker through an experimental laboratory and both men were accidentally exposed to a device that temporarily swapped their personalities. The Joker, imprisoned in Batman's body, engaged in all sorts of new nefarious pursuits, while Batman, stuck in the Joker's body, worried about two very important things: how to fight crime while trapped in the body of the world's most wanted felon... and how to prevent his foe from doffing the Bat-cowl and

revealing his Bruce Wayne alter ego to every man, woman, and child in Gotham City.

The decade limped to an end with a few mundane Joker appearances, such as "The Joker's Practical Jokes," an eight-pager drawn by Dick Sprang and Charles Paris from BATMAN #123 that was later re-edited into a Prell Shampoo mini-comic giveaway, and "Batman's Super-Partner" (BATMAN #127), in which the Caped Crusader was assisted against the Joker by a new, flying super-doer called The Eagle — in reality, Alfred the butler. Don't ask.

Now, mentioned earlier, the 1960s marked a different period. The difference, sadly, lay exclusively in quality. While the Joker stories from the 1950s ranged from remarkable to soporific, they at least tended to be of a kind... generally noteworthy for their well-thought-out weirdness, if nothing else. Alas, with the two exceptions printed herein, the early '60s Joker stories were by all measures completely uninspired. In more than one instance, literally any criminal could have stood in for the Crime Jester. Among the stories one will *not* find in a collection of the greatest Joker stories, for example, is "The Son of Joker" from BATMAN #145, one of a series of Alfred's speculative tales of a future in which Batman would marry Batwoman and retire, passing the Batman-Robin mantle along to a grown Dick Grayson and Bruce Wayne, Jr. How cute.

Fortunately, the Joker — indeed, the entire Batman cast — received a serious shot in the arm when, in June of 1964, Julius Schwartz took over the editorial reins of BATMAN and DETECTIVE, bringing aboard several new writers and artists, including Gardner Fox, John Broome, and Carmine Infantino, all of whom contributed to what has become known as the "New Look" Batman.

At first, Schwartz's staff started with contemporary and straightforward detective adventures; within a year, Schwartz began re-introducing Batman villains into the books, beginning with "The Joker's Last Laugh" (DETECTIVE #332). While not spectacular, this story, which centered around the villain's new "laughing dust," was better-written than most of the previous dozen or so Joker tales and bode well for the future.

John Broome penned the next Joker story, "The Joker's Comedy Capers" from DETECTIVE #341. Here, the Mirthful Montebank staged a series of crimes, each one while dressed as an old-time movie comedian. Oddly enough, this 16-pager was adapted less than a year later into a Riddler story called "Death in Slow Motion." Strange plagiarism? Not really, because you won't find it in any Batman *comic* of the time. You might, however, recognize it from the mid-'60s *BATMAN* TV show...

All in all, you might say that the Joker's biggest career break came in 1966, when he became a household word thanks to ABC-TV. The third two-part *BATMAN* episode, "The Joker Is Wild," was a loose adaptation of "The Joker's Utility Belt" and starred Cesar Romero as the Clown Prince of Crime in a role originally written for actor José Ferrer. Romero's Joker was the star of 18 half-hour *BATMAN*s, appearing in more episodes than any other Bat-villain save the Penguin (who also had 18 shows under his rather large belt). Moreover, Romero joined Catwoman, Penguin, and Riddler as one of the Fearsome Foursome who terrorized Adam (Batman) West and Burt (Robin) Ward in the August, 1966 *BATMAN* theatrical release.

BRIAN BOLLAND

Through the run of the show, the Joker battled Batman and Robin time and again, both as a solo villain and in tandem with the Penguin, the Catwoman, and others. He wired them to electric chairs, trapped them in gas-filled industrial chimneys, fed them to giant clams, and even tried to crush them

with comic-book printing presses. Scary? Lethal? Menacing? Forget it. How could the Joker of the 1940s hope to stack up against the villain who tried to best Batman in a surfing contest ("Surf's Up! Joker's Under!," November 16, 1967)? Really, how is it possible that Batman could keep *this* Joker from plundering Gotham at whim? The show's producers couldn't even talk him into *shaving his mustache before donning his make-up in every show...*

At any rate, as innocuous and incidental as this humorous treatment made the Joker, it was certainly a boost for his career. The *BATMAN* show sparked an unprecedented nationwide Bat-fad. Batman was *everywhere*, and so were his arch-foes. The Joker showed up on toys, coloring books, 45 rpm records, beach towels, posters — any and all forms of Bat-merchandising. He even made the break into prose novels with the publication of *BATMAN VS. THE THREE VILLAINS OF DOOM*, penned by longtime comics writer Bill Woolfolk under the name "Winston Lyon."

More important, as the Batman line of books began to reflect the TV program, the Jeering Jester once more became a regular player therein. And while we would like to say that his comics appearances during that time ranged from the ridiculous to the sublime, it would be untrue. They simply ranged from the ridiculous to the goofy. Not bad... just goofy.

For instance, in the first of DC's attempts to take advantage of the "look" of the show, writer Bob Haney made Joker, Riddler, and Penguin the heavies of "Alias the Bat-Hulk," a Batman/Metamorpho team-up in the November, 1966 issue of THE BRAVE AND THE BOLD. Then, the Joker and his new sidekick, a dwarf named Gaggy — yes, a dwarf named Gaggy — battled the Dynamic Duo in "The Joker's Original Robberies" (BATMAN #186). The Joker enlisted the aid of Bizarro duplicates of Superman and Batman in WORLD'S

FINEST #156. And — believe it or not — there was the matter of the December, 1966 issue of THE ADVENTURES OF JERRY LEWIS.

It seemed that a new crook named the Kangaroo had the Joker, the Riddler, and the Penguin in a lather: his bumbling antics were, by association, giving Gotham's premier criminals a bad name. As if appearing in THE ADVENTURES OF JERRY LEWIS wasn't. Meanwhile, Jerry and his nephew Renfrew, inspired by their television heroes, donned costumes to become Ratman and Rotten, the Boy Blunder, only to be defeated by the Kangaroo. Eventually, they were saved by the real Batman and Robin, who complained incessantly about that damned TV show. Not only were they exhausted from rescuing Catman and Kitten, Fatman and Tubbin, Flatman and Ribbon (the Taped Crusaders), and all their other imitators, they were sick to death of stupid criminals:

JERRY: Look, here's a clue that the Kangaroo dropped!
BATMAN: "What's got four wheels and flies?"
ROBIN: A garbage truck. (Yawn)
BATMAN: "What's black and white and read all over?"
ROBIN: A newspaper. (Sigh)
BATMAN: "What's big and red and eats rocks?"
ROBIN: A big, red rock-eater. (Yawn) (Sigh)
JERRY: What do those clues mean?
BATMAN: They're not clues — just old riddles! That's another thing that TV show did to us! Crooks keep throwing riddles at us — terrible, awful riddles!
ROBIN: Where will it all end?

Everything eventually came to a tumultuous conclusion at the Batman-Land Amusement Park, and everybody lived happily ever after. And we're sorry for giving such lengthy coverage to this one story, but quite frankly, if the legal department had looked the other

BRIAN BOLLAND

way, we would have put it in this book in a nanosecond. Believe us — they loved it in France.

The rest of the decade gave forth a half-dozen Joker appearances in several different titles: the Joker acted solo in DETECTIVE's "The House the Joker Built" and "Public Lunatic Number One"; fought alongside other Bat-villains in BATMAN; dueled with his two-time partner Lex Luthor in WORLD'S FINEST #177; and exposed to the world the location of the Justice League's first secret headquarters in JUSTICE LEAGUE OF AMERICA #77.

That JLA story was the first Joker tale written by Dennis O'Neil — but, thankfully, not the last. The Clown Prince of Crime vanished for nearly four years before resurfacing in O'Neil's brilliant "The Joker's Five-Way Revenge," which took the Joker back to his original conception as an insane killer, and that portrayal has stayed true ever since. In "This One'll KILL You, Batman" (BATMAN #260), the Batman had to overcome the effects of a lethal drug that threatened to make him literally laugh himself to death; in BRAVE & BOLD #118, the Joker armed the Gotham Guardian and Wildcat with spiked gloves and forced them into a brutal boxing match. And if anyone needed further proof that the Joker was being defined as the Batman's number one nemesis, it was confirmed in May of 1975… when the Joker received his very own series.

While it would be nice to say that the nine issues of THE JOKER were outrageously good, it wouldn't be right; even editor Julius Schwartz admitted that it became very tough very quickly to do anything with the "hero," particularly since the Comics Code wanted him imprisoned at the end of each story. The stories weren't bad, but they soon fell into a pattern: beginning with issue #3, the Joker matched wits with a different hero or villain in each story. Arguably, the best of these was #7's

"Luthor — You're Driving Me Sane," but since it was almost completely a Luthor story, we opted for "The Last Ha Ha" instead.

As evidenced by the selection of stories included in this book, the 1970s marked a golden period for the Crime Clown. As the 1980s began, a wider variety of good artists were drawing Batman stories, including "The Joker's Rumpus Room Revenge," by Gerry Conway, Don Newton, and Dan Adkins, which had Batman battling an army of deadly Joker-controlled children's toys (DETECTIVE #504).

In 1983, Doug Moench penned one of the longest Joker stories ever done, a 62-page tale that stretched over two issues of BATMAN and one of DETECTIVE. Here, the Harlequin of Hate would have slain Batman and overthrown an entire South American country had not Batman's new partner, an innocent youngster named Jason Todd, stepped in and saved the day; but for its length, it would have made this book as well.

DANGEROUS
DO NOT APPROACH

BRIAN BOLLAND

The popularity of the Joker has yet to wane. In the last five years, he has appeared in nearly every corner of the DC Universe. He has taken time out from fighting the Batman to travel to Metropolis in hopes of ridiculing that city's hometown crimefighter (SUPERMAN #9) and has even taken on the entire Justice League in a humorous tale slightly more representative of those of the mid-1950s.

Two of the most important Joker stories have seen publication over the past couple of years. In the pages of the award-winning THE DARK KNIGHT RETURNS, the story of a Caped Crusader who has been retired for a full decade, Frank Miller set forth possibly the grimmest portrayal of the Clown Prince of Crime to date when he made the Joker the prime instigator behind the final case of the Batman. The Joker took hundreds upon hundreds of lives in his most lethal rampage ever... until the Dark Knight ended his murderous career for good.

And in last year's THE KILLING JOKE, Alan Moore and Brian Bolland used elements of "The Man Behind the Red Hood" to weave the backstory behind the most intense vision of the Joker yet seen. The Joker's scheme to drive his arch-enemy as insane as he, a scheme that involved the brutalization of Batgirl and Commissioner Gordon, took a backseat to the narrative interludes that showed readers bits and pieces of the events that led up to the creation of the Ace of Knaves. In THE KILLING JOKE, we learned that the Joker was originally a pathetic would-be comedian who was driven to the brink of sanity when his beloved wife perished in a freak accident... and was pushed over the edge when he fell victim to the circumstances that transformed him into a chalk-faced harlequin.

Most recently, the Joker enacted his most bitter revenge on his nemesis yet, in the four-part BATMAN miniseries titled "A Death in the Family," by doing what no other criminal has ever been able to do: slay the partner of the Batman. And if any doubt remained in anyone's mind that the Joker is the Batman's number one foe, it was dispelled in the summer of 1989, when the Darknight Detective battled the Clown Prince of Crime for the lives of all Gotham in the *BATMAN* movie.

His place in popular fiction is assured, just as it has been for half a century. For as long as there is a Batman, there will be a Joker for him to fight.

— Mark Waid
former Associate Editor, DC Comics

CREATING THE GREATEST
THE MEN BEHIND THE MASK

BRIAN BOLLAND

NEAL ADAMS

"The Joker's Five-Way Revenge"

Neal Adams began his comics career assisting on and occasionally pencilling the *Bat Masterson* syndicated comic strip. At the same time, Adams was doing advertising illustration and began to develop the realistic art style that would become his trademark. From there, Neal went on to a brief stint at Archie Comics and to his own newspaper strip, *Ben Casey*, based on the popular television series. Adams joined DC in 1967. His work on such books as WORLD'S FINEST, SUPERMAN, THE SPECTRE, GREEN LANTERN-GREEN ARROW and *DEADMAN* won him much acclaim and many fans, but it is his tenure on The Batman that is most fondly remembered. Working with writer Dennis O'Neil and editor Julius Schwartz, Adams returned him to his roots as the Darknight Detective. Adams's other credits include work at Marvel, Warren and National Lampoon. He currently heads Continuity Studios, an art production studio and comics publisher.

DAN ADKINS

"Last Laugh"

Learning his trade at the elbow of classic comics artist Wally Wood uniquely qualified Dan Adkins for his career in comic art. Breaking in as a penciller and inker on Wood's *T.H.U.N.D.E.R. Agents* for Tower Comics, Adkins' work soon began appearing in many publications. Adkins did many well-remembered art jobs for Warren Publications' *Creepy* and *Eerie*; for Marvel, Dan drew a handful of features including *Dr. Strange* and *The Sub-Mariner*. It is as an inker that Adkins is best known, however, having worked on virtually every Marvel comic and many DC comics, including SUPERMAN over Curt Swan's pencils.

MURPHY ANDERSON

"The Joker's Happy Victims"

Influenced by artists Lou Fine and Will Eisner, Anderson broke into comics in 1944 drawing many features for Fiction House publishing. After a tour of duty in the Navy during World War II, Murphy returned to comics, drawing a host of features for many publishers. In 1947, Murphy assumed the art chores on the *Buck Rogers* syndicated comic strip. Though he would return to the *Rogers* strip ten years later, Murphy left it in 1949 and once again turned his attentions exclusively to comic books. Joining DC in 1950, Anderson's work graced many science fiction and super-hero strips. He is best remembered for his artwork on *CAPTAIN COMET, THE ATOMIC KNIGHTS*, HAWKMAN and THE SPECTRE, and for his inking on *ADAM STRANGE*, THE ATOM and a long, celebrated run on SUPERMAN, over Curt Swan's pencils. Today, most of his time is taken up with the running of Murphy Anderson Visual Concepts, a publishers' support service company providing color separations and typesetting for the comics industry.

JIM APARO

"Death Has the Last Laugh"

A graduate of the Hartford Art School, Jim Aparo spent his early career primarily as an advertising illustrator, with an occasional assignment from Charlton Comics. In the mid-'60s Aparo started drawing comics on a regular basis. Moving to DC in 1968 Aparo quickly made his mark on several popular, long-running features like AQUAMAN, THE PHANTOM STRANGER and, with writer Michael Fleisher, the controversial *SPECTRE* series in ADVENTURE COMICS. As the regular artist on THE BRAVE AND THE BOLD, the Batman team-up title, Aparo was deemed heir-apparent to Neal Adams as *the* Batman artist. This popularity led to assignments as the artist on both BATMAN and DETECTIVE COMICS. Aparo went on to the art chores of the popular super-team comic, THE OUTSIDERS. Aparo currently lends his fluid line and solid story-telling to one of the monthly BATMAN titles.

TERRY AUSTIN

"The Laughing Fish," "The Sign of the Joker"

Being a student and assistant to Dick Giordano is one of the better ways to break into comics, and that's exactly the route chosen by inker Terry Austin. He developed an inking style all his own, though, becoming known for his highly effective use of texture and his decorative pen line. Among his earliest work was at DC inking penciller Mike Nasser on a series of Martian Manhunter stories and teamed with Marshall Rogers on various strips, which eventually led to their assignment as the regular team on Batman in DETECTIVE COMICS. The popular inker has worked with many of comics' best pencillers, most notably with John Byrne on a long, acclaimed run on Marvel's *X-Men*.

MIKE W. BARR

"Catch As Catscan," "The Last Laugh"

A fan and student of classic mystery detectives such as Sherlock Holmes and Ellery Queen, Ohio native Mike Barr was an ideal choice to bring that element back to the adventures of the world's greatest detective. With artists Alan Davis and Paul Neary, Barr produced some of the more memorable modern Batman tales, including the acclaimed "Batman: Year Two" in DETECTIVE COMICS. With artist Jerry Bingham, he produced the best-selling graphic novel, BATMAN: SON OF

THE DEMON. Mike has created and written many other popular DC titles, including fondly remembered work on CAMELOT 3000 and THE OUTSIDERS. Currently, Barr writes his own creation, the independent comic *The Maze Agency*, which features — not surprisingly — stories of mystery in the classic style.

E. NELSON BRIDWELL
"The Joker's Happy Victims"

Perhaps the first of the "comics fans turned comics pro," Edward Nelson Bridwell began as a writer for *Mad Magazine* in 1957. In 1965 he joined DC as an assistant editor, working primarily with SUPERMAN editor Mort Weisinger. As an editor, Nelson specialized in reprint titles, putting together creatively chosen, popular collections. This expertise extended to several hardcover volumes tracing the careers of Superman, Batman, and Captain Marvel. Bridwell's writing credits include various features in SUPERMAN FAMILY, the original Captain Marvel in SHAZAM!, THE INFERIOR FIVE, SUPER FRIENDS, and the cult favorite, THE SECRET SIX, which he also created. Possessed of an incredible memory for detail, Bridwell became an unofficial "continuity cop" at DC, fact-checking various comics for historical accuracy. E. Nelson Bridwell passed away in 1987. His spirit and enthusiasm are greatly missed.

JACK BURNLEY
"The Joker and the Sparrow"

Hardin "Jack" Burnley started his career as a newspaper sports cartoonist in 1929. In the late '30s, Burnley joined the newly formed Joe Shuster art studio, assisting in the production of Superman. Through the early '40s Jack worked on a great variety of features at DC. In addition to SUPERMAN, Burnley's stamp can be seen on BATMAN, The Justice Society in ALL-STAR and on the Golden Age Starman, which he co-created with writer Gardner Fox. Burnley also worked on the syndicated Superman Sunday strip as well as the Sunday Batman strip. Burnley left comics work in 1946, returning to newspaper cartooning, spending nearly 25 years as a staff artist and layout designer with *The San Francisco Examiner*.

ERNIE CHAN
"The Last Ha-Ha"

Philippine artist Ernesto Chan began his career as an assistant to fellow Filipino artist Tony De-Zuñiga. Chan moved to the U.S. in the late 1960s to pursue a career in American comics. At DC, Chan worked on many titles, including CLAW, SWAMP THING, THE SECRET SOCIETY OF SUPER-VILLAINS, BATMAN and of course, THE

JOKER. Ernie was also the chief cover artist at DC through the mid '70s. For Marvel, Chan (or, alternately, Chua) toiled on a wide variety of features for both their color and black-and-white comics. Chan was the most frequent inker for John Buscema's Conan work in both formats. Chan has also pencilled and inked many Conan stories for *The Savage Sword of Conan* magazine.

GERRY CONWAY
"Last Laugh"

Breaking into comics writing at the tender age of sixteen, Gerry Conway quickly established an impressive list of credentials. At Marvel, Conway had long and definitive stints on many of their major titles including *Spider-Man*, *Thor* and *The Fantastic Four*. He also created one of Marvel's most popular characters, The Punisher. At one time, Conway was also Marvel's Editor-in-Chief. For DC Comics, Conway wrote the adventures of BATMAN and SUPERMAN, while also creating FIRESTORM with artist Al Milgrom. Conway is also an accomplished novelist, television and film writer. Among his credits is the screenplay (with Roy Thomas) for *Conan the Destroyer*. Currently Gerry is back at Marvel where, among other work, he once again chronicles the adventures of Spider-Man.

ALAN DAVIS
"Catch As Catscan," "The Last Laugh"

The British-born artist first gained international notice for his work on Marvelman, a revival of a classic British super-hero for *Warrior* magazine (the work has been reprinted in the U.S. as Miracleman, for obvious legal reasons). Additionally, Alan drew the adventures of the revitalized Captain Britain for Marvel U.K. and recently co-created the popular Marvel title *Excalibur* with writer Chris Claremont. At DC, Alan's work appeared in THE OUTSIDERS and in DETECTIVE COMICS. Soon, Alan's art will grace the Batman graphic novel FULL CIRCLE, the sequel to the acclaimed "Batman: Year Two," written by Mike W. Barr.

STEVE ENGLEHART
"The Laughing Fish," "The Sign of the Joker"

It is not generally known that comics writer Englehart began his career as a comics artist. Early art credits include a few stories for Warren and some romance stories for Marvel, both in the very early '70s. Since then, Englehart has concentrated his efforts on writing. His credits include a wide range of Marvel work including notable stints on *The Avengers*, *The Defenders* and *Master of Kung-Fu*, which he co-created with Jim Starlin. Working on DETECTIVE COMICS with artists Marshall

Rogers and Terry Austin, Steve produced moody, atmosphere-drenched stories worthy of the Darknight Detective. In the process he reinstated elements of menace to old Bat-villains Hugo Strange, Deadshot, the Penguin and, most effectively, the Joker. Englehart was the writer of DC's highly popular miniseries MILLENNIUM, and he recently scripted Marvel's *Silver Surfer*.

BILL FINGER

"Batman Meets the Joker,"
"The Case of the Joker's Crime Circus"

Heralded for his work on Batman by none other than Bob Kane, Finger's contribution to the character is immeasurable. Finger was the primary, though uncredited writer of the majority of Batman comics stories through the early 1960s. During his long tenure he created or contributed to many of the core characters in the Batman mythos, including the Penguin, Catwoman, Two-Face and the Riddler. Finger always endeavored to instill his scripts with fast-paced action and moody *film noir* atmosphere. He plied his craft on a handful of other DC comics, including work on GREEN LANTERN, SUPERMAN, *WILDCAT*, and the Robin solo stories in STAR-SPANGLED COMICS, and also contributed to Timely/Marvel, Quality and Fawcett, among other publishers. Finger retired from comics in 1968, although he went on to write many of the scripts for the Superman cartoon show of the late '60s. Bill Finger passed away in 1974.

JOSÉ LUIS GARCIA-LOPÉZ

"The Last Ha-Ha," "The Last Laugh"

The Spanish-born artist can boast of a distinguished 20-year comics career, most of that time spent working for DC comics. José's expressive, dynamic art style has brightened many titles for DC, including work on virtually every character including Superman, Hawkman, Batman, Batgirl and Robin, Jonah Hex, and Hercules in the HERCULES UNBOUND title. In addition to occasional work on the short-lived THE JOKER solo series, Garcia-Lopéz did the art chores on the Marvel/DC co-produced special, BATMAN VS. THE HULK, which co-starred the crazed crime clown. Recently, José illustrated the CINDER AND ASHE miniseries and has just completed work on an upcoming new miniseries entitled TWILIGHT, written by Howard Chaykin.

DICK GIORDANO

"The Joker's Five-Way Revenge"

In a career spanning more than 35 years, Dick Giordano has worked on virtually every major comics character, as artist, inker or editor. Dick concentrated his early efforts at Charlton Comics, and was named Editor-in-Chief in 1965. Giordano began revamping the line and added an emphasis on action heroes like The Blue Beetle, The Question, and Sarge Steel. His success did not go unnoticed, for he was soon offered an editorial job at DC by then-publisher Carmine Infantino. Working with many of the creators he had employed at Charlton — Jim Aparo, Dennis O'Neil, Steve Skeates, and Steve Ditko — Dick edited a string of truly innovative titles, including HAWK & DOVE, THE CREEPER, and a revamped AQUAMAN. Returning to the freelance life, Dick joined with Neal Adams to produce the art for the much acclaimed GREEN LANTERN-GREEN ARROW series, as well as the definitive 1970s Batman stories. Today, Dick continues to ink various series, including the hit comic GREEN ARROW. That he finds time is amazing, considering that he is also DC's Vice President/Editorial Director.

BOB HANEY

"Death Has the Last Laugh"

A journeyman comics scripter, Bob Haney's career began in 1948. Working for nearly every publisher of the time on virtually every genre — war, horror, crime, westerns and super-heroes — Haney settled at DC in 1953, writing a wide range of material that included REX THE WONDER DOG, SEA DEVILS, METAMORPHO and the original TEEN TITANS. Haney has also scripted the Batman team-ups in THE BRAVE AND THE BOLD and the Superman/Batman team-ups in WORLD'S FINEST. Haney's credits also include scripts for the *SUPERMAN-AQUAMAN ADVENTURE HOUR* animated TV series of the late-'60s.

CARMINE INFANTINO

"The Joker's Happy Victims"

A versatile and creative artist, Carmine Infantino has produced exciting, dynamic comics since the 1940s. At DC, his early credits include the original FLASH and GREEN LANTERN, western hero JOHNNY THUNDER, PHANTOM STRANGER and many science-fiction and mystery tales. Infantino's style always stressed movement — so he was a perfect choice to revitalize the super-fast hero, the Flash. In 1964 he was charged with a similar task, this time giving a "new look" to Batman, a successful trend that continued into the late-'60s. At the end of that decade, Infantino became first Art Director, then Editorial Director, and finally Publisher at DC, a post he held until 1976, when he returned to full-time freelance artwork. Among Infantino's other credits are the fondly remembered *ELONGATED MAN* and *ADAM STRANGE* series.

BOB KANE

"Batman Meets the Joker,"
"The Case of the Joker's Crime Circus"

Inspired by the drawings of Leonardo da Vinci and the 1931 film version of Mary Roberts Rinehart's *The Bat*, a young cartoonist sketched his vision of an ominous, brooding, batwinged night-creature, and the rest is history. Teaming with writer Bill Finger, the young artist fashioned that nightmare vision into one of the most enduring fictional characters of all time — The Batman. Heading a studio that included artists Jerry Robinson, Dick Sprang and many others, Kane produced Batman art for several decades. Retiring from comics in 1967, Kane went into television and animation. Confining his artwork to painting, Bob Kane has had many one-man art shows and many of his Batman paintings have been nationally displayed. Appropriately enough, Kane served as technical consultant for the 1989 *BATMAN* film.

STAN KAYE

"Superman's and Batman's Greatest Foes"

Trained primarily as a cartoonist in the funny "big-foot" style, Stan Kaye nonetheless made the transition to more serious comic art beautifully. His loose cartooning style can be seen on a score of humor features for DC in the early '40s. Kaye's clean fluid ink line emboldened a handful of DC's finest pencillers, including Dick Sprang on WORLD'S FINEST, and Curt Swan and Wayne Boring on SUPERMAN. Stan also inked the syndicated Superman newspaper strip in the late '40s and early '50s.

SHELDON MOLDOFF

"The Man Behind the Red Hood," "The Great Clayface-Joker Feud," "The Joker Jury"

Shelly Moldoff's long, diverse career at DC began in 1938, with the young artist learning his craft by doing whatever filler and back-up he could stake out. He soon "graduated" to regular features, most notably *HAWKMAN* in FLASH COMICS. Moldoff drew many other adventure and humor strips at DC and other companies throughout the '40s and early '50s. In 1943 he began a 25-year tenure on the Batman feature in both BATMAN and DETECTIVE COMICS. The prolific penciller and inker's style was so prevalent that it was his look that defined the character throughout the '50s. Moldoff left comics in the late '60s to concentrate on animation storyboards.

JIM MOONEY

"The Joker Jury"

Contributing to many Batman stories throughout the '40s and '50s, Jim Mooney is best remembered for his art on the Robin solo feature appearing in STAR-SPANGLED COMICS and for countless Superman and Batman team-up stories appearing in WORLD'S FINEST into the '60s. Mooney's art was also a large part of the success of long running features such as *SUPERGIRL* and *TOMMY TOMORROW*, both for DC. Jim's credits also include many features for Marvel, particularly a long run on *Spider-Man*. Now in semi-retirement, Mooney still finds time to do an occasional comics art job.

PAUL NEARY

"Catch As Catscan," "The Last Laugh"

Paul Neary's artwork has appeared in many different publications on both sides of the Atlantic, including work for the Warren horror magazines in the U.S. More recently, the English-born artist drew the miniseries, *Nick Fury vs S.H.I.E.L.D.* for Marvel. For the past several years, Neary has been working most with Alan Davis, inking Davis' art on *Excalibur* for Marvel, and THE OUTSIDERS and Batman in DETECTIVE COMICS for DC.

DENNIS O'NEIL

"The Joker's Five-Way Revenge,"
"The Last Ha-Ha"

Dennis O'Neil's 20-plus year comics career started almost by accident. Offered the Stan Lee writer's test by fellow Missourian Roy Thomas, Dennis accepted on a lark. After passing with flying colors, O'Neil decided to give comics writing a "brief fling" — one that lasts to this day. Working at Marvel on features ranging from *Millie the Model* to *The Two-Gun Kid* to *S.H.I.E.L.D.* and *Dr. Strange*, O'Neil then moved to Charlton and then to DC. Teamed with artists Neal Adams and Dick Giordano, O'Neil wrote the critically acclaimed GREEN LANTERN-GREEN ARROW and the dramatic revitalization of Batman back into the dark figure of mystery he once was. Dennis' credits at DC also include scripting stints on SUPERMAN, WONDER WOMAN, and JUSTICE LEAGUE OF AMERICA. After a short term as an editor and writer at Marvel, O'Neil returned to DC where he is currently the writer of THE QUESTION and editor of BATMAN and DETECTIVE COMICS.

CHARLES PARIS

"The Joker and the Sparrow," "The Joker's Crime Costumes," "The Joker's Utility Belt," "The Crazy Crime Clown," "Crime-of-the-Month Club," "The Great Clayface-Joker Feud"

From 1947 until 1964, Charles Paris spent virtually his every working moment inking the Batman. His fluid ink line lent solidity and consistency to a wide variety of Batman artists including Jack Burnley, Fred Ray, Sheldon Moldoff and, most memorably, Dick Sprang. Paris began his career inking Mort Meskin on Johnny Quick and Vigilante. After his stint on Batman, Charlie went on to ink a handful of other DC features including METAMORPHO, various BRAVE AND BOLD team-ups and the very first appearance of the Teen Titans. Paris retired in 1968 to paint and travel.

JERRY ROBINSON

"Batman Meets the Joker,"
"The Case of the Joker's Crime Circus"

Legend has it that Bob Kane "discovered" the young Robinson on a New York street. Noticing an intricately hand-decorated jacket that the young art student was wearing, Kane approached him, praising the artwork and offered Robinson a job as an assistant on BATMAN. More than any other artist, Jerry Robinson set the visual tone for the Batman feature. His crisp line, dynamic figure drawing and daring page layout made the stories come alive. Robinson lent his name and youthful exuberance to Batman's sidekick and helped create the visual for the greatest of Batman's foes — the Joker, inspired by a playing card and the nightmare countenance of actor Conrad Veidt in the film *The Man Who Laughs*. Robinson worked on numerous other features for various publishers until the early 1950s, then turned his attention to syndicated strip work and advertising illustration. Today, the artist is a nationally syndicated political cartoonist.

MARSHALL ROGERS

"The Laughing Fish," "The Sign of the Joker"

A former architecture student, Marshall Rogers made his early appearances as an artist on a number of second features at DC in the late '70s. In the back of DETECTIVE COMICS, he teamed with inker Terry Austin on a series of connected back-up features that pitted a succession of heroes, including Batman, against a common foe, the Calculator. The series and the art proved popular enough to secure for the artists the slot as lead art team on the book. With writer Steve Englehart, Rogers and Austin produced a version of the Batman that is still held by many to be among the best of a character that has no shortage of "bests." Since then, Rogers' art has been featured on many titles from several publishers.

GEORGE ROUSSOS

"The Man Behind the Red Hood"

George Roussos was one of the first artists to join Bob Kane's Batman studio in 1940. Lettering and inking over the pencils of Kane, Robinson, and many other Batman artists over many years, Roussos also illustrated a number of other DC features, including *AIRWAVE*. George's inking can be found over many different pencillers, such as Mort Meskin on several DC features. Roussos has also been a highly innovative comics colorist, pioneering many of today's most commonly used color effects. George Roussos is currently the chief cover colorist at Marvel.

WALTER SIMONSON

"Dreadful Birthday, Dear Joker—!"

Illustrating a myriad of short war, fantasy and science-fiction stories for DC in the 1970s, Walt Simonson moved up the art chores on THE METAL MEN and HERCULES UNBOUND. It was while he teamed with writer Archie Goodwin on *MANHUNTER* that Simonson attracted the most notice. Manhunter's climactic finale was the first of several Simonson renditions of The Batman. Walt has gone on to many other assignments, mostly for Marvel, where he wrote and drew a popular run of *Thor*, and where he currently does the same honors on *The Fantastic Four*.

DICK SPRANG

"The Joker's Crime Costumes," "The Joker's Utility Belt," "The Crazy Crime Clown," "Superman's and Batman's Greatest Foes," "Crime-of-the-Month Club"

A master among many masters of Batman art, Dick Sprang was, and still is to many, *the* Batman artist. His fluid art and powerful layouts presented stories that leaped, flew, and seethed with energy. Sprang's razor-jawed Batman swung across an almost surreal cityscape, facing truly bizarre villains, including a delightfully deranged Joker. Considered the definitive Batman artist of the '50s, Sprang drew the character until his own retirement in 1962. Sprang's style remains vital 30 years later, continuing to influence later Batman artists like Marshall Rogers and Norm Breyfogle. Dick and his wife reside in Arizona, where he paints and relaxes. His occasional special Batman drawings prove the master still has it.

LEN WEIN

"Dreadful Birthday, Dear Joker—!"

A veteran of numerous comics titles, Len Wein did double duty on the Batman, serving as scripter for several years in the late 1970s and early '80s, and following that with a tenure as editor on the Batman line, Wein is perhaps best known as the creator, with artist Berni Wrightson, of the enduring and extremely popular SWAMP THING. Wein has contributed scripts on many titles for Marvel, including *Spider-Man, Thor*, and the first several issues of the new *X-Men*. Wein's most recent writing work at DC was BLUE BEETLE.

— Brian Augustyn
Editor, DC Comics

351

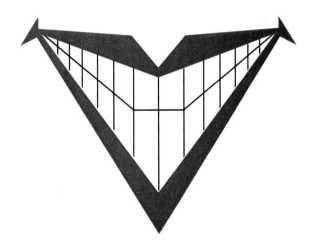